ROBIN McKINLEY
THE HERO AND THE CROWN

ACE BOOKS, NEW YORK

THE HERO AND THE CROWN

An Ace Book / published by arrangement with
the author

PRINTING HISTORY
Greenwillow edition published 1984
Berkley edition / April 1986
Second printing / October 1986
Ace edition / April 1987

The Penguin Putnam Inc. World Wide Web site address is
http://www.penguinputnam.com

ISBN: 0-441-32809-1

ACE®
Ace Books are published by
The Berkley Publishing Group, a division of Penguin Putnam Inc.,
375 Hudson Street, New York, New York 10014.
The name "ACE" and the "A" design are trademarks
belonging to Penguin Putnam Inc.

PRINTED IN THE UNITED STATES OF AMERICA

35 34 33 32 31 30 29 28 27 26

TO TERRI

The Hero and the Crown takes place some considerable span of years before the time of *The Blue Sword*. There are a few fairly dramatic topographical differences between the Damar of Aerin's day and that of Harry's.

THE HERO AND THE CROWN

PART ONE

❧ CHAPTER 1 ❧

SHE COULD NOT REMEMBER a time when she had not known the story; she had grown up knowing it. She supposed someone must have told her it, sometime, but she could not remember the telling. She was beyond having to blink back tears when she thought of those things the story explained, but when she was feeling smaller and shabbier than usual in the large vivid City high in the Damarian Hills she still found herself brooding about them; and brooding sometimes brought on a tight headachy feeling around her temples, a feeling like suppressed tears.

She brooded, looking out over the wide low sill of the stone windowframe; she looked up, into the Hills, because the glassy surface of the courtyard was too bright at midday to stare at long. Her mind ran down an old familiar track: Who might have told her the story? It wouldn't have been her father who told her, for he had rarely spoken more than a few words together to her when she was younger; his slow kind smiles and slightly preoccupied air had been the most she knew of him. She had always known that he was fond of her, which was something; but she had only recently begun to come into focus for him, and that, as he had told her himself, in an unexpected fashion. He had the best—the only—right to have told her the story of her birth, but he would not have done so.

Nor would it have been the hafor, the folk of the household;

3

they were polite to her always, in their wary way, and reserved, and spoke to her only about household details. It surprised her that they still remembered to be wary, for she had long since proven that she possessed nothing to be wary about. Royal children were usually somewhat alarming to be in daily contact with, for their Gifts often erupted in abrupt and unexpected ways. It was a little surprising, even, that the hafor still bothered to treat her with respect, for the fact that she was her father's daughter was supported by nothing but the fact that her father's wife had borne her. But then, for all that was said about her mother, no one ever suggested that she was not an honest wife.

And she would not have run and told tales on any of the hafor who slighted her, as Galanna would—and regularly did, even though everyone treated her with the greatest deference humanly possible. Galanna's Gift, it was dryly said, was to be impossible to please. But perhaps from the hafor's viewpoint it was not worth the risk to discover any points of similarity or dissimilarity between herself and Galanna; and a life of service in a household that included Galanna doubtless rendered anyone who withstood it automatically wary and respectful of anything that moved. She smiled. She could see the wind stir the treetops, for the surface of the Hills seemed to ripple beneath the blue sky; the breeze, when it slid through her window, smelled of leaves.

It might very well have been Galanna who told her the story, come to that. It would be like her; and Galanna had always hated her—still did, for all that she was grown now, and married besides, to Perlith, who was a second sola of Damar. The only higher ranks were first sola and king; but Galanna had hoped to marry Tor, who was first sola and would someday be king. It was no matter that Tor would not have had Galanna if she had been the only royal maiden available—"I'd run off into the Hills and be a bandit first," a much younger Tor had told his very young cousin, who had gone off in fits of giggles at the idea of Tor wearing rags and a blue headband and dancing for luck under each quarter of the moon. Tor, who at the time had been stiff with terror at Galanna's very determined attempts to ensnare him, had relaxed enough to grin and tell her she had no proper respect and was a shameless hoyden. "Yes," she said unrepentantly.

Tor, for whatever reasons, was rather over-formal with everyone but her; but being first sola to a solemn, twice-widowed king of a land with a shadow over it might have had that effect on a far more frivolous young man than Tor. She suspected that he was as grateful for her existence as she was for his; one of her earliest memories was riding in a baby-sack over Tor's shoulders while he galloped his horse over a series of hurdles; she had screamed with delight and wound her tiny hands in his thick black hair. Teka, later, had been furious; but Tor, who usually took any accusation of the slightest dereliction of duty with white lips and a set face, had only laughed.

But whenever she decided that it must have been Galanna who first told her the story, she found she couldn't believe it of her after all. Having told it for spite and malice, yes; but the story itself had too much sad grandeur. But perhaps she only felt that way because it was about her mother; perhaps she had changed it in her own mind, made a tragedy of nothing but sour gossip. But that Galanna would deliberately spend enough time in her company to tell her the story was out of character; Galanna preferred whenever possible to look vaguely over the head of the least of her cousins, with an expression on her face indicating that there was a dead fly on the windowsill and why hadn't the hafor swept it away? When Galanna was startled into speaking to her at all, it was usually from a motive of immediate vengeance. The tale of Arlbeth's second wife would be too roundabout for her purposes. Still, that it had been one of the cousins was the best guess. Not Tor, of course. One of the others.

She leaned out of the window and looked down. It was hard to recognize people from the tops of their heads, several stories up. Except Tor; she always knew him, even if all she had to go on was an elbow extending an inch or two beyond a doorframe. This below her now was probably Perlith: that self-satisfied walk was distinctive even from above, and the way three of the hafor, dressed in fine livery, trailed behind him for no purpose but to lend to their master's importance by their presence pretty well assured it. Tor went about alone, when he could; he told her, grimly, that he had enough of company during the course of his duties as first sola, and the last thing he wanted was an unofficial entourage for any gaps in the official ones. And she'd like to see her father pulling velvet-covered flunkeys in his wake, like a child with a toy on a string.

Perlith's head spoke to another dark head, the hafor waiting respectfully several arms' length distant; then someone on a horse—she could not distinguish voices but she heard the click of hoofs—emerged from around a corner. The rider wore the livery of a messenger, and the cut of his saddle said he came from the west. Both heads turned toward him and tipped up, so she could see the pale blur of their faces as they spoke to him. Then the horseman cantered off, the horse placing its feet very delicately, for it was dangerous to go too quickly across the courtyard; and Perlith and the other man, and Perlith's entourage, disappeared from her view.

She didn't have to hear what they said to each other to know what was going on; but the knowledge gave her no pleasure, for it had already brought her both shame and bitter disappointment. It was either the shame or the disappointment that kept her mewed up in her rooms, alone, now.

She had hardly seen her father or Tor for the week past as they wrestled with messages and messengers, as they tried to slow down whatever it was that would happen anyway, while they tried to decide what to do when it had happened. The western barons—the fourth solas—were making trouble. The rumor was that someone from the North, either human or human enough to look it, had carried a bit of demon-mischief south across the Border and let it loose at the barons' council in the spring. Nyrlol was the chief of the council for no better reason than that his father had been chief; but his father had been a better and a wiser man. Nyrlol was not known for intelligence, and he was known for a short and violent temper: the perfect target for demon-mischief.

Nyrlol's father would have recognized it for what it was. But Nyrlol had not recognized anything; it had simply seemed like a wonderful idea to secede from Damar and the rule of Damar's King Arlbeth and Tor-sola, and set himself up as King Nyrlol; and to slap a new tax on his farmers to support the raising of an army, eventually to take the rest of Damar away from Arlbeth and Tor, who didn't run it as well as he could. He managed to convince several of his fellow barons (demon-mischief, once it has infected one human being, will usually then spread like a plague) of the brilliance of his plan, while the mischief muddled their wits. There had been a further rumor, much fainter, that Nyrlol had, with his wonderful idea, suddenly developed a mesmerizing ability to sway those who heard him speak; and this rumor was a much more worrying one, for, if true, the demon-mischief was very strong indeed.

Arlbeth had chosen to pay no attention to the second rumor; or rather to pay only enough attention to it to discount it, that none of his folk might think he shunned it from fear. But he did declare that the trouble was enough that he must attend to it personally; and with him would go Tor, and a substantial portion of the army, and almost as substantial a portion of the court, with all its velvets and jewels brought along for a fine grand show of courtesy, to pretend to disguise the army at its back. But both sides would know that the army was an army, and the show only a show. What Arlbeth planned to do was both difficult and dangerous, for he wished to prevent a civil war, not provoke one. He would choose those to go with him with the greatest care and caution.

"But you're taking Perlith?" she'd asked Tor disbelievingly, when she met him by chance one day, out behind the barns, where she could let her disbelief show.

Tor grimaced. "I know Perlith isn't a very worthwhile human being, but he's actually pretty effective at this sort of thing—because he's such a good liar, you know, and because he can say the most appalling things in the most gracious manner."

No women rode in Arlbeth's army. A few of the bolder wives might be permitted to go with their husbands, those who could ride and had been trained in cavalry drill; and those who could be trusted to smile even at Nyrlol (depending on how the negotiations went), and curtsy to him as befitted his rank as fourth sola, and even dance with him if he should ask. But it was expected that no wife would go unless her husband asked her, and no husband would ask unless he had asked the king first.

Galanna would certainly not go, even if Perlith had been willing to go to the trouble of obtaining leave from Arlbeth (which would probably not have been granted). Fortunately for the peace of all concerned, Galanna had no interest in going; anything resembling hardship did not appeal to her in the least, and she was sure that nothing in the barbaric west could possibly be worth her time and beauty.

A king's daughter might go too; a king's daughter who had, perhaps, proved herself in some small ways; who had learned to keep her mouth shut, and to smile on cue; a king's daughter who happened to be the king's only child. She had known they would not let her; she had known that Arlbeth would not dare give his permission even had he wanted to, and she did not know if he had wanted to. But he could not dare take the witchwoman's daughter to confront the workings of demon-mischief; his people would never let him, and he too sorely needed his people's good will.

But she could not help asking—any more, she supposed, than poor stupid Nyrlol could help going mad when the demon-mischief bit him. She had tried to choose her time, but her father and Tor had been so busy lately that she had had to wait, and wait again, till her time was almost gone. After dinner last night she had finally asked; and she had come up here to her rooms afterward and had not come out again.

"Father." Her voice had gone high on her, as it would do when she was afraid. The other women, and the lesser court members, had already left the long hall; Arlbeth and Tor and a few of the cousins, Perlith among them, were preparing for another weary evening of discussion on Nyrlol's folly. They paused and all of them turned and looked at her, and she wished there were not so many of them. She swallowed. She had decided against asking her father late, in his own rooms, where she could be sure to find him alone, because she was afraid he would only be kind to her and not take her seriously. If she was to be shamed—and she knew, or she told herself she knew, that she would be refused—at least let him see how much it meant to her, that she should ask and be refused with others looking on.

Arlbeth turned to her with his slow smile, but it was slower and less of it reached his eyes than usual. He did not say, "Be quick, I am busy," as he might have done—and small blame to him if he had, she thought forlornly.

"You ride west—soon? To treat with Nyrlol?" She could feel Tor's eyes on her, but she kept her own eyes fixed on her father.

"Treat?" said her father. "If we go, we go with an army to witness the treaty." A little of the smile crept into his eyes after all. "You are picking up courtly language, my dear. Yes, we go to 'treat' with Nyrlol."

Tor said: "We have some hope of catching the mischief"—one did not say *demon* aloud if one could help it—"and bottling it up, and sending it back where it came from. Even now we have that hope. It won't stop the trouble, but it will stop it getting worse. If Nyrlol isn't being pricked and pinched by it, he may subside into the subtle and charming Nyrlol we all know and revere." Tor's mouth twisted up into a wry smile.

She looked at him and her own mouth twitched at the corners. It was like Tor to answer her as if she were a real part of the court, even a member of the official deliberations, instead of an interruption and a disturbance. Tor might even have let her go with them; he wasn't old enough yet to care so much for his people's good opinion as Arlbeth did; and furthermore, Tor was stubborn. But it was not Tor's decision. She turned back to her father.

"When you go—may I come with you?" Her voice was little more than a squeak, and she wished she were near a wall or a door she could lean on, instead of in the great empty middle of the dining-hall, with her knees trying to fold up under her like an hour-old foal's.

The silence went suddenly tight, and the men she faced went rigid: or Arlbeth did, and those behind him, for she kept her face resolutely away from Tor. She thought that she could not bear it if her one loyal friend forsook her too; and she had never tried to discover the extent of Tor's stubbornness. Then the silence was broken by Perlith's high-pitched laughter.

"Well, and what did you expect from letting her go as she would these last years? It's all very well to have her occupied and out from underfoot, but you should have thought the price you paid to be rid of her might prove a little high. What did you expect when our honored first sola gives her lessons in swordplay and she tears around on that three-legged horse like a peasant boy from the Hills, with never a gainsay but a scold from that old shrew that serves as her maid? Might you not have thought of the reckoning to come? She needed slaps, not encouragement, years ago—she needs a few slaps now, I think. Perhaps it is not too late."

"Enough." Tor's voice, a growl.

Her legs were trembling now so badly that she had to move her feet, shuffle in her place, to keep the joints locked to hold her up. She felt the blood mounting to her face at Perlith's words, but she would not let him drive her away without an answer. "Father?"

"Father," mimicked Perlith. "It's true a king's daughter might be of some use in facing what the North has sent us; a king's daughter who had true royal blood in her veins. . . ."

Arlbeth, in a very unkinglike manner, reached out and grabbed Tor before anyone found out what the first sola's sudden move in Perlith's direction might result in. "Perlith, you betray the honor of the second sola's place in speaking thus."

Tor said in a strangled voice, "He will apologize, or I'll give *him* a lesson in swordplay he will not like at all."

"Tor, don't be a—" she began, outraged, but the king's voice cut across hers. "Perlith, there is justice in the first sola's demand."

There was a long pause while she hated everyone impartially: Tor for behaving like a farmer's son whose pet chicken has just been insulted; her father, for being so immovably kingly; and Perlith for being Perlith. This was even worse than she had anticipated; at this point she would be grateful just for escape, but it was too late.

Perlith said at last, "I apologize, Aerin-sol. For speaking the truth," he added venomously, and turned on his heel and strode across the hall. At the doorway he paused and turned to shout back at them: "Go slay a dragon, lady! Lady Aerin, Dragon-Killer!"

The silence resettled itself about them, and she could no longer even raise her eyes to her father's face.

"Aerin—" Arlbeth began.

The gentleness of his voice told her all she needed to know, and she turned away and walked toward the other end of the hall, opposite the door which Perlith had taken. She was conscious of the length of the way she had to take because Perlith had taken the shorter way, and she hated him all the more for it; she was conscious of all the eyes on her, and conscious of the fact that her legs still trembled, and that the line she walked was not a straight one. Her father did not call her back. Neither did Tor. As she reached the doorway at last, Perlith's words still rang in her ears: "A king's daughter who had true royal blood in her veins . . . Lady Aerin, Dragon-Killer." It was as though his words were hunting dogs who tracked her and nipped at her heels.

✣ CHAPTER 2 ✣

HER HEAD ACHED. The scene was still so vividly before her that the door of her bedroom was half open before she heard it. She spun round, but it was only Teka, bearing a tray; Teka glanced once at her scowling face and averted her eyes. She was probably first chosen for my maid for her skill at averting her eyes, Aerin thought sourly; but then she noticed the tray, and the smell of the steam that rose from it, and the worried mark between Teka's eyebrows. Her own face softened.

"You can't not eat," Teka said.

"I hadn't thought about it," Aerin replied, realizing this was true.

"You shouldn't sulk," Teka then said, "and forget about eating." She looked sharply at her young charge, and the worried mark deepened.

"Sulking," said Aerin stiffly.

Teka sighed. "Hiding. Brooding. Whatever you like. It's not good for you."

"Or for you," Aerin suggested.

A smile touched the corners of the worry. "Or for me."

"I will try to sulk less if you will try to worry less."

Teka set the tray down on a table and began lifting napkins off of plates. "Talat missed you today."

"He told you so, of course." Teka's fear of anything larger than the smallest pony, and therefore the fact that she gave a

12

very wide berth to the stables and pastures beyond them, was well known to Aerin. "I'll go down after dark." She turned back to the window. There were more comings and goings across the stretch of courtyard that her bedroom overlooked; she saw more messengers, and two men racing by on foot in the uniform of the king's army, with the red divisional slash on their left forearms which meant they were members of the supply corps. Equipping the king's company for its march west was proceeding at a pace presently headlong and increasing toward panicky. Under normal circumstances Aerin saw no one from her bedroom window but the occasional idling courtier.

Something on the tray rattled abruptly, and there was a sigh. "Aerin—"

"Whatever you're going to say I've thought of already," Aerin said without turning around.

Silence. Aerin finally looked round at Teka, standing with head and shoulders bowed, staring at the tray. The plates were heavy earthenware, handsome and elegant, but easily replaced if Aerin managed to break one, as she often did; and she had not the small Gift to mend them. She stared at the plates. Tor had mended her breakages when she was a baby, but she was too proud to ask now she was far past the age when she should have been able to fit the bits together, glower at them with the curious royal Gifted look, and have them grow whole again. It did not now help her peace of mind or her temper either that she had been an unusually large and awkward child who seemed able to break things simply by being in the same room with them; as if fate, having denied her something that should have been her birthright, wanted her never to forget it. Aerin was not a particularly clumsy young woman, but she was by now so convinced of her lack of coordination that she still broke things occasionally out of sheer dread.

Teka had silently exchanged the finer royal plates for these earthenware ones several years ago, after Galanna had found out that the red-and-gold ones that should only be used by members of the first circle of the royal house—which included Aerin—were slowly disappearing. She had one of her notorious temper tantrums over this, caused crisis and dismay in the whole hierarchy of the hafor, and turned off three of the newest and lowliest servant girls on suspicion of stealing—and then, when no one could possibly overlook the commotion she was making, contrived to discover that the disappearances were merely the result of Aerin being clumsy. "You revolting child," she said to a mutinous Aerin; "even if you are *incapable*"—there was inexpressible malice lurking behind the word—"of mending the settings yourself, you might save the pieces and let one of *us* do it for you."

"I'd hang myself first," spat Aerin, "and then I'd come back and haunt you till you were haggard with fear and lost all your looks and people pointed at you in the streets—"

At this point Galanna slapped her, which was a tactical error. In the first place, it needed only such an excuse for Aerin to jump on her and roll her over on the floor, bruise one eye, and rip most of the lace off her extremely ornate afternoon dress—somehow both the court members and the hafor witness to this scene were a little slow in dragging Aerin off her —and in the second place, both the slap and its result quite ruined Galanna's attempted role of great lady dealing with contemptible urchin. It was generally considered—Galanna was no favorite—that Aerin had won that round. Of the three serving girls, one was taken back, one was given a job in the stables, which she much preferred, and one, declaring that she wouldn't have any more to do with the royal house if saying so got her beheaded for treason, went home to her own village, far from the City.

Aerin sighed. Life had been easier when her ultimate goal had been murdering Galanna with her bare hands. She had continued to use the finer ware when she ate with the court, of course; when she was younger she had rarely been compelled to do so, fortunately, since she never got much to eat, but sat rigidly and on her guard (Galanna's basilisk glare from farther down the high table helped) for the entire evening. But at least she didn't break anything either, and Teka could always be persuaded to bring her a late supper as necessary. On earthenware plates.

She lifted her eyes to Teka, who was still standing motionless behind the tray. "Teka, I'm sorry I'm so tiresome. I can't seem to help it. It's in my blood, like being clumsy is— like everything else isn't." She walked over and gave the older woman a hug, and Teka looked up and half smiled.

"I hate to see you . . . fighting everything so."

Aerin's eyes rose involuntarily to the old plain sword hanging at the head of her tall curtained bed.

"You know Perlith and Galanna are horrid because they're horrid themselves—"

"Yes," said Aerin slowly. "And because I'm the only daughter of the witchwoman who enspelled the king into marrying her, and I'm such a desperately easy butt. Teka," she said before the other had a chance to break in, "do you suppose it was Galanna who first told me that story? I've been trying to remember when I first heard it."

"Story?" said Teka, carefully neutral. She was always carefully neutral about Aerin's mother, which was one of the reasons Aerin kept asking about her.

"Yes. That my mother enspelled my father to get an heir that would rule Damar, and that she turned her face to the wall and died of despair when she found she had borne a daughter instead of a son, since they usually find a way to avoid letting daughters inherit."

Teka shook her head impatiently.

"She did die," Aerin said.

"Women die in childbed."

"Not witches, often."

"She was not a witch."

Aerin sighed, and looked at her big hands, striped with callus and scarred with old blisters from sword and shield and pulling her way through the forest tangles after her dragons— *Dragon-Killer*—and from falling off the faithful Talat. "You would certainly think she wasn't from the way her daughter goes on. If he was going to turn out like me, it wouldn't have done my poor mother any good to have had a son." She paused, brooding over her last burn scar, where a dragon had licked her and the ointment hadn't gone on quite evenly. "What was my mother like?"

Teka looked thoughtful. She too looked toward Aerin's sword and dragon spears, but Aerin was pretty sure she did not see them, for Teka did not approve of her first sol's avocation. "She was much like you but smaller—frail almost." Her shoulders lifted. "Too frail to bear a child. And yet it was rather as though something was eating her from the inside; there was a fire behind that pale skin, always burning. I think she knew she had only a little time and she was fighting for enough time to bear her baby."

Teka's eyes refocused on the room, and she looked hastily away from the dragon spears. "You were a fine strong child from the first."

"Do *you* think she enspelled my father?"

Teka looked at her, frowning. "Why do you ask so silly a question?"

"I like to hear you tell stories."

Teka laughed involuntarily. "Well. No, I don't think she enspelled your father—not the way Galanna and her lot mean, anyway. She fell in love with him, and he with her; that's a spell if you like."

They had had this conversation before; many times since Aerin was old enough to talk and ask questions. But over the years Teka sometimes let fall one more phrase, one more adjective, as Aerin asked the same questions, and so Aerin kept on asking. That there was a mystery she had no doubt. Her father wouldn't discuss her mother with her at all, beyond telling her that he still missed her, which Aerin did find reassuring as far as it went. But whether the truth behind the mystery was known to everyone but her and was too terrible to speak of, particularly to the mystery's daughter, or whether it was a mystery that no one knew and therefore everyone blamed her for endlessly reminding them of, she had never been able to make up her mind. On the whole she inclined to the latter; she couldn't imagine anything so awful that Galanna would recoil from using it against her. And if there were something quite that awful, then Perlith wouldn't be able to resist ceasing to ignore her long enough to explain it.

Teka had turned back to the tray and poured a cup of hot malak, and handed it to Aerin, who settled down cross-legged on her bed, the hanging scabbard just brushing the back of her neck.

"I brought mik-bars too, for Talat, so you need not go to the kitchens if you don't wish to."

Aerin laughed. "You know me too well. After sulking, I sneak off to the stables after dark—preferably after bedtime—and talk to my horse."

Teka smiled and sat down on the red-and-blue embroidered cushion (her embroidery, not Aerin's) on the chair by Aerin's bed. "I have had much of the raising of you, these long years."

"Very long years," agreed Aerin, reaching for a leg of turpi. "Tell me about my mother."

Teka considered. "She came walking into the City one day. She apparently owned nothing but the long pale gown she wore; but she was kind, and good with animals, and people liked her."

"Until the king married her."

Teka picked up a slab of dark bread and broke it in half. "Some of them liked her even then."

"Did you?"

"King Arlbeth would never have chosen me to nurse her daughter else."

"Am I so like her as folk say?"

Teka stared at her, but Aerin felt it was her mother Teka looked at. "You are much like what your mother might have been had she been well and strong and without hurt. She was no beauty, but she . . . caught the eye. You do too."

Tor's eye, thought Aerin, for which Galanna hates me even more enthusiastically than she would anyway. She is too stupid to recognize the difference between that sort of love and the love of a friend who depends on the particular friendship—or a farmer's son's love for his pet chicken. I wonder if Perlith hates me because his wife hoped to marry Tor, or merely for small scuttling reasons of his own. "That's just the silly orange hair."

"Not orange. Flame-colored."

"Fire is orange."

"You are hopeless."

Aerin grinned in spite of a large mouthful of bread. "Yes. And besides, it is better to be hopeless, because—" The grin died.

Teka said anxiously: "My dear, you can't have believed your father would let you ride in the army. Few women do so—"

"And they all have husbands, and go only by special dispensation from the king, and only if they can dance as well as they can ride. And none at all has ridden at the king's side since Aerinha, goddess of honor and of flame, first taught *men* to forge their blades," Aerin said fiercely. "You'd think Aerinha would have had better sense. If we were still using slingshots and magic songs, I suppose we'd still all be riding with them.

They needed the women's voices for the songs to work—"

"That's only a pretty legend," said Teka firmly. "If the singing worked, we'd still be using it."

"Why? Maybe it got lost with the Crown. They might at least have named me Cupka or Marli or—or Galanna or something. Something to give me fair warning."

"They named you for your mother."

"Then she has to have been Damarian," Aerin said. This was also an old argument. "Aerinha was Damarian."

"Aerinha is Damarian," said Teka, "and Aerinha is a goddess. No one knows where she first came from."

There was a silence. Aerin stopped chewing. Then she remembered she was eating, swallowed, and took another bite of bread and turpi. "No, I don't suppose I ever thought the king would let his only, and she somewhat substandard, daughter ride into possible battle, even though sword-handling is about the only thing she's ever gotten remotely good at—her dancing is definitely not satisfactory." She grunted. "Tor's a good teacher. He taught me as patiently as if it were normal for a king's child to have to learn every sword stroke by rote, to have to practice every maneuver till the muscles themselves know it, for there is nothing that wakes in this king's child's blood to direct it." Aerin looked, hot-eyed, at Teka, remembering again Perlith's words as he left the hall last night. "Teka, dragons aren't that easy to kill."

"I would not want to have to kill one," Teka said sincerely. Teka, maid and nurse, maker of possets and sewer of patches, scolder and comforter and friend, who saw nothing handsome in a well-balanced sword and who always wore long full skirts and aprons.

Aerin burst out laughing. "No, I am not surprised."

Teka smiled comfortably.

Aerin ate several of the mik-bars herself before dusk fell and she could slip privately out of the castle by the narrow back staircase that no one else used, and into the largest of the royal barns where the horses of the first circle were kept. She liked to pretend that the ever observant men and women of the horse, the sofor, did not notice her every time she crept in at some odd hour to visit Talat. Anyone else of the royal blood could be sure of not being seen, had they wished to be unseen; Aerin could only tiptoe through the shadows, when there were shadows, and keep her voice down; and yet she knew she was simply recognized and permitted to pass. The sofor accepted that when she came thus quietly she wished to be left alone, and they respected her wishes; and Hornmar, the king's own groom, was her friend. All the sofor knew what she had done for Talat, so the fact that they were being kind by ignoring her hurt her less than similar adaptations to the first sol's deficiencies did elsewhere in the royal court.

Talat had been wondering what had become of her for almost two days, and she had to feed him the last three milk-bars before he forgave her; and then he snuffled her all over, partly to make sure she was not hiding anything else he might eat, partly to make sure she had in fact returned to him. He rubbed his cheek mournfully along her sleeve and rolled a reproachful eye.

Talat was nearly as old as she was; he had been her father's horse when she was small. She remembered the dark grey horse with the shining black dapples on his shoulders and flanks, and the hot dark eye. The king's trappings had looked particularly well on him: red reins and cheekpieces, a red skirt to the saddle, and a wide red breastplate with a gold leaf embroidered on it; the surka leaf, the king's emblem, for only one of the royal blood could touch the leaves of the surka plant and not die of its sap.

He was almost white now. All that remained of his youth were a few black hairs in his mane and tail, and the black tips of his ears.

"You have not been neglected; don't even try to make me think so. You are fed and watered and let out to roll in the dirt every day whether I come or not." She ran a hand down his back; one of Hornmar's minions had of course groomed him to a high gloss, but Talat liked to be fussed over, so she fetched brushes and groomed him again while he stretched his neck and made terrible faces of enjoyment. Aerin relaxed as she worked, and the memory of the scene in the hall faded, and the mood that had held for the last two days lightened and began to break up, like clouds before a wind.

❧CHAPTER 3❧

THE YOUNG AERIN had worshipped Talat, her father's fierce war-stallion, with his fine lofty head and high tail. She thought it very impressive that he would rear and strike at anyone but Hornmar or her father, rear with his ears flat back, so that his long wedge-shaped head looked like a striking snake's.

But when she was twelve years old her father had gone off to a Border battle: a little mob of Northerners had slipped across the mountains and set fire to a Damarian village. Something of the sort happened not infrequently, and in those days Arlbeth or his brother Thomar attended to such occurrences, riding out hopefully and in haste to chop up a few Northerners who had stayed to loot instead of scrambling back across the Border again at once. The Northerners knew Damarian reprisals were invariably swift, and yet always there were a few greedy ones who lingered. It was Arlbeth's turn this time; and there had been more Northerners than usual. Three men had been killed outright, and one horse; two men injured—and Talat.

Talat had been slashed across the right flank by a Northern sword, but he had carried Arlbeth safely through the battle till its end. Arlbeth was appalled when at last he was free to dismount and attend to it; there were muscles and tendons severed; the horse should have fallen when he took the blow. Arlbeth's first thought was to end it then; but he looked at his

20

favorite horse's face, with the lips curled back from the teeth and the white showing around the eye: Talat was daring his master to kill him, and his master couldn't do it. Arlbeth thought, If he is stubborn enough to walk home on three legs, I am stubborn enough to let him try.

Aerin had been one of the first to run out of the City and meet the returning company. They were slow coming home, for Talat had set the pace, and while Aerin knew that if anything had happened to her father a messenger would have been sent on ahead, still their slowness had worried her—and she felt an awful fear squeeze her belly when she first saw Talat, his head hanging nearly to his knees, put three legs slowly down one after the other, and hop for the fourth. She only then saw her father walking on the horse's far side.

Somehow Talat climbed the last hill to the castle, and crept into his own stall, and with a terrible sigh, lay slowly down in the straw there, the first time he had been off his feet since the sword struck him. "He's made it this far," said Aerin grimly, and sent for the healers; but when they came to corner Talat in his stall, he surged to his feet and threatened them, and when they tried to pour a narcotic down his throat, it took four of the hafor and a chain twisted around his jaw to hold him still.

They sewed the leg up, and it healed. But he was lame, and he would always be lame. They turned him out into a pasture of his own, green with chest-high grass, cool with trees, with a brook to drink from and a pond to soak in, mud at the edge of the pond for rolling, and a nice big dry shed for rain; and Hornmar brought him grain morning and evening, and talked to him.

But Talat only grew thin and began to lose his black dapples; his coat stared and he didn't eat his grain, and he turned his back on Hornmar, for Hornmar was taking care of Arlbeth's new war-horse now.

Arlbeth had hoped Talat might sire him foals; he would like nothing better than to ride Talat again. But Talat's bad leg was too weak; he could not mount the mares, and so he savaged them, and turned on his handlers when they tried to prevent him. Talat was sent back to his pasture in disgrace. Had he been any horse but the king's favorite, he would have been fed to the dogs.

It had been over two years since Arlbeth had led Talat home

from his last battle, and Aerin was fifteen when she ate some
leaves from the surka. While they had been trying to breed
Talat, Aerin had been turning corners that weren't there and
falling downstairs and being haunted by purple smoke billowing from scarlet caves.

It began with a confrontation with Galanna, as so much of
Aerin's worst trouble did. Galanna was the youngest of the
royal cousins, but for Aerin, and she had been about to turn
seven when Aerin was born. Galanna had become quite accustomed to being the baby of the family, petted and indulged;
and she was a very pretty child, and learned readily how best
to play up to those likeliest to spoil her. Tor was nearest her in
age, only four years her elder, but he was always trying to pretend that he was just as grown up as the next lot of cousins,
Perlith and Thurny and Greeth, who were six, seven, and ten
years older than he was. Tor was no threat. The next-youngest
girl cousin was fifteen years older than Galanna, and she, poor
Katah, was plain. (She was also, very shortly after Aerin's
birth, married off to one of the provincial barons, where,
much to Galanna's disgust, she thrived and became famous
for settling a land dispute in her husband's family that had
been the cause of a blood feud for generations.)

Galanna was not at all pleased by Aerin's birth; not only
was Aerin a first sol, which Galanna would never be unless
she managed to marry Tor, but her mother died bearing her,
which made Aerin altogether too interesting a figure within
the same household that Galanna wished to continue to re-
volve around herself.

Aerin was by nature the sort of child who got into trouble
first and thought about it later if at all, and Galanna, in her
way, was quite clever. Galanna it was who dared her to eat a
leaf of the surka; she dared her by saying that Aerin would be
afraid to touch the royal plant, because she was not really of
royal blood: she was a throwback to her mother's witch breed,
and Arlbeth was her father in name only. If she touched the
surka, she would die.

At fifteen Aerin should already have shown signs of her
royal blood's Gift; usually the Gift began to make its presence
known—most often in poltergeist fits—years younger. Galanna had contrived to disguise her loathing for her littlest
cousin for several years after her temper tantrums upon
Aerin's birth had not been a complete success; but lately it had

occurred to an older Galanna that if Aerin really was a throwback, a sport, as she began to appear truly to be, Galanna had excellent reason to scorn and dislike her: her existence was a disgrace to the royal honor.

They made a pair, facing off, standing alone in the royal garden, glaring at each other. Galanna had come to her full growth and beauty by that time: her blue-black hair hung past her hips in heavy waves, and was artfully held in place by a golden webwork of fine thread strung with pearls; her cheeks were flushed becomingly with rage till they were as red as her lips, and her huge black eyes were opened their widest. Her long eyelashes had almost grown back since the night Aerin had drugged her supper wine and crept into her bedroom later and cut them off. Everyone had known at once who had done it, and Aerin, who in general held lying in contempt, had not bothered to deny it. She had said before the gathered court—for Galanna, as usual, had insisted on a public prosecution—that Galanna should have been grateful she hadn't shaved her head for her; she'd been snoring like a pig and wouldn't have wakened if she'd been thrown out her bedroom window. Whereupon Galanna had gone off in a fit of strong hysterics and had to be carried from the hall (she'd been wearing a half-veil that covered her face to her lips, that no one might see her ravaged features), and Aerin had been banished to her private rooms for a fortnight.

Aerin was as tall as Galanna already, for Galanna was small and round and compact, and Aerin was gangly and awkward; and Aerin's pale skin came out in splotches when she was angry, and her fiercely curly hair—which when wet from the bath was actually longer than Galanna's—curled all the more fiercely in the heat of her temper, and for all the pins that attempted to keep it under control. They were alone in the garden; and whatever happened Galanna had no fear that Aerin would ever tale-bear (which was another excellent reason for Galanna to despise her), so when Aerin spun around, pulled half a branch off the surka, and stuffed most of it into her mouth, Galanna only smiled. Her full lips curved most charmingly when she smiled, and it brought her high cheekbones into delicate prominence.

Aerin gagged, gasped, turned a series of peculiar colors which ended with grey, and fell heavily to the ground. Galanna noticed that she was still breathing, and therefore waited a few minutes while Aerin twitched and shook, and then went composedly to find help. Her story was that she had gone for a walk in the garden and found Aerin there. This, so far as it went, was true; but she had been planning to find Aerin alone in the garden for some time, that she might say certain things to her. She had thought of those certain things while she had been keeping to her rooms while her eyelashes grew out again.

Aerin was sick for weeks. Her mouthful had given her mad hallucinations of men with translucent blue skin and six-legged riding beasts, and of a pale face terribly like her own with a dull grey band wound about its temples, bending down at her through clouds of smoke, and of a cave with five walls that glittered as though it were walled with rubies. The worst of these then began to wear off, and she could again see the walls of her own room around her, and Teka's face bending over her, half angry and half frightened; but she still had dizzy spells and stomachaches, and these lasted a very long time. She knew this was not how it should be for a king's daughter, just as Galanna had said; and a depression she would not admit further slowed her recovery.

"You idiot!" Tor yelled at her. "You bonehead, you mud-brain, you oozog, you stzik! How could you do such a thing?" He tried to remind her of the stories of the surka; he said did she remember by chance that the stuff was dangerous even to those of the royal house? True, it did not kill them; true, a leaf of it bestowed superhuman strength and the far-seeing eyes of a bird of prey to one of royal blood, or, if the Gift were strong enough, true visions; although this last was very rare. But when the effect wore off, in several hours or several days, the aftereffects were at best mortal exhaustion and blurred sight—sometimes permanent. Had she forgotten the tale of King Merth the Second, who kept himself on the battlefield for a fortnight, never resting, by the virtue of the surka, pausing only to chew its leaves at need? He won the battle, but he died even as he proclaimed his victory. He looked, when they buried him, like an old, old man, though he was only a year past twenty.

"You must have eaten half the tree, from the size of the scar of the branch you took off. Enough for two or three Merths. Are you really trying to kill yourself?" Here his voice almost broke, and he had to get up and stamp around the room, and kick over a handy chair, which he then picked up again so that

Teka wouldn't notice and ban him from the sickroom. He sat on the edge of Aerin's bed and brooded. "It must have been Galanna. It always is Galanna. What did she do this time?"

Aerin stirred. "Of course it's Galanna. I've been desperate to think of an excuse to get out of attending her wedding. It's only a little over a season away, you know. This was the best that occurred to me."

Tor laughed—grudgingly, but it was a laugh. "Almost I forgive you." He reached out and grabbed one of her hands. She refrained from telling him that his bouncing on the edge of her bed was making her feel sick, and that every time he moved she had to refocus her eyes on him and that made her feel more sick, and she squeezed his hand. "I guess she dared you to eat a leaf. I guess she told you you weren't royal and wouldn't dare touch it." He looked at her sternly. She looked back, her face blank. He knew her too well, and he knew she knew, but she wouldn't say anything; he knew that too, and he sighed.

Her father visited her occasionally, but he always sent warning ahead, and as soon as she could creak out of bed without immediately falling down in a heap, she began receiving him in her sitting-room, bolt upright in a straight chair and hands crossed in her lap. To his queries she answered that she was feeling quite well now, thank you. She had learned that no one could tell how badly her vision wandered in and out of focus, so long as she kept still where the dizziness couldn't distract her; and she kept her eyes fixed on the shifting flesh-colored shadows where she knew her father's face was. He never stayed long, and since she closed her eyes when he came near to stoop over her and kiss her cheek or forehead (other people's movements were almost as dizzying as her own) she never saw the anxious look on his face, and he didn't shout at her, like Teka or Tor.

When she was enough better to totter out of bed for a longer stretch than into a chair in her sitting-room, or rather when she hated her bed so thoroughly that Teka could no longer keep her in it, she had to make her way around the castle by feeling along the walls, for neither her eyes nor her feet were trustworthy. Creeping about like one of her father's retired veterans escaped from the grace-and-favor apartments in the rear of the castle did nothing for her morale, and she avoided everyone but Teka, and to some extent Tor, even more single-mindedly than usual; and she stayed out of the court's way altogether.

Especially she avoided the garden at the center of the castle. The surka stood by the main gate, wrapped around one of the tall white pillars. Its presence was symbolic only; anyone might pass the gate without danger of touching its leaves, and there were several other ways into the garden. But she felt that the surka exhaled hallucinations into the very air around it, waiting gleefully for her to breathe them in, and that it clattered its leaves at her if she came too near. She heard it mocking her if she even dared step out on one of the balconies that overlooked the garden from three or four stories up. Her protracted illness more nearly proved Galanna's contention about her heritage than her own, whatever Tor said, but she saw no reason to remind herself of it any oftener than she had to.

It was a kind of trapped restlessness combined with a feeling of kinship for the equally trapped and restless Talat that drew her to his pasture. She had visited him before, or tried to, in the last three years, but he was no politer to her than he was to Hornmar, and it hurt her so much just to look at him that out of cowardice she had stopped going. Now she felt she no longer cared; she couldn't see clearly two feet beyond the end of her nose anyway. But it was a somewhat laborious process to carry out even so simple a plan as to walk to one of the smaller pastures beyond the royal barns. First she wanted a cane, that she might have something to tap her way with; so she persuaded Tor to open the door of the king's treasure house for her, which required a lock-relaxing charm she couldn't perform any more than she could mend plates.

She told Tor only that she wanted to borrow a walking stick to help her up and down stairs. Tor knew perfectly well that she had something further on her mind, but he did it anyway. She chose a cane with a pleasantly lumpy head, since her sense of touch was sometimes a little vague too.

Talat's first impulse had been to charge her. She'd not moved, just looked at him, leaning on her cane and swaying gently. "If I try to run away from you, the earth will leap up and throw me down." Two tears rolled silently down her cheeks. "I can't even walk properly. Like you." Talat dropped his head and began grazing—without much interest, but it gave him something to pretend to be doing while he kept an eye on her.

She went back the next day, and the next. The exercise, or the fresh air, or both, seemed to do her some good; her vision began to clear a bit. And it was quiet and peaceful in Talat's pasture, where no one came, and she went back to the swarming castle more and more reluctantly. Then the thought of the royal library occurred to her. Galanna would never set foot in the library.

She went there the first time only to escape her own rooms, which had begun to seem the size of shoeboxes, and for some of the same imprecise restlessness that had inspired her to visit Talat. But, idly, she ran her fingers over the spines of the books lined up on the shelves, and pulled down one that had an interestingly tooled binding. More idly still she opened it, and found that her poor muddled eyes focused quite nicely on a printed page held not too far from her nose—found that she could read. The next day she took it with her to Talat's pasture.

He didn't exactly meet her with an eager whinny of greeting, but he did seem to spend most of his time on the unmuddy shore of the pool, where she leaned against the bole of a convenient tree and read. "It's funny," she said, chewing a grass stem, "you'd think if I couldn't walk I couldn't read either. You'd think eyes would be at least as hard to organize as feet." She leaned over, and laid a mik-bar down on the ground as far away from her as she could reach, and sat up again, looking only straight before her. Thoughtfully she hefted the big book in her lap and added, "Even carrying it around is useful. It sort of weighs me down, and I don't stagger so much." She could hear his hoofbeats: thunk-thunk-thunk-drag. "Maybe what I need for my feet is the equivalent of the muscular concentration of reading." The hoofbeats paused. "Now if only someone could tell me what that might be."

The mik-bar had disappeared.

❧ CHAPTER 4 ❧

TEKA FOUND HER OUT very soon; she'd been keeping a very sharp eye on her wayward sol since she first crawled out of bed after the surka episode. She'd been appalled when she first discovered Aerin under the tree in the vicious stallion's paddock; but she had a bit more sense than Aerin gave her credit for ("Fuss, fuss, fuss, Teka! Leave me *alone*!") and with her heart beating in her mouth she realized that Talat knew that his domain had been invaded and didn't mind. She saw him eat his first mik-bar, and when they thereafter began disappearing at an unseemingly rate from the bowl on Aerin's windowseat, Teka only sighed deeply and began providing them in greater quantity.

The book with the interesting binding was a history of Damar. Aerin had had to learn a certain amount of history as part of her royal education, but this stuff was something else again. The lessons she'd been forced to learn were dry spare things, the facts without the sense of them, given in the simplest of language, as if words might disguise the truth or (worse) bring it to life. Education was one of Arlbeth's pet obsessions; before him there hadn't been a king in generations who felt much desire for book learning, and there was no precedent for quality in royal tutors.

The book was faded with age, and the style of lettering was strange to her, so she had to puzzle out some of the words; and some of the words were archaic and unfamiliar, so she had to puzzle out the meanings. But it was worth it, for this book told her stories more exciting than the ones she made up for herself before she fell asleep at night. And so, as she read, she first learned of the old dragons.

Damar had dragons still; little ones, dog-sized, nasty, mean-tempered creatures who would fry a baby for supper and swallow it in two gulps if they could; but they had been beaten back into the heavy forest and the wilder Hills by Aerin's day. They still killed an occasional unwary hunter, for they had no fear, and they had teeth and claws as well as fire to subdue their prey, but they were no longer a serious threat. Arlbeth heard occasionally of one—or of a family, for they most often hunted in families—that was harassing a village or an outlying farm, and when that happened a party of men with spears and arrows—swords were of little use, for if one were close enough to use a sword, one was close enough to be badly burned—went out from the City to deal with them. Always they came back with a few more unpleasant stories of the cunning treachery of dragons; always they came back nursing a few scorched limbs; occasionally they came back a horse or a hound the less.

But there was no glamour in dragon-hunting. It was hard, tricky, grim work, and dragons were vermin. The folk of the hunt, the thotar, who ran the king's dogs and provided meat for the royal household, would have nothing to do with dragons, and dogs once used for dragons were considered worthless for anything else.

There were still the old myths of the great dragons, huge scaled beasts many times larger than horses; and it was sometimes even said that the great dragons flew, flew in the air, with wingspreads so vast as to blacken the sun. The little dragons had vestigial wings, but no one had ever seen or heard of a dragon that could lift its thick squat body off the ground with them. They beat their wings in anger and in courtship, as they raised their crests; but that was all. The old dragons were no more nor less of a tale than that of flying dragons.

But this book took the old dragons seriously. It said that while the only dragons humankind had seen in many years were little ones, there were still one or two of the great ones hiding in the Hills; and that one day the one or two would fly out of their secret places and wreak havoc on man, for man

would have forgotten how to deal with them. The great
dragons lived long; they could afford to wait for that forget-
fulness. From the author's defensive tone, the great dragons
even in his day were a legend, a tale to tell on festival days,
well lubricated with mead and wine. But she was fascinated, as
he had been.

"It is with the utmost care I have gathered my information;
and I think I may say with truth that the ancient Great Ones
and our day's small, scurrilous beasts are the same in type.
Thus anyone wishing to learn the skill to defeat a Great One
can do no better than to harry as many small ones as he may
find from their noisome dens, and see how they do give
battle."

He went on to describe his information-gathering tech-
niques, which seemed to consist of tirelessly footnoting the
old stories for dragonish means and methods; although,
thought Aerin, that could as well be from the oral tale-tellers
adapting the ancient dragons to the ways of the present ones as
from the truth of the author's theory. But she read on.

Dragons had short stubby legs on broad bodies; they were
not swift runners over distance, but they were exceedingly
nimble, and could balance easily on any one foot the better to
rip with any of the other three, as well as with the barbed tail.
The neck was long and whippy, so that the dragon might spray
its fire at any point of the circle; and they often scraped their
wings against the ground to throw up dust and further con-
found their enemies, or their prey.

"It is customary today to hunt the dragon with arrow and
thrown spear; but if one of the Great Ones comes again, this
will avail his attacker little. As their size has diminished, so
has their armament; a well-thrown spear may pierce a small
dragon anywhere it strikes. The Great Ones had only two vul-
nerable spots that might be depended upon: at the base of the
jaw, where the narrow head joins the long neck; and behind
the elbow, from whence the wings spring. Dragons are, as I
have said, nimble; it is most unlikely that a Great One would
be so foolish as to lower its head or its wings to make an easy
mark. A great hero only may slay a Great One; one who by
skill and courage may draw close enough to force the fatal
blow.

"It is fortunate for all who walk the earth that the Great
Ones bred but rarely; and that mankind has borne enough

heroes to vanquish the most of them. But it is this writer's most fervid belief that at least one more hero must stand forth from his people to face the last of the Great Ones.

"Of this last—I have said one or two; perhaps there are three or four; I know not. But of one I will make specific remark: Gorthold, who slew Crendenor and Razimtheth, went also against Maur, the Black Dragon, and it he did not slay. Gorthold, who was himself wounded unto death, said with his last strength that the dragon would die of its wounds as he would die of his; but this was never known for a certainty. The only certainty is that Maur disappeared; and has been seen by no man—or none that has brought back the tale to tell—from that day to this."

In the back of the book Aerin found an even older manuscript: just a few pages, nearly illegible with age, sewn painstakingly into the binding. Those final ancient pages were a recipe, for an ointment called kenet. An ointment that was proof against dragonfire—it said.

It had a number of very peculiar ingredients; herbs, she thought, by the sound of them. She knew just enough of the Old Tongue to recognize a few syllables; there was one that translated as "red-root." She frowned; there was a thing called redroot that showed up in boring pastoral poems, but she'd always thought it belonged to that classic category known as imaginary, like nymphs and elephants. Teka might know about redroot; she brewed a uniquely ghastly tea or tisane for every ailment, and when Aerin asked what was in the awful stuff, Teka invariably rattled off a list of things that Aerin had never heard of. She had been inclined to assume that Teka was simply putting her off with nonsense, but maybe not.

An ointment against dragonfire. If it worked—one person, alone, could tackle a dragon safely; not a Great One, of course, but the Black Dragon probably did die of its wounds . . . but the little ones that were such a nuisance. At present the system was that you attacked with arrows and things from a distance, with enough of you to make a ring around it, or them, so if they bolted at someone he could run like mad while the other side of the ring was filling them full of arrows. They couldn't run far, and usually a family all bolted in the same direction. It was when they didn't that horses died.

Aerin had been sitting under the convenient tree by Talat's

pond most afternoons for several weeks when she found the
recipe for dragon salve. It made her thoughtful, and she was
accustomed to pacing while she thought. The surka was slowly
losing its grip on her, and while she couldn't exactly pace, she
could amble slowly without her cane. She ambled around
Talat's pool.

Talat followed her. When she stopped, or grabbed a tree
limb for balance, he moved a step or two away and dropped
his nose to the ground and lipped at whatever he found there.
When she moved on, he picked up his head and drifted after
her. On the third afternoon since finding the recipe she was
still pacing, not only because she was a slow thinker, but
because her four-legged shadow with the dragging hind foot
intrigued her. It was on the third day that when she put her
hand out to steady herself against the air, a horse's neck in-
sinuated itself under her outstretched fingers. She let her hand
lie delicately on his crest, her eyes straight ahead, ignoring
him; but when she took another step forward, so did he.

Two days later she brought a currycomb and some brushes
to Talat's meadow; they belonged to Kisha, her pony, but
Kisha wouldn't miss them. Kisha was the ideal young sol's
mount: fine-boned and delicate and prettier than a kitten. She
was also as vain as Galanna, and loved nothing better than a
royal procession, when the horses of the first circle would be
all decked out in gilt and tassels. The sols' horses further
would have ribbons braided into their manes and tails, and
Kisha had a particularly long silky tail. (She would doubtless
be cross at missing the mounted salute at Galanna and Perlith's wedding.) She never shied at waving banners and flap-
ping velvet saddle skirts; but if Aerin tried to ride her out in
the countryside, she shied sulkily at every leaf, and kept trying
to turn and bolt for home. They thoroughly detested each
other. Galanna rode her full sister, Rooka. Aerin was convinced that Rooka and Kisha gossiped together in the stable at
night about their respective mistresses.

Kisha had dozens of brushes. Aerin rolled up a few in a bit
of leather and hid them in an elbow of her reading tree by the
pond.

Talat was still too much on his dignity to admit how thoroughly he enjoyed being groomed; but his ears had a tendency
to lop over, his eyes to glaze and half shut, and his lips to
twitch, when Aerin rubbed the brushes over him. White hairs

flew in a blizzard, for Talat had gone white in the years since he was lamed.

"Hornmar," she said, several days later, trying to sound indifferent, "do you suppose Talat's leg really hurts him any more?"

Hornmar was polishing Kethtaz, Arlbeth's young bay stallion, with a bit of soft cloth. There wasn't a dust mote on the horse's hide anywhere. Aerin looked at him with dislike: he was fit and shining and merry and useful, and she loved Talat. Hornmar looked at Arlbeth's daughter thoughtfully. All of the sofor knew by now of the private friendship between her and the crippled stallion. He was glad for Talat and for Aerin both, for he knew more than she would have wished about what her life was like. He was also, deep down, a tiny bit envious; Kethtaz was a magnificent horse, but Talat had been a better. And Talat now turned away from his old friend with flattened ears.

"I imagine not much any more. But he's gotten into the habit of favoring that leg, and the muscles are soft, and stiff too, from the scarring," he said in a neutral voice. He buffed a few more inches of Kethtaz's flank. "Talat is looking good, this season." He glanced at Aerin and saw the blood rising in her face, and turned away again.

"Yes, he's getting fat," she said.

Kethtaz sighed and flicked his tail; Hornmar had tied it up so it wouldn't slap him in the face. He worked his way round the stallion's quarters and started the other side; Aerin was still leaning against the stable wall, watching. "Talat might come back a little more," Hornmar said at last, cautiously. "He'd never be up, say, to a man's weight again, though."

"Oh," said Aerin, still indifferent. Kethtaz had a black dapple on one shoulder; she rubbed it with a finger, and he turned his head around and poked her with his nose. She petted him for a moment, and then she quietly slipped away.

The next day she rode her crippled stallion. She brushed him first, and when she was done, she dropped the grooming things together in a pile. She ran a finger along one wide cheek; Talat, nothing loath for a little more attention, rested his nose against her stomach so she could stroke the other cheek with the other hand. After a moment she worked down his left side, and placed her hands on his withers and loins, and leaned on them. He was smaller than most of the royal war-horses, but still too tall for her to put much of her weight into her hands. He flicked his ears at her. "Well," she said. She rested one hand on his shoulder and he followed her to a rock she had picked out for the purpose some days before. She stepped up on it, and he stood quietly as she slowly eased one leg over his back.

She was sitting on him. Nothing happened. Well, she said to herself crossly, what was supposed to happen? He was broken to saddle while I was still learning to walk. The first time.

Talat cocked his ears back toward her, his head bowed as if he felt the bit in his mouth again. She nudged him with her legs, and he walked away from the mounting stone: thunk-thunk-thunk-drag. He was bigger than she expected, and her legs ached spanning a war-stallion's broad back. For all that Talat had done nothing but stand in a field for over two years, the shoulders under her hands were hard with muscle.

She rode him every day after that. At first it was once around his field, starting and stopping at the mounting stone; then it was two and three times: thunk-thunk-thunk-drag, thunk-thunk-thunk-drag. He walked when she squeezed with her legs, and went right or left when she bumped him with the outside knee; and after a few tries he realized she meant him to stop when she dug her hipbones into his back. She ran her hands over the bad leg every day after she dismounted: there was no heat, no swelling, no tenderness. One day she banged the long ugly scar with her closed fist, said, "Very well, it really doesn't hurt, I hope," got back on him again and wrapped her legs around him till, his ears flicking surprise at her, he broke into a shuffling trot. He limped six steps and she let him stop. Tears pricked at her eyes, and she fed him mik-bars silently, and left early that day.

Nonetheless she returned the next afternoon, though she looked glum, and tried to pick up her book after she'd done grooming him. But he went so expectantly to the mounting stone and stood watching her that she sighed, and climbed on him again, and sent him forward with her legs. But he broke at once into the shuffling trot, and at the end of the six steps he did not stumble to a halt, but strode out a little more boldly; a quarter of the way around the field, halfway—Aerin sat into him and he obediently subsided into a walk, but his ears spoke to her: You see? It was that day that a small but terrible hope first bloomed in Aerin's heart.

❧ CHAPTER 5 ❧

AERIN WAS GOING to have to take part in Galanna's wedding after all. The surka was indisputably wearing off—"It's lasted this long, why couldn't it have hung on just a little longer?" Aerin said irritably to Tor.

"It tried, I'm sure," said Tor. "It just wasn't expecting Galanna."

Galanna had contrived to have the great event put off an extra half-year because, she said coyly, she wanted everything to be perfect, and in the time remaining it was not possible to drag a sufficient number of things up to meet that standard. Meanwhile Aerin had resignedly begun to take her old place in her father's court; her presence was not a very necessary one, but her continued absence was noted, and the surka hadn't killed her after all. "I wonder if I could at least convince her that I'm too woozy to carry a rod and a veil or throw flowers and sing. I could maybe get away with just standing with my father and looking pale and invalid. Probably. She can't possibly want me around any more than I want to be around."

"She should have thought more exactingly of the timing involved when she goaded you into eating the surka in the first place."

Aerin laughed.

Tor said ruefully, "I almost wish I'd had the forethought to eat a tree myself."

Perlith had asked Tor to stand behind him at the ceremony. The first companion was supposed to hold a sola's badge of rank during his wedding; but in this particular case there were some interesting politics going on. Perlith was required by tradition to ask the king and the first sola to stand by him for the ceremony, and the king and the first sola by tradition were required to accept the invitation. The first companion's place was, as attendants go, the most important, but it was also the most attentive; the slang for the first companion's position was rude, and referred to the companion's location near his sola's backside. Asking Tor to stand first companion was a token of Perlith's unrivaled esteem for his first sola, as the first companion's place should go to Perlith's dearest friend. It would also be Perlith's only chance ever to have the first sola waiting on him.

"You should drop the badge with a clatter just as the chant gets to the bit about family loyalty and the unending bliss of being a member of a family. Ugh," said Aerin.

"Don't tempt me," Tor said.

Fortunately Galanna did not have her future husband's sense of humor, and she was glad to excuse Aerin from participation on the grounds of the continuing unreliability of the first sol's health. Galanna was incapable of plotting much of anything over a year in advance, and the surka incident had had nothing to do with the predictable approach of her wedding day. It had had to do with the loss of her eyelashes just when she knew Perlith had decided to offer for her—which offer had then had to be put off till they were long enough again for her to look up at him through them. (She had actually been weak enough to wonder if Aerin was Gifted after all, her timing in this case being no less than diabolical.) But it had occurred to her lately that it would be a boon to find a way to keep Aerin out of the ceremony itself, without giving visible public offense (and since the surka hadn't killed her off, which, to give Galanna what little credit she deserves, she had not been attempting). Galanna understood as well as Perlith did why Tor had been asked, and would stand as first companion; but Tor was reliable, for all his disgusting sympathy for his youngest cousin. He believed in his first sola's place as Aerin had no reason to believe in her place as first sol; and Aerin, if dragooned into performing some ceremonial role, would by fair means or foul mess things up. Nothing was going to spoil Galanna's wedding day. She and Aerin understood each other very well when Aerin, formal and smiling, offered her apologies and regrets, and Galanna, formal and smiling, accepted them.

Galanna and Perlith's wedding was the first great state event since the celebration of Tor's coming to manhood, and thus his taking his full place at his uncle's right hand, less than two years after his own father died. Aerin had been a part of that ceremony, and she had been determined to perform her role with both dignity and accuracy, that Tor would not be embarrassed in front of all the people who had told him not to ask her to be in it. The result was that she remembered very little of the day-long rites. She did remember frantically running her responses through her mind (which she had so firmly committed to memory that she remembered them all her life). When the priests finished naming the three hundred and ten sovereigns before Arlbeth (not that all of them had ruled quite the same country, but the sonorous recitation of all the then-who-came-afters had an impressive ring to it), she had to rename the last seven of them, seven being the perfect number because of the Seven Perfect Gods, and name their Honored Wives or queens (there hadn't been a ruling queen in a very long time) and any full brothers or sisters. The finish was: And then who came after was Tor, son of Thomar, own brother to Arlbeth; Tor came next. And she had to not squeak, and she had to not squeak three times, for they went through it all once at dawn, once at midday, and once at sunset. She also had to hold his swordbelt, and by the evening she had blisters across both palms from gripping it too hard. But she had done everything right.

Tor had been busier since then, often away from the City, showing himself to the Hillfolk who came rarely or never to the City, that they might one and all know the face and voice of the man who would be their king someday; and it had also been soon after Tor's coming of age that Aerin had eaten the surka. While it lay heavily on her she had not wished to see much of him even when he was at home, though he had come often to sit by her when she was too sick to protest and even, without her knowledge, put off one or two trips that he might stay near her. But as she got enough better to be surly about not being well, and as his absences of necessity increased, a barrier began to grow up between them, and they were no

longer quite the friends they had once been. She missed him,
for she had been accustomed to talking to him nearly every
day, but she never said she missed him, and she told herself
that it was as well, since the surka had proved Galanna three-
quarters right about her, that the first sola not contaminate
himself with her company too often. When she did see him,
she was painstakingly bright and offhand.

A few days after Talat had trotted halfway round his
pasture with Aerin on his back, she asked Hornmar what had
become of Talat's tack. She knew that each of the court horses
had its own, and Kethtaz would never be insulted by wearing
bits of his predecessor's gear; but she was afraid that Talat's
might have been destroyed when his leg had doomed him.
Hornmar, who had seen Talat jogging around his field with
Aerin at attention on his back, brought out saddle and girth
and bridle, for while he had thought they would never be used
again, he had not had the heart to get rid of them. If Aerin
noticed that they appeared to have been freshly cleaned and
oiled, she said nothing but "Thank you." The same day that
she carried Talat's gear up to her room and hid it in her wardrobe (where Teka, finding it later, also found that it had left oil
spots on Aerin's best court dress), she saw from her window
Tor riding in from one of his rounds of political visits; and she
decided it was time to waylay him.

"Aerin," he said, and hugged her gladly. "I have not seen
you in weeks. Have you your dress made yet for the wedding
of the century? Who won, you or Teka?"

She pulled a face. "Teka has won more ground than I, but I
refused to wear it in yellow at all, so at least it's going to be a
sort of leaf green, and there's less lace. It's still quite awful."

Tor looked amused. When he looked amused she almost
forgot she had decided that it was better that they weren't such
good friends any more. "Have supper with me," he said. "I
must have dinner in the hall—I suppose you are still pleading
ill health and dining peacefully with Teka? But supper I may
have alone in my rooms. Will you come?"

"Pleading ill health indeed," she said. "Do you really want
me to have a dizzy moment and drop a full goblet of wine in
the lap of the esteemed guest at my right—or left? I'm less
likely to cause civil war if I stay away."

"A very convenient excuse. I sometimes think if I have to
look at Galanna purring over the latest detail of the upcoming

event I shall throw an entire cask at her. You'd think we were declaring bloody independence from a genocidal tyrant, the way she goes on about the significance of the seating of the barons' third cousins twice removed. Did you know that Katah doesn't want to come at all? Her husband says he may have to put a bag over her head and tie her to her horse. Katah says that she knows Galanna and he doesn't. Will you come to supper?"

"Of course, if you'll shut up long enough for me to accept." She grinned at him.

He looked at her, feeling a twitch of surprise; in her smile for the first time he saw that which was going to trouble his sleep very soon; something very unlike the friendship they'd enjoyed all their lives thus far; something that would raise the barrier between them much faster than anything else could; the barrier that thus far Aerin alone saw growing.

"What's wrong?" she said; some of the old familiarity still worked, and she saw the shadow pass over his face, although she had no clue to what caused it.

"Nothing. I'll see you tonight, then."

She laughed when she saw the place settings for their supper: gold. The golden goblets were fishes standing on their tails, their open mouths waiting for the wine to be poured; the plates were encircled by leaping golden deer, the head of each bowed over the quarters of the one before, and their flying tails made a scalloped edge; the spoons and knives were golden birds, their long tails forming handles. "Highly unbreakable. I can still spill the wine."

"We'll have to make do."

"Where in Damar did you get these?"

Something like a flush crept up his face. "Four settings of the stuff was one of my coming-of-age gifts; it's from a town in the west known for its metalwork. I only just brought it back, this trip." It had been given him for his bride, the town's chief had told him.

Aerin looked at him, trying to decide about the flush; he was brown to begin with, and copper-colored from sunburn, and it was hard to tell. "It must have been a long and gaudy ceremony, and they covered you with glory you don't feel you've earned."

Tor smiled. "Near enough."

She didn't spill anything that evening, and she and Tor reminded each other of the most embarrassing childhood moments they could think of, and laughed. Galanna and Perlith's wedding was not mentioned once.

"Do you remember," she said, "when I was very young, almost a baby still, and you were first learning to handle a sword, how you used to show me what you'd learned—"

"I remember," he said, smiling, "that you followed me around and wheedled and wept till I was forced to show you."

"Wheedled, yes," she said. "Wept, never. And *you* started it; I didn't ask to get put in a baby-sack while you leaped your horse over hurdles."

"My own fault, I admit it." He also remembered, though he said nothing of it, how their friendship had begun. He had felt sorry for his young cousin, and had sought her first out of dislike for those who wished to ostracize her, especially Galanna, but soon for her own sake: for she was wry and funny even when she could barely speak, and loved best to find things to be enthusiastic about; and did not remind him that he was to grow up to be king. He had never quite learned to believe that she was always shy in company, nor that the shyness was her best attempt at a tactful acknowledgement of her precarious place in her father's court; nor that her defensive obstinacy was quite necessary.

It was to watch her take fire with enthusiasm that he had made a small wooden sword for her, and shown her how to hold it; and later he taught her to ride a horse, and let her ride his own tall mare when the first of her pretty, spoiled ponies had made her wish to give up riding altogether. He had shown her how to hold a bow, and to send an arrow or a spear where she wished it to go; how to skin a rabbit or an oozog, and how best to fish in running streams and quiet pools. The complete older brother, he thought now, and for the first time with a trace of bitterness.

"I can still hunt and fish and ride," she said. "But I miss the swordplay. I know you haven't much spare time these days—" She hesitated, calculating which approach would be likeliest to provoke the response she desired. "And I know there's no reason for it, but—I'm big enough now I could carry one of the boys' training swords. Would you—"

"Train you?" he said. He was afraid he knew where her thoughts were tending, although he tried to tell himself that this was no worse than teaching her to fish. He knew that even if he did grant her this it would do her no good; it didn't matter that she was already a good rider, that she was, for whatever inbred or circumstantial reasons, less silly than any of the other court women; that he knew from teaching her other things that he could probably teach her to be a fair swordswoman. He knew that for her own sake he should not encourage her now.

The gods prevent her from asking me anything I must not give, he thought, and said aloud, "Very well."

Their eyes met, and Aerin's dropped first.

The lessons had to be at infrequent intervals because of Tor's ever increasing round of duties as first sola; but lessons still Aerin had, as she wished, and after several months' time and practice she could make her teacher pant and sweat as they danced around each other. Her lessons were only a foot soldier's lessons; horses were not mentioned, and she was wise enough, having gained so much, not to protest.

She took pride, in a grim sort of way, in learning what Tor taught her; and he need not know the hours of drill she put in, chopping at leaves and dust motes, when he was not around. She made what she considered to be obligatory protests about the regular hiatuses in her progress when Tor was sent off somewhere, but in truth she was glad of them, for then she had the time to put in, grinding the lessons into her slow, stupid, Giftless muscles. But she was always eager for her next meeting with the first sola, and what he guessed about her private practice sessions was not discussed, any more than the fact that he had not fought unhorsed since he was a little boy and learning his first lessons in swordplay. A sola always led cavalry. Aerin knew pretty well when the time came that if she had been in real training she would have been put on a horse; but this moment too passed in silence.

But there was one good thing that also passed in silence, for Aerin was too proud, for different reasons, to mention it: the specific muscular control and coordination of learning to wield a sword finally sweated the last of the surka out of her system. It had been two years since her meeting with Galanna in the royal garden.

Tor and Aerin's meetings on the farthest edge of the least used of the practice fields also gave them an excuse to be together, as they had always been together, without having to acknowledge the new restraint between them, without discovering that conversation between them was growing awkward.

Aerin knew that Tor was careful not to use his real strength when he forced her back; but at least, as she learned, he had to be quick to keep her off; and strength, she hoped, would come. She was growing like a weed; her seventeenth birthday had come and gone, with the tiresome pomp necessary to a king's daughter, and the stiff courtesy inspired by an unsatisfactory king's daughter, and she was far too old to be suddenly growing taller. Not that she minded towering over Galanna; Galanna's perfect profile, when seen from above, seemed to beetle slightly at the brows and narrow slightly around the eyes. Aerin also had hopes that she would outgrow the revolting Kisha and be given a real horse.

A real horse. She began to have to close her lips tighter over her determination not to mention horses to Tor. A mounted man's strength was his horse—or a mounted woman's. But if she asked Tor to teach her to fight from horseback he would have to admit to knowing how much it meant to her, that it was not only an amusing private game she was playing; and she knew he was troubled about what they were doing already. His curious silence on the cause of her eagerness to learn told her that; and he could still read as many of her thoughts as she could of his.

❧ CHAPTER 6 ❧

TALAT GREW FIT and shining. He was always a little short with
the right hind when she mounted, but it took less and less time
for him to work out of it. She rode him without gear for
weeks, while the saddle and bridle shed oil all over the inside
of her wardrobe, for she found herself superstitiously reluctant to use it—as if something would be spoiled, or a gift
would become a duty, once tack officiated over their rides
together. "I suppose even the pleasantest convalescence must
come to an end someday," she said to him one evening; and
the next day she brought all his gear and her boy's sword out
to the pasture. He sniffled them all over, slowly and then with
enthusiasm, and danced with impatience while she tacked him
up, till she pounded on his shoulder with her fist and yelled at
him to behave.

He moved off proudly and obeyed each command at once;
and yet she found the jingling of the various bits and buckles
annoying, and the reins took up too much of her hands and
her concentration. "How does one deal with a sword and
these thrice-blasted reins?" she said to the small white ears.
"There must also be a way to hang the rotten thing so it
doesn't bang into you when you're not using it. I carry the
reins in my teeth—and accidentally strangle myself in them—
and meanwhile I can't shout blood-curdling war cries of *Victory!* and *For Damar!* to bring terror into the hearts of my

43

enemies, with my mouth full of reins.'' As they stood, she pulled the sword from its scabbard and swung it experimentally just as Talat turned his head to snap at a fly on his shoulder, and the sword tangled itself in the reins till Talat could not straighten his neck again, but remained with his head bent around and one reproachful dark eye fixed on his rider, and the blunt blade snuggled along his cheek.

"Ah, *hells*," she said, and yanked the sword free. One rein parted. Talat stood, either waiting for directions or afraid to move; the short end of the cut rein dangled a few inches beneath his chin, and he ducked his head and grabbed it, and chewed it thoughtfully.

"We did just fine without," she said furiously, dismounted, tore the bridle off and dumped it on the ground, holding her unwieldy sword in the other hand like a marauding bandit. She remounted and dug her legs into Talat's sides—harder than she meant for the saddle skirts muddled her. Talat, delighted, set off on his first gallop since the day he was wounded; and Aerin had wrought better than she knew, for he had the strength and stamina now to gallop quite a distance.

He tore across his pasture. Aerin failing to collect either her wits or her stomach, which seemed to be lying back on the ground with the bridle; and then she discovered that just as the saddle had made her misjudge how hard to squeeze, so now its bulk made it very easy for Talat to ignore her as she tried to tell him to stop by sitting heavily on his back. The fence loomed up before them; "Oh no," moaned Aerin, dropped her sword, and grabbed two handfuls of mane; and they were up and over. The take-off was a lurch, but they came down lightly, and Aerin discovered that while her exconvalescent was still disinclined to stop, he was willing to listen to her legs again; and eventually the circles got smaller, and the gallop more like a canter, and finally when she sat back he came down docilely to a walk.

But his head and tail were still up, and he reared suddenly, and Aerin frantically clutched him around the neck. He neighed, and struck out with his forelegs. Aerin had seen him do this years before, when her father rode him, for war-horses were trained to do battle as well as to carry their riders into it; and she had seen them and others of the cavalry on the practice fields, and at the laprun trials. But it was a lot different, she found, when one was on the horse performing.

"Shh," she said. "If someone notices we're out here, there will be trouble." Talat bounced stiff-legged once or twice and subsided. "And how am I supposed to get you back into your pasture again, dimwit?" she addressed him, and his ears flicked back for her voice. "The gate is right under anyone's eyes watching from the barn; and there's always someone in the barn." His ears twitched. "No, we will not jump back in." She was shaking all over; she felt that her legs were clattering against Talat's sides.

She turned him back toward the far side of the pasture again, feeling that anything was better than being seen; and they made their way to the place where Talat had made his leap. Aerin dismounted. "You stay right here or I'll chop your other three legs," she told him. He stood still, watching her, as she clambered cautiously up the low rock wall and the wooden rails above it. She cast around a few minutes, and found her discarded sword; came back to the fence and began banging the end of the top rail with the hilt till it slid protestingly out of the post and fell to the ground. The other followed. Aerin examined her blisters grimly, and wiped her sweating face. Talat was still watching her intently, and had not stirred a hoof. Aerin grinned suddenly. "Your war-horse training is no joke, hey? Only the best carries the king." He wrinkled his nose at her in a silent whicker. "Or even a third-rate first sol, now and then."

She stepped back from the fence. "Now, you. Come here." She beckoned him as if he were one of the king's hunting dogs. He bunched his feet together and sprang over the low stones, the stirrups clanging against his sides. She ground the rails back into the post holes again, picked up the sword, and with Talat following—she felt she'd had enough of riding for one day—they walked back to the pool and the mounting stone, and the heap of bridle and scabbard.

Talat was very lame the next day, and Aerin chased him on foot for three days to make him trot and work the soreness out before mounting him again. She reverted to riding him without saddle or bridle, but she took her sword with her, and slashed at dangling leaves and cobwebs—and fell off occasionally when a particularly wicked swing overbalanced her—and learned to hang on with her legs when Talat reared. They also cantered endlessly to the left to strengthen the weak leg, although some days she had to yell and thump on his shoulders and flanks to make him pick up the left lead at all.

She asked Tor, idly, what cues the war horses knew for their leaps and plunges, and Tor, who did not know about Talat and feared what she might be doing, warily told her. Talat nearly unseated her the first time she asked him these things, and didn't settle down again for days, hoping for more signals to do what he loved best, going off in curvettes when she only wanted him to trot.

The bridle she did not return to her wardrobe, but instead only threw it under her bed out of sight. (Teka, who had rearranged the wardrobe to allow for saddle oil, wondered about this new arrangement, but on the whole found it preferable, since court dresses were not kept under the bed.) She pulled the stirrups off the saddle and began to wrench the stitching out of its bottom, pulled most of the stuffing out, and sewed what remained back together again.

She put the resulting wreck on Talat's back, sat on it, said hells, took it off, pulled it entirely to bits, and began painstakingly to redesign it to follow exactly the contours of Talat's back and her legs, which meant that for several weeks she was putting it on him and climbing into it maybe half a dozen times in an afternoon, and Talat was a bit cross about it. She also had to borrow leather-working tools from Hornmar. Her heart was in her mouth for the questions Hornmar had never asked her but might yet someday; but he gave her the tools silently and willingly.

Her saddle was finished at last. She had left the breastplate links on it so that Talat could still wear the royal insignia; and when she put the saddle and breastplate on him she was surprised at how handsome it looked.

"I did a good job on this," she said, staring at her handiwork; and she blushed, but only Talat was there to see.

Meanwhile the long-awaited wedding of Galanna and Perlith finally occurred, with Tor performing the functions of first companion to Perlith with a blank and sober face, and Galanna almost transcendent with gratified vanity, for the eyes of the entire country were upon her. She was as beautiful as summer dawn, in rose and gold and turquoise, her black hair bound only with flowers, pink and white and pale blue; but she made up for this uncommon self-restraint by wearing rings on every finger and two on each thumb, so that when she made the ritual gestures her hands seemed on fire as the gems caught the sunlight.

But it was also at this wedding that a new and troubling rumor about the king's daughter began, a rumor that Galanna did not have to start, for more eyes than hers observed and drew conclusions similar to hers without the spur of wounded pride and jealousy. The king's daughter, Aerin-sol, stood at her father's left hand, as was proper; she wore green, a long dress, the skirts nearly as full as Galanna's, but this was only to show her cousin proper respect. The lace of her bodice was modest, and she wore but two rings, one of the house of the king, and one her father had given her on her twelfth birthday; her hair was bound primly to the back of her neck, and she carried only a small yellow-and-white posy of ringaling flowers. Aerin would not have wished to outshine Galanna even if she could, and had argued with Teka over every stitch of the dress and every braid of her bound hair, and tried to get out of carrying flowers at all.

The king and his daughter stood to the right of the wedding pair, and the first companions stood across from them; and it was obvious to many pairs of eyes that Perlith's first companion's gaze rested not on the bride but on the king's daughter; and the irony was that had he not been standing first companion he would have been on the king's right hand, where he could not look at Aerin-sol whether he wished to or not, and so his secret might have been kept a little longer.

The rumor began that day, for the people at the wedding feast passed it among themselves, and took it home with them afterward, that the first sola was in love with the king's daughter; and that the witch's daughter would entrap the next king of Damar as her mother had entrapped her father; and a little breath of fear was reawakened—for Aerin's Giftlessness had been reassuring—and accompanied the rumor.

Galanna, who had hoped to make Tor just a little sorry after all that he had not married her, had her day of glory almost ruined when at last she noticed where her new husband's first companion's eyes were tending; but anger became her, so long as she kept her tongue between her lips. It was almost worth it, for a few days later one of her dumber but most well-meaning ladies mentioned, worriedly, to her that someone had said that Tor was falling under the spell of the witchwoman's daughter, and that history was to repeat itself. "I don't quite

know what she meant, do you?" said the lady, frowning.
"Aerin-sol's mother was queen; it would be a most suitable
match."

Galanna laughed her most light-hearted laugh. "You are so
young," she said caressingly. "It was a terrible scandal when
Arlbeth married Aerin's mother. Didn't you know that
Aerin's mother was from the North?"

The lady, who had grown up in a small town to the south,
did not know, and her eyes opened wide; Galanna could read
her eagerness to have an interesting fresh slice of gossip to slip
into the conversation the next time she and her friends
gathered together. "Oh, Arlbeth certainly married her," Galanna said gently, "but she wasn't exactly queen." She made
it sound as if Arlbeth's only excuse for such a liaison was
misguided passion and, blinded by that passion, perhaps he
hadn't quite married her at all. She let this sink in a moment—
the lady was very stupid, and had to be played carefully—and
then, seeing dawning comprehension in the lady's eyes, sent
her gently and kindly, that the comprehension would not be
joggled loose again, about her business.

Aerin herself bore up under the wedding and the feast afterward as best she could, but as this meant that she withstood
them stoically as a martyr might withstand torture, she did not
notice either Tor's eyes or Galanna's fury—she was only too
accustomed to ignoring Galanna whenever possible; the one
thing she did observe about the bride was the twelve rings,
which were hard to miss—nor did she notice any more than
usual stiffness in the courtesy that those around her offered
her. And Tor, who was either viewed as dangerously enamored
and therefore to be treated with caution, or as pitiably
misguided and thus to be protected—or, as a few implausibly
simple souls believed, capable of deciding his own fate—did
not know till much later all that he had betrayed.

Aerin peeled out of her fancy clothes and fancy manners
and pelted off to the barns at the first opportunity, and
thought no more about weddings.

She had taken some time away from her leather-working to
begin experimenting with the fire ointment. Most of the ingredients she found easily, for they were common things, and a
first sol's education included a little basic herb-lore—which
Aerin had learned gladly as an escape from deportment and

history. One or two things she asked Hornmar for, from his stock of horse cures; and he, thinking she wished perhaps to try some sort of poultice on Talat's weak leg, granted her the run of his medicines as he had his tool chest, and again asked no questions. She was aware of the great boon he offered her, and this time she couldn't help but look at him a little wonderingly.

He smiled at her. "I love Talat too, you know," he said mildly. "If I can aid you, you need only to ask."

Teka and the redroot were a little more difficult.

"Teka, what is redroot?" Aerin asked one afternoon as she applied an uneven patch to a skirt she had always detested, and glowered at the result.

"If you spent a quarter of the time about your mending that you have over that old saddle, you would be better turned out than Galanna," said Teka with asperity. "Rip that out and do it again."

Aerin sighed, and began to pick at the irregular stitches. "I suppose there's no point in mentioning that I have no desire to be better turned out than Galanna." She picked a moment in silence and added, "For that matter, Galanna never wears anything that has a patch or a tear."

Teka grinned. "No. She takes out a great gash and puts in a whole new panel of different cloth, and it's a new dress."

"I would like to make a new floor mop out of this thing," replied Aerin.

Teka lifted it out of Aerin's hands and squinted at it. "The color has not worn well," she explained, "but the cloth is sound. We could redye it." Aerin did not show any marked access of enthusiasm for this plan. "Blue perhaps, or red. Don't overwhelm me with your gladness, child. You're always wanting to wear red, in spite of your flaming hair—"

"Orange," murmured Aerin.

"You could do quite well with this skirt in red, and a golden tunic over—*Aerin!*"

"It would still have to be patched," Aerin pointed out.

Teka sighed heavily. "You would try the patience of Gholotat herself. If you will do something useful with that wretched bridle that has been lying under the bed for the last fortnight, I will redye your poor skirt, and put a patch on it that not even Galanna will notice—as if you cared."

Aerin reached out to hug Teka, and Teka made a noise that

sounded like "Hmmph." Aerin fell off the windowseat and made her way over to the bed on her hands and knees and began to scrabble under it. She re-emerged only slightly dusty, for the hafor were dutiful floor-sweepers, held the bridle at arm's length and looked at it with distaste. "Now what do I do with it?" she inquired.

"Put it on a horse," Teka suggested in a much-tried tone.

Aerin laughed. "Teka, I am inventing a new way to ride. I don't use a bridle."

Teka, who still occasionally watched Aerin and Aerin's white stallion in secret to reassure herself that Talat would do her beloved child no harm, shuddered. It was the luck of the gods that Teka had not been watching the day Talat had jumped the fence. "I don't want to hear about it."

"Someday," Aerin went on with a bold sweep of her empty hand, "I shall be famous in legend and story—" She stopped, embarrassed to say such things even to Teka.

Teka, holding the skirt to the light as she made deft invisible stitches around the patch, said quietly, "I have never doubted it, my dear."

Aerin sat down on the edge of the bed with the bridle in her lap and looked at the fringe on the bedcurtains, which were the long golden manes of the embroidered horseheads on the narrow canopy border, and thought of her mother, who had died in despair when she found she had borne a daughter instead of a son.

"What is redroot?" she asked again.

Teka frowned. "Redroot. That's—um—astzoran. Redroot's the old term for it—they used to think it was good for some things."

"What things?"

Teka glanced at her and Aerin bit her lip. "Why do you want to know?"

"I—oh—I read a lot in the old books in the library while I wasn't . . . feeling quite well. There was some herb-lore, and they mentioned redroot."

Teka considered, and some of her thoughts were similar to Tor's when Aerin had asked him to teach her swordplay. Teka had never thought about whether Aerin's fate had more to do with what Aerin was or what Damar was, or for reasons beyond either; Teka merely observed that Aerin's fate was unique. But she knew, knew better even than the cousin who loved her, that Aerin would never be a court lady; not like Galanna, who was a beautiful termagant, but neither like Arlbeth's first wife, Tatoria, whom everyone had loved. None of the traditions of Arlbeth's court could help the king's daughter discover her fate; but Teka, unlike Aerin herself, had faith that the destiny was somewhere to be found. She hesitated, but she could remember nothing dangerous about the no longer valued redroot.

"Astzoran doesn't grow around here," said Teka; "it is a low weedy plant that prefers open meadows. It spreads by throwing out runners, and where the runner touches the earth a long slender root strikes down. That is the redroot." Teka pretended great concentration upon her patch. "I might take a few days to ride into the meadows beyond the City and into the Hills; I am reminded that there are herbs I need, and I prefer to gather my own. If you wish to come, I will show you some astzoran."

Teka asked no questions when Aerin rolled up a small herb bundle of her own and tied it to Kisha's saddle during their journey, a bundle that included several long thready roots of astzoran, and if any of the outriders noticed (for Teka only rode at all under duress, and even on her slow, sleepy, elderly pony she felt much safer with several other people around), they said nothing either.

The ointment recipe, Aerin found, was not as exact as it might be. She made one mixture, spread some of it on one finger, and thrust the finger into a candle flame—and snatched it out again with a yelp. Three more mixtures gained her three more burnt fingers—and a terrific lecture from Teka, who was not, of course, informed as to the details of why Aerin seemed intent on burning her fingers off. After that she used bits of wood to smear her trial blends on; when they smoked and charred, she knew she had not yet got it right.

After the first few tries she sighed and began to keep careful notes of how each sample was made. It was not an exercise natural to her, and after she'd filled several sheets of parchment with her tiny exact figures—parchment was expensive stuff, even for kings' daughters—she began to lose heart. She thought: If this mess really worked, everyone would know of it; they would all use it for dragon-hunting, and would have been using it all along, and dragons would no longer be a risk

—and that book would be studied and not left to gather dust. It is foolish to think I might have discovered something everyone before me had overlooked. She bowed her head over her burnt twig, and several hot tears slipped down her face onto her page of calculations.

❧ CHAPTER 7 ❧

ON HER EIGHTEENTH BIRTHDAY there was a banquet for the
first sol, despite all she could do to prevent it. Galanna shot
her glances like poisoned arrows and clung curiously near
Tor's side for someone else's wife of so few seasons. Perlith
made witty remarks at Aerin's expense in his soft light tenor
that always sounded kind, whatever he might be saying. The
king her father toasted her, and the faces around the tables in
the great hall glittered with smiles; but Aerin looked at them
sadly and saw only the baring of teeth.

Tor watched her: she was wearing a golden tunic over a long
red skirt; the tunic had embroidered flowers wound round its
hem, and petals of many colors stitched drifting down the full
sleeves; she wore the same two rings she had at Galanna's wedding. Her flame-colored hair was twisted around her head,
and a golden circlet was set upon it, and over her forehead
three golden birds held green stones in their beaks. He saw
her wince away from the courtiers' smiles, and he shook Galanna's hand from his arm impatiently, and then Galanna no
longer even pretended to smile.

Aerin did not notice this, for she never looked at Galanna if
she could help it, and if Galanna were near Tor she didn't look
at Tor either. But Arlbeth noticed. He knew what it was that
he saw, for better or for worse, and it was not often that he did

not know what was best done about the things he saw; but in this case he did not know. What he read in Tor's face tore at his heart, for it would be his heart's fondest wish that these two might wed, and yet he knew his people had never loved the daughter of his second wife, and he feared their mistrust, and he had reason to fear it. Aerin felt her father's arm around her shoulders, and turned to smile up at him.

After the banquet she went to sit in her windowseat, staring into the dark courtyard; the torches around its perimeter left great pools of shadow near the castle walls. Her bedroom was dark as well, and Teka had not yet come to be sure she had hung her good clothes up as she should instead of leaving them on the floor where she would step on them. There was a light knock on the door. She turned and said, "Come in," with surprise; if she had thought about it, she would have been silent and let the visitor leave without finding her. She wished to be alone after the hall full of food and talk and bright smiles.

It was Tor. She could see him outlined in the light from the hall, and she had been sitting in the dark long enough to see clearly. But he blinked and looked around, for her figure was only a part of the heavy curtains that hung around the deep window alcove. She stirred, and he saw the flicker of her red skirt.

"Why do you sit in the dark?"

"There was too much light in the hall tonight."

Tor was silent. After a moment she sighed, and reached for a candle and flint. It seemed to Tor that the shadows it cast upon her face made her briefly old: a woman with grandchildren, for all her brilliant hair. Then she set the candle on a small table and smiled at him, and she was eighteen again.

She saw that he carried something in his arms: a long narrow something, wrapped in dark cloth. "I have brought you your birthday present—privately, as I thought you might prefer." And so that I need not do any explaining, he thought.

She knew at once what it was: a sword. She watched with rising excitement as he unrolled the wrappings, and from them, gleaming, came her sword, her very own sword. She reached for it eagerly, and slid it out of its scabbard. It was plain but for some work on the hilt to make the grip sure; but she felt it light and true and perfect in her hand, and her hand trembled with the pride of it.

"Thank you," she said, her eyes still fixed on the sword, so she did not see the look of hope and pity on Tor's face as he watched her.

"At dawn you shall try it out," said Tor, and the tone of his voice shook her out of her reverie, and she raised her eyes to his. "I will meet you at our usual place," he said, and tried to speak as if this were a lesson like any other lesson; and if he failed, Aerin still did not guess why he failed.

"This is ever so much better than another dressing gown," she said lightly, and was pleased to see him smile.

"It was a very beautiful dressing gown."

"If it had been less beautiful, I would not have disliked it so much. You were as bad as Teka, trying to keep me in bed, or trailing about my rooms in a dressing gown forever."

"And a lot of good it did us, despite the fact that you could not stand on your feet without either fainting or falling over."

"It was concentrating on my lessons with you that finally sweated the last of the surka out of me," Aerin said, waving her birthday present gently under his nose.

"I almost believe you," he replied sadly.

So they were standing, looking at each other, with the naked blade upheld between them, when Teka come through the open door behind them. "Gholotat protect us," said Teka, and closed the door behind her.

"Is my birthday present not beautiful?" said Aerin, and turned the blade back and forth quickly so that it winked at her old nurse as she stood by the door. Teka looked at her face and then at Tor's, and then back at Aerin's, and said nothing.

"I will bid you good night," said Tor, and because Teka was there he dared reach out his hands to Aerin, and put them on her shoulders, as she slid her sword into its scabbard, and kiss her cheek as a cousin might; which he would not have dared had they been alone. He bowed to Teka, and left them.

Perhaps it was having a real sword of one's own. Perhaps it was being eighteen—or that eighteen years' practice of being stubborn was finally paying off. If she still stumbled over the corners of rugs or bumped into doorways while she was thinking about other things, she no longer bothered looking around anxiously to find out if anyone had seen her: either they had or they hadn't, and she had other things on her mind; she reveled in those other things. They meant that she did not blush automatically when she caught sight of Perlith, knowing that he would have thought of something to say to her since the last time she had failed to avoid him, and that his little half smile beneath half-lidded eyes would make whatever he said worse. She walked through the halls of the castle and the streets of the City the most direct way instead of the way she would meet the fewest people; and she avoided the surka in the royal garden, but only that it might not make her sick again. She did not cringe from the thought of its presence, or from the shame that she had to avoid it in the first place; nor did she any longer feel that breathing the garden air was synonymous with breathing Galanna's malice.

She had discovered how to make the dragonfire ointment.

It was, she knew, sheer obstinacy that had kept her at it—over two years of making fractional changes in her mixtures, learning how to find and prepare all the ingredients for the mixtures, for she could not continue raiding Hornmar's and Teka's supplies; finding small apothecary shops in the City that might sell the odder ones, and riding out on the reluctant Kisha for the herbs that grew nearby.

At first she had wondered if anyone would try to stop her, and her first visits to shopkeepers, and beyond the City gates, gave her stomachaches of dread. But the shopkeepers attended her respectfully and even helpfully, and slowly the visits stopped seeming so awful. There was no sense in trying to disguise herself; she was the only person in the City with orange hair, and any Damarian who had never in fact seen her would know instantly who she was. She had tried the effect of a scarf over the give-away hair, but as soon as she looked in a mirror she realized this wouldn't work: the scarf was obviously there to hide her hair, and she still had orange eyebrows. There was stuff Galanna used to blacken her brown lashes, but Aerin had no idea how to get hold of it, and thought that while Teka seemed willing to let her and her peculiar errands alone at present, she would probably throw a fit and spoil everything if she caught her royal charge creeping around with her hair hidden and her brows blackened. And as she wasn't stopped, her confidence grew, and she swept into the shops she frequented with her head high as a first sol should, and made her purchases, and swept out again.

She felt tremendously grand, but the shopmen and women found her charmingly unpretentious, being accustomed to the Perliths and Galannas who never looked anyone in the eye and were never satisfied (it was widely held that the woman who supplied Galanna with her brow-darkener more than earned the fancy price she charged), and who always had lackeys to handle the money and the purchases themselves while they fingered their jewels and looked into the distance. Arlbeth would have been pleased to hear the small new thread of gossip that began to circulate in the City about the witchwoman's daughter, and how the daughter (like the mother, a few folk now recalled) had a smile for everyone; and this view of the king's daughter almost eased the fear of her that had begun with the rumor that she was enspelling the first sola. A few of her new supporters decided that Tor, as first sola and king to be, understandably wanted a quiet family life; and the king's daughter, of all those court ladies, looked the likeliest to give it to him.

There were even those, especially among the older folk, who shook their heads and said that they shouldn't keep the young first sol mewed up in that castle the way they did; it'd be better if she were let out to mingle with her people. If Aerin could have heard, she would have laughed.

And the things she bought were such harmless things, even if some of them were odd, and even though, as the months passed, she did buy quite a quantity of them. Nothing there that could cause any . . . mischief. Hornmar had mentioned, very quietly, to one or two of his particular friends the first sol's miraculous cure of old Talat; and somehow that tale got around too, and as the witchwoman's easy smile was remembered, so did some folk also begin to remember her way with animals.

It was a few months before her nineteenth birthday that she put a bit of yellowish grease on a fresh bit of dry wood, held it with iron pincers, and thrust it into the small candle flame at the corner of her work table—and nothing happened. She had been performing this particular set of motions—measuring, noting down, mixing, applying and watching the wood burn— for so long that her movements were deft and exact with long practice even while her brain tended to go off on its own and contemplate her next meeting of swords with Tor, or the nagging Teka was sure to begin within the next day or two for her to darn her stockings since they all had holes in them and lately she had perforce always to wear boots when she attended the court in the great hall so that the holes wouldn't show. She was thinking that the green stockings probably had the smallest and most mendable holes, and she had to have dinner in the hall tonight. Since she'd turned eighteen she'd been expected to take part in the dancing occasionally, and there was sure to be dancing tonight since the dinner was in honor of Thorped and his son, who were here from the south; one of Thorped's daughters was one of Galanna's ladies. It was difficult dancing in boots and she needed all the help she could get. At this point she realized that her arm was getting tired—and that the bit of yellow-slick wood was peacefully ignoring the fire that burned around it, and that the iron tongs were getting hot in her hand.

She jumped, and knocked over the candlestick and dropped the hot tongs, and the greasy bit of wood skittered over the dusty, woodchip-littered floor, picking up shreds and shavings till it looked like a new sort of pomander. She had set up shop in a deserted stone shed near Talat's pasture that had once held kindling and things like old axe handles and sticks of wood that might make new axe handles, and she had never gotten around to sweeping the floor. Her hands were shaking so badly that she dropped the candle again when she tried to pick it up, and missed when she went to stamp out the thread of smoke that rose from the floor where the candle had fallen.

She sat down on a pile of axe handles and took a few deep breaths, and thought fixedly about green stockings. Then she stood up, lit the candle again, and set it quietly back in its holder. She'd learned in the long months past not to waste her time and the apothecaries' wares by making more than a tiny trial bit of each mixture, and the marble bowl where the final mashing and mixing went on before the experiment with the candle flame was no bigger than an eggcup. There was just enough in the bottom of the cup now to grease one fingertip. She chose the left index finger, which had been the one to get burnt with the result of her very first fire-ointment attempt, what seemed centuries ago. She held the fingertip steadily in the flame, and watched it; the pointed blue-and-yellow oval of the fire parted smoothly around her finger and rejoined above it to prick the shadows of the stone ceiling. She felt nothing. She withdrew the finger and stared at it with awe—touched it with another finger. Skin-heat, no more; and while it had remained stickily apparent on the surface of the wood, the ointment was not greasy on her finger. Kenet. It existed.

She checked her notes to be sure she could read what she had written about the proportions of this particular attempt; then blew out the candle and went off in a daze to darn stockings.

Teka asked her twice, sharply, what was the matter with her, as she tried to help her dress for the court dinner. Aerin's darns were worse than usual—which was saying a good deal, and Teka had said even more when she saw them, but as much out of worry for her sol's extraordinary vagueness as from straightforward exasperation at yet another simply homely task done ill. Usually, big court dinners made Aerin clumsy and rather desperately here-and-now. Teka finally tied ribbons around both of Aerin's ankles to hide the miserable lumps of mending and was even more appalled when Aerin did not object. Ankle ribbons were all the fashion among the higher-born young ladies this year; when this first became apparent Teka had had a difficult time convincing Aerin not to lengthen all her skirts eight inches, that they might drag on the floor and render all questions of ankle adornment academic; and Teka was fairly sure the only reason she'd won the argument was that Aerin couldn't face the thought of all the sewing such a project would entail.

Teka hung a tassel at the front of one ankle, to fall gracefully over the high arch of Aerin's long foot (not that it would stay there; Galanna and the others had developed a coy little hitch and skip to their walk, to make their tassels fall forward as they should), and pinned a small silver brooch bearing the royal crest on the other, and Aerin didn't even fidget. She was dreamily staring into space; she was even wearing a slight smile. Could she have fallen in love? Teka wondered. Who? Thorped's son—what was his name? Surely not. He was half a head shorter than she and wispy.

Teka sighed and stood up. "Aerin—are you sure you're not ill?" she said.

Aerin came back to herself with a visible jerk and said, "Dear Teka, I'm fine. Truly I am." Then she looked down with a scowl and wiggled her ankles. "Ugh."

"They hide your—dare I call them—darns," Teka said severely.

"There's that," said Aerin, and smiled again, and Teka thought, What ails the girl? I will look for Tor tonight; his face will tell me something.

❧ CHAPTER 8 ❧

TOR THOUGHT that night she looked radiant and wished, wistfully, that it had something to do with him, while he was only too certain it did not. When, daring greatly, he told her as they spun through the figures of the dance that she was beautiful, she laughed at him. Truly she has grown up, he thought; even six months ago she would have blushed scarlet and turned to wood in my arms. "It's the ribbons round my ankles," she said. "My darning surpassed itself in atrocity today, and Teka said it was this or going barefoot."

"I am not looking at your feet," said Tor, looking into her green eyes; and she said without flinching: "Then you should be, dearest cousin, for you have never seen me thus bedecked previously, nor likely are ever to see me so again."

Thorped's wispy son could barely take his eyes off her. He remarked to his father that Aerin-sol was so splendidly large. Thorped, who liked a woman of the size to throw over a shoulder and run lightly off with—not that the opportunity had ever presented itself, but it was an appealing standard of measurement—said ah, hmm. Galanna, who didn't like wispy men, was still furious that anyone should waste time looking at Aerin, and snuggled relentlessly with Perlith. She was about resigned to being married to him; Tor was truly hopeless. If only Perlith would play up a bit more; a little mock despair over her being the center of attention at every gathering (well, nearly); a little jealousy when beautiful young men wrote her poems, as she was able occasionally to persuade them to do. But he had the infuriating attitude that his carefully chosen offer for her hand had conferred upon her a favor. By the gods! She was a good match, after all.

But then so was he. Neither of them would ever forget it for a moment.

Aerin floated through the evening. Since she was first sol, she never had the embarrassment (or the relief) of being able to sit out. She wasn't particularly aware that—most unusually—she had stepped on no one's feet that night; and she was accustomed to the polite protests, at the end of each set when partners were exchanged, of what a pleasure it was to dance with her, and her thoughts were so far away that she failed to catch the unusual ring of truth in her dancing partners' voices. She didn't even mind dancing three figures with Thorped's son (what was his name again?), for while his height did not distress her, his chinlessness, on another occasion, would have.

She did notice when she danced with Perlith that there was an unwonted depth of malignance in his light remarks, and wondered in passing what was biting him. Does the color of my gown make his skin look sallow? But Perlith too had noticed Thorped's son's admiration of the king's only daughter, and it irritated him almost as much as it irritated Galanna. Perlith knew quite well that when Galanna had stopped playing hard to get back in the days when he was punctiliously courting her it was because she had decided to make a virtue of necessity after it became apparent that a second sola was the best she was going to get. But a second sola was an important personage, and Perlith wanted everyone to envy him his victory to the considerable extent that his blue blood and irresistible charm—and of course Galanna's perfect beauty—deserved. How dare this common runt admire the wrong woman?

Being Perlith, he had, of course, timed his courtship to coincide with the moment that Galanna admitted defeat on the score of future queenship; but he'd never been able to bring himself to flirt with Aerin. He had as much right to the king's daughter as anyone—what a pity she had to have orange hair and enormous feet—and while he would never have married her, king's daughter or no, with that commoner for a mother, it might have been amusing to make her fall in love with him. In his conscious mind he preferred to think that he hadn't made her fall in love with him by choice; in a bleaker moment it had occurred to him that Aerin probably wouldn't like being flirted with, and that his notorious charm of manner (when he cared to use it) might have had no effect on her whatsoever. He had banished the thought immediately, and his well-trained self-esteem had buried it forever.

He could admit that she looked better than usual tonight; he'd never seen her in the fashionable ribbons before, and she had nice trim ankles, in spite of the feet. This realization did not soften his attitude; he glared at his dancing partner, and Aerin could feel the glare, though she knew that if she looked into his face his expression would be one of lazy pleasure, with only a deep glint in his heavy-lidded eyes to tell her what he was thinking. At a pause in the dance he plucked several golden specks out of the air that were suddenly there for him when he reached for them. He closed his fingers around them, smiled, and opened his hand again, and a posy of yellow and white ringaling flowers—the flowers Aerin had carried at his wedding—sprang up between his thumb and first finger.

"For the loveliest lady here tonight," he said, with a bow, to Aerin.

Aerin turned white and backed up a step, her hands behind her. She bumped into the next couple as they waited for the music for the next figure to begin, and they turned, mildly irritated, to see what was happening; and suddenly the entire hall was watching. The musicians in the gallery laid down their instruments when they should have played their first notes; it didn't occur to them to do anything else. Perlith, especially when he was feeling thwarted, was formidably Gifted.

A little space cleared around Perlith and Aerin, and the focal point of the vast hall was a little bouquet of yellow and white flowers. Tor muttered something, and dropped his partner's hand, much to that lady's annoyance (she would feel resentful of the orange-haired sol for weeks after); but he was on the far side of the hall from Aerin and Perlith, and it was as though the company were frozen where they stood, for he had difficulty threading his way through them, and no one tried to make room.

Aerin knew if she touched the magic flowers they would turn to frogs, or burst in an explosion that anyone who might not have noticed the frogs couldn't help but notice; or, worst of all, make her sick on the floor at Perlith's feet. Perlith knew it too. Magic had made her queasy since early adolescence, when her Gift should have been asserting itself and wasn't; and since her illness her reaction to anything to do with other royal Gifts was much more violent. She stood helpless and could think of no words to say; even if she asked him to return the flowers to dust motes, the whiff of magic about his hands and face would remain, and she dared not dance with him again immediately.

Perlith stood, smiling gently at her, his arm gracefully raised and his hand curled around his posy; the glint in his eye was very bright.

And then the flowers leaped from his fingers and grew wings, and became yellow and white birds which sang "Aerin, Aerin" as sweetly as golden harps, and as they disappeared into the darkness of the ceiling the musicians began playing again, and Tor's arms were around her, and Perlith was left to make his way out of the circle of dancers. Aerin stepped on Tor's feet several times as he helped her off the dancing-floor, for the magic was strong in her nostrils, and though what Tor had done had been done at a distance, it still clung to him too. He held her up by main force till she said, a little shakily, "Let go, cousin, you're tearing the waistband right out of my skirt."

He released her at once, and she put a hand out—to a chair, not to his outstretched arm. He let the arm drop. "My pardon, please. I am clumsy tonight."

"You are never clumsy," she said with bitterness, and Tor was silent, for he was wishing that she would lean on him instead of on the chair, and did not notice that most of the bitterness was for Perlith, who had hoped to embarrass her before the entire court, and a little for herself, and none at all for him. She told him he might leave her, that she was quite all right. Two years ago he would have said, "Nonsense, you are still pale, and I will not leave you"; but it wasn't two years ago, and he said merely, "As you wish," and left her to find his deserted partner and make his excuses.

Perlith came to Aerin as she sat in the chair she had been

leaning on, sipping from a glass of water a woman of the hafor had brought her. "I beg most humbly for forgiveness," he said, closing his eyes till only the merest glitter showed beneath his long lashes. "I forgot that you—ah—do not care for such—ah—tokens."

Aerin looked at him levelly. "I know perfectly well what you were about this evening. I accept your apology for precisely what it is worth."

Perlith blinked at this unexpected intransigence and was, very briefly, at a loss for a reply. "If you accept my apology for what it is worth," he said smoothly, "then I know I need have no fear that you will bear me a grudge for my hapless indiscretion."

Aerin laughed, which surprised her as much as it surprised him. "No indeed, cousin; I shall bear you no grudge for this evening's entertainment. Our many years of familiar relationship render us far beyond grudges." She curtsied hastily and left the hall, for fear that he would think of something else to say to her; Perlith never lost verbal skirmishes, and she wanted to keep as long as she could the extraordinary sensation of having scored points against him.

Later, in the darkness of her bedroom, she reconsidered the entire evening, and smiled; but it was half a grimace, and she found she could not sleep. It had been too long a day, and she was too tired; her head always spun from an evening spent on display in the great hall, and tonight as soon as she deflected her thoughts from Perlith and Tor and yellow birds they immediately turned to the topic of the dragonfire ointment.

She considered creeping back to her laboratory, but someone would see a light where only axe handles should be. She had never mentioned that she had taken over the old shed, but she doubted anyone would care so long as lights didn't start showing at peculiar hours—and how would she explain what she was doing?

At last she climbed wearily out of bed and wrapped herself in the dressing gown Tor had given her, and made her way through back hallways and seldom-used stairs to the highest balcony in her father's castle. It looked out to the rear of the courtyard; beyond were the stables, beyond them the pastures, and beyond them all the sharp rise of the Hills. From where she stood, the wide plateau where the pastures and training grounds were laid out stretched directly in front of her; but to her left the Hills crept close to the castle walls, so that the ground and first-floor rooms on that side got very little sunlight, and the courtyard wall was carved out of the Hills themselves.

The castle was the highest point in the City, though the walls around its courtyard prevented anyone standing at ground level within them from seeing the City spread out on the lower slopes. But from the third- and fourth-story windows and balconies overlooking the front of the castle the higher roofs of the City could be seen, grey stone and black stone and dull red stone, in slabs and thin shingle-chips; and chimneys rising above all. From fifth- and sixth-story windows one could see the king's way, the paved road which fell straight from the castle gates to the City gates, almost to its end in a flat-stamped earth clearing cornered by monoliths, a short way beyond the City walls.

But from any point in the castle or the City one might look up and see the Hills that cradled them; even the break in the jagged outline caused by the City gates was narrow enough not to be easily recognizable as such. The pass between Vasth and Kar, two peaks of the taller Hills that surrounded the low rolling forested land that lay before the City and circled round to meet the Hills behind the castle, was not visible at all. Aerin loved the Hills; they were green in spring and summer, rust and brown and yellow in the fall, and white in the winter with the snow they sheltered the City from; and they never told her that she was a nuisance and a disappointment and a halfblood.

She paced around the balcony and looked at the stars, and the gleam of the moonlight on the glassy smooth courtyard. Somehow the evening she'd just endured had quenched much of her joy in her discovery of the morning. That a bit of yellow grease could protect a finger from a candle flame said nothing about its preventive properties in dealings with dragons; she'd heard the hunters home from the hunt say that dragonfire was bitter stuff, and burned like no hearthfire.

On her third trip around the balcony she found Tor lurking in the shadow of one of the battlemented peaks. "You walk very quietly," he said.

"Bare feet," she said succinctly.

"If Teka should catch you so and the night air so chill, she would scold."

"She would; but Teka sleeps the sleep of the just, and it is long past midnight."

"So it is." Tor sighed, and rubbed his forehead with one hand.

"I'm surprised you've escaped so early; the dancing often goes on till dawn."

In spite of the dimness of the light she could see Tor make a face. "The dancing may often go on till dawn, but I rarely last half so long—as you would know if you ever bothered to stay and keep me company."

"Hmmph."

"Hmmph threefold. Has it ever occurred to you, Aerin-sol, that I am not a particularly good dancer either? It's probably just as well we don't dance together often or we would do ourselves a serious injury. Nobody dares mention it, of course, because I am first sola—"

"And a man of known immoderate temper."

"Flattery will get you nowhere. But I leave the dance floor as soon as I've tramped around once with every lady who will feel slighted if I don't."

His light-heartedness seemed forced. "What's wrong?" she said.

Tor gave a snort of laughter. "Having exposed one of my most embarrassing shortcomings in an attempt to deflect you, you refuse to be deflected."

Aerin waited.

Tor sighed again, and wandered out of the shadows to lean his elbows against the low stone wall surrounding the balcony. The moonlight made his face look pale, his profile noble and serene, and his black hair the stuff of absolute darkness. Aerin rather liked the effect, but he spoiled it by rubbing one hand through his hair and turning the corners of his mouth down, whereupon he reverted to being tired and confused and human. "There was a meeting, of sorts, this afternoon, before the banquet." He paused again, but Aerin did not move, expecting more; he glanced at her and went on. "Thorped wanted to talk about the Hero's Crown."

"Oh." Aerin joined him, leaning her elbows on the wall next to his, and he put an arm around her. She discovered that she was cold and that she was rather glad of the arm and the warmth of his side. "What did he want to know about it?"

"What does anybody ever want to know about it? He wants to know where it is."

"So do we all."

"Yes. Sorry. I mean he wants to know if we're looking for it now and if not why not and if so by what means and what progress we've made. And if we know how important it is, and on and on."

"I see that you spent a less than diverting afternoon."

"How does he *think* we're supposed to look for it? By the Seven Gods and Aerinha's foundry! Every stone in Damar has been turned over at least twice looking for it, and there was a fashion there for a while to uproot trees and look for it underneath. We've had every seer who ever went off in a fit or brewed a love potion that didn't work try to bring up a vision of its whereabouts for us."

Including my mother? thought Aerin.

"Nothing. Just a lot of dead trees and misplaced rocks."

Galanna had told her once that there was a Crown that kept mischief away from Damar, and that if Arlbeth had had it when he met Aerin's mother he would never have married her, and if he had found it any time since Aerin was born Galanna would no longer have to put up with having her eyelashes cut off; exactly how the Crown performed its warding functions she did not describe. Aerin also knew that the more strongly Gifted royalty were expected to chew a surka leaf at least once and try to cast their minds toward a sighting of the Crown. She assumed Tor had done so, though it was not something he would have told her about. And all her history lessons had told her was that the current sovereigns of Damar had gone crownless for many generations, in honor of a Crown that was lost long ago.

Aerin said slowly. "I've heard of it, of course, but I'm not entirely sure what the Crown is, or is supposed to do."

There was a silence. "Neither am I," said Tor. "It's been lost . . . a long time. I used to think it was only a legend, but old Councillor Zanc mentioned it a few weeks ago—that's when Arlbeth told me that when he was a boy they were looking under trees for it. Zanc's father's father used to tell the story of how it was lost. Zanc thinks the increase of the Border raids is somehow due to its absence; that Northern . . . mischief . . . did not trouble us when the Hero's Crown lay in the City. And Thorped apparently agrees with him, although he's not quite so outspoken about it.''

He shrugged, and then settled her more securely in the curve of his arm. ''The Hero's Crown holds much of what Damar is; or at least much of what her king needs to hold his people together and free of mischief. Aerinha was supposed to have done the forging of it. Here we get into the legend, so maybe you know this bit. Damar's strength, or whatever it is about this land that makes it Damar and us Damarians, was thought to be better held, more strongly held, in a Crown, which could be handed from sovereign to sovereign, since some rulers are inevitably better or wiser in themselves than others. Of course this system runs the risk of the Crown's being lost, and the strength with it, which is what eventually happened. Zanc's story is that it was stolen by a black mage, and that he rode east, not north, or the Northerners would have fallen on us long since. Arlbeth thinks . . .'' His voice trailed away.

''Yes?''

''Arlbeth thinks it has come into the hands of the Northerners at last.'' He paused a moment before he said slowly, ''Arlbeth at least believes in its existence. So must I, therefore.''

Aerin asked no more. It was the heaviest time of the night; dawn was nearer than midnight, but the sky seemed to hold them in a closing hand. Then suddenly through the weight of the sky and of her new knowledge, she remembered her dragon ointment, and somehow neither the missing Crown nor Perlith's malice, the reason she had come up to stare at the sky in the middle of the night, mattered quite so much; for, after all, she could do nothing about either Perlith or the Crown, and the recipe for kenet was hers. If she got no sleep, she'd botch making a big trial mixture tomorrow. ''I must go to bed,'' she said, and straightened up.

''I too,'' said Tor. ''It will be very embarrassing to the dignity of the royal house if the first sola falls off his horse tomorrow. Lady, that's a very handsome dressing gown.''

''It is, isn't it? It was given me by a friend with excellent taste.'' She smiled up at him, and without thinking he bent his head and kissed her. But she only hugged him absently in return, because she was already worrying whether or not she had enough of one particular herb, for it would spoil the whole morning if she had to fetch more and she'd be mad with impatience and would botch the job after all. "A quiet sleep to you," she said.

"And to you," said Tor from the shadows.

❧ CHAPTER 9 ❧

SHE HAD ALMOST enough of the herb she had been worrying about. After dithering awhile and muttering to herself she decided to go ahead and make as much ointment as she had ingredients for, and fetch more tomorrow. It was a messy business, and her mind would keep jumping away from the necessary meticulousness; and she knocked over a pile of axe handles and was too impatient to pile them up again and so spent several hours tripping over them and stubbing her toes and using language she had picked up while listening to the sofor, and the thotor, who were even more colorful. Once she was hopping around on one foot and yelling epithets when her other foot was knocked out from under her as well by a treacherous rear assault from a fresh brigade of rolling lumber, and she fell and bit her tongue. This chastened her sufficiently that she finished her task without further incident.

She stared at the greasy unpleasant-looking mess in the shallow trough before her and thought, Well, so what do I do now? Build a fire and jump in? The only fireplaces big enough are all in heavily used rooms of the castle. Maybe a bonfire isn't such a bad idea after all; but it will have to be far enough away that no one will come looking for the source of the smoke.

Meanwhile she did have enough of the kenet to fireproof both hands, and she made a small fire in the middle of the shed floor (out of broken axe handles) and held both hands, trembling slightly, in its heart—and nothing happened. The next day she went to fetch more herbs.

She decided at once that she would have to leave the City to try her bonfire; and she decided just as quickly that she had to take Talat. Kisha would be worse than a nuisance under such circumstances; at very least she would find the bonfire excuse enough to break either her halter rope or her neck in a declared panic attempt to bolt back toward the City.

Teka, however, did not like this plan at all. Teka was willing to accept that Aerin was a good rider, and might be permitted to leave the City alone for a few hours on her pony; but that she should want to go alone, overnight, with that vicious stallion—such an idea she was not willing to entertain. First she declared that Talat was too lame to go on such a journey; and when Aerin, annoyed, tried to convince her otherwise, Teka changed her ground and said that he was dangerous and Aerin couldn't be certain of her ability to control him. Aerin was ready to weep with rage, and after several weeks of this (she having meanwhile made vast quantities of her kenet and almost set her hair on fire trying to test its effectiveness on various small bits of her anatomy), Teka had to realize that there was more to this than whim.

"You may go if your father says you may," she said at last, heavily. "Talat is still his horse, and he has a right to decide what his future should be. I—I think he will be proud of what you've done with him."

Aerin knew how much it cost Teka to say so, and her anger ebbed away and she felt ashamed of herself.

"The journey itself—I do not like it. It is not proper"—and here a smile touched the corners of Teka's sad mouth—"but you will always be unusual, as your mother was, and she traveled alone as she chose, nor did your father ever try to hinder her. You are a woman grown, and past needing a nursemaid to judge your plans. If your father says you may go—well, then."

Aerin went off and began to worry about how best to approach her father. She had known she would have to ask his permission at some point, but she had wanted to get Teka on her side first, and had misjudged how alarming the horse-shy Teka would find a war-stallion like Talat, even an elderly, rehabilitated, and good-natured war-stallion. Aerin's own attitude toward Talat hadn't been rational for years.

She brooded for days after Teka had withdrawn from the field of combat; but she brooded not only about how to tackle her father, but also about what, precisely, she was setting out to do. Test the fire-repellent properties of her discovery. Toward killing dragons. Did she really want to kill dragons? Yes. Why? Pause. To be doing something. To be doing something better than anyone else was doing it.

She caught her father one day at breakfast, between ministers with tactical problems and councillors with strategic ones. His face lit up when he saw her, and she made an embarrassed mental note to seek him out more often; he was not a man who had ever been able to enter into a child's games, but she might have noticed before this how wistfully he looked at her. But for perhaps the first time she was recognizing that wistfulness for what it was, the awkwardness of a father's love for a daughter he doesn't know how to talk to, not shame for what Aerin was, or could or could not do.

She smiled at him, and he gave her a cup of malak, and pushed the bun tray and the saha jam toward her. "Father," she said through crumbs, "do you know I have been riding Talat?"

He looked at her thoughtfully. Hornmar had brought him this information some months back, adding that Talat had looked like pining away and dying before Aerin took him over. Arlbeth had wished that she might bring him the story herself; the sort of fears Teka had did not occur to him.

"Yes," he said. "And I would have guessed something was up sooner or later when you stopped nagging me to get rid of Kisha and find you a real horse."

Aerin had the grace to blush. "It's been . . . quite a while. I didn't think about what I was doing at first."

Arlbeth was smiling. "I should like to see you ride him."

Aerin swallowed. "You . . . would?"

"I would."

"Er—soon?"

"As it pleases you, Aerin-sol," he said gravely.

She nodded wordlessly.

"Tomorrrow, then."

She nodded again, picked up a second bun and looked at it.

"I have guessed that there is some purpose to your joining me at breakfast," Arlbeth said, as she showed no sign of

breaking the silence, "a purpose beyond telling me of something that has been going on for years without your troubling
me with it. It has perhaps to do further with Talat?"

She looked up, startled.

"We kings do develop a certain ability to recognize objects
under our noses. Well?"

"I should like to ride Talat out of the City. A day's ride
out—sleep overnight, outside. Come back the next day." She
was sorry about the bun, now; it made her mouth dry.

"Ah. I recommend you go east and south—you might
follow the Tsa, which will provide you with water as well as
preventing you from getting lost."

"The river? Yes. I'd thought—I'd already thought of that."
Her fingers were crumbling the rest of the bun to tiny bits.

"Good for you. I assume you planned to go soon?"

"I—yes. You mean you'll let me?"

"Let you? Of course. There's little within a day's ride of the
City that will harm you." Momentarily his face hardened.
Time had once been, before the loss of the Crown, that any
sword drawn in anger within many miles of the City would re-
bound on the air, twist out of its wielder's hands, and fall to
the earth. "Talat will take care of you. He took excellent care
of me."

"Yes. Yes, he will." She stood up, looked at the mess on
(and around) her plate, looked at her father. "Thank you."

He smiled. "I will see you tomorrow. Mid-afternoon."

She nodded, gave him a stricken smile, and fled. One of the
hafor appeared to remove her plate and brush the crumbs
away.

Aerin was early at Talat's pasture the next morning. She
groomed him till her arms ached, and he loved every minute of
it; he preferred being fussed over even to eating.

Maybe she should hang a bridle on him. She'd mended the
cut rein on his old bridle the night before, and brought it with
her today. But when she offered the bit to him—he who had so
eagerly seized it two years before, knowing that it meant he
would be really ridden again—he looked at it and then at her
with obvious bewilderment, and hurt feelings. He suffered her
to lift the bar into his mouth and pull the straps over his ears,
but he stood with his head drooping unhappily.

"All *right*," she said, and ripped the thing off him again, and dropped it on the ground, and picked up the little piece of padded cloth that passed for a saddle and dropped it on his back. He twisted his head around and nibbled the hem of her tunic, rolling his eye at her to see if she was really angry. When she didn't knock his face away he was reassured, and waited patiently while she arranged and rearranged the royal breast-plate to her liking.

Arlbeth came before she expected him. Talat had felt the tension in her as soon as she mounted, but he had cheered her into a good mood again by being himself, and they were weaving nonchalantly around several tall young trees at a canter when she noticed Arlbeth standing on the far side of the stream that ran through the meadow. They forded the water and then halted, and Arlbeth gave them the salute of a soldier to his sovereign, and she blushed.

He nodded at Talat's bare head. "I'm not sure this would be such a good idea with another horse, but with him . . ." He paused and looked thoughtful, and Aerin held her breath for fear he would ask her how it had begun, for she hadn't decided what to tell him. He said only: "It could be useful to have no reins to handle; but I'm not sure even our best horses are up to such a level of training." His eyes then dropped to Aerin's feet. "That's a very pretty way to ride, with your legs wrapped around his belly, but the first pike that came along would knock you right out of the saddle."

"You're not in battle most of the time," Aerin said boldly, "and you could build a special war saddle with a high pommel and cantle."

Arlbeth laughed, and Aerin decided that they had passed their test. "I can see he likes your new way."

Aerin grinned. "Pick up the bridle and show it to him."

Arlbeth did, and Talat laid back his ears and turned his head away. But when Arlbeth dropped it, Talat turned back and thrust his nose into the breast of his old master, and Arlbeth stroked him and murmured something Aerin could not hear.

Talat did not like the fire ointment at all. He pranced and sidled and slithered out of reach and flared his nostrils and snorted, little rolling huff-huff-huffs, when she tried to rub it on him, "It smells like herbs!" she said, exasperated; "And it will probably do your coat good; it's just like the oil Hornmar put on you to make you gleam."

He continued to sidle, and Aerin said through clenched teeth: "I'll tie you up if you're not good." But Talat, after several days of being chased, step by step and sidle by sidle, around his pasture, decided that his new master was in earnest; and the next time Aerin ran him up against the fence, instead of eluding her again, he stood still and let his doom overtake him.

They went on their overnight journey a fortnight after Arlbeth had watched them work together, by which time Talat had permitted Aerin—sometimes with more grace than other times—to rub her yellow grease all over him. Aerin hoped it would be a warm night since most of what looked like a roll of blankets hung behind her saddle was a sausage-shaped skin of kenet.

They started before dawn had turned to day, and Aerin pushed Talat along fairly briskly, that they might still have several hours of daylight left when they made camp. There was a trail beside the little river, wide enough for a horse but too narrow for wagons, and this they followed; Aerin wished to be close to a large quantity of water when she tried her experiment; and not getting lost was an added benefit.

She made camp not long after noon. She unrolled the bundle that had looked like bedding and first removed the leather tunic and leggings she'd made for herself and let soak in a shallow basin of the yellow ointment for the last several weeks. She'd tried setting fire to her suit yesterday, and the fire, however vigorous it was as a torch, had gone out instantly when it touched a greasy sleeve. The suit wasn't very comfortable to wear; it was too sloppy and sloshy, and as she bound up her hair and stuffed it into a greasy helmet she thought with dread of washing the stuff off herself afterward.

She built up a big bonfire, and then smeared kenet over her face, and last pulled on her gauntlets. She stood by the flames, now leaping up over her head, and listened to her heart beating too quickly. She crept into the fire like a reluctant swimmer into cold water; first a hand, then a foot. Then she took a deep breath, hoped that her eyelashes were greasy enough, and stepped directly into the flame.

Talat came up to the edge of the fire and snorted anxiously.

The fire was pleasantly warm—*pleasantly*. It tapped at her face and hands with cheerful friendliness and the best of good will; it murmured and snapped in her ears; it wrapped its flames around her like the arms of a lover.

She leaped out of the fire and gasped for breath.

She turned back again and looked at the fire. Yes, it was a real fire; it burned on, unconcerned, although her booted feet had disarranged it somewhat.

Talat thrust a worried nose into her neck. "Your turn," she said. "Little do you know."

Little did he know indeed, and this was the part that worried her the most. Talat was not going to walk into a bonfire and stand there till she told him to come out again. She'd already figured out that for her future dragon-slaying purposes, since dragons were pretty small, Talat could get away with just his chest and legs and belly protected. But she would prefer to find out now—and to let him know—that the yellow stuff he objected to did have an important use.

She reached up to feel her eyelashes and was relieved to discover that they were still there. Talat was blowing at her anxiously—she realized, light-headedly, that in some odd way she now smelled of fire—and when she swept up a handful of kenet he eluded her so positively that for a bad moment she thought she might have to walk home. But he let her approach him finally and, after most of his front half was yellowish and shiny, permitted her to lead him back to the fire.

And he stood unmoving when she picked up a flaming branch and walked toward him. And still stood when she held the branch low before him and let little flames lick at his knees.

Kenet worked on horses too.

❧ CHAPTER 10 ❧

SHE RODE HOME in a merry mood. The time and the soap (fortunately she had thought to bring a great chunk of the harsh floor-scrubbing soap with her) it had taken to get the yellow stuff out of her hair could not dampen her spirits, any more than had the cold night, and she with only one thin blanket.

Even another dreadful court affair, with an endless diplomatic dinner after it, could not completely quell her happiness, and when the third person in half an hour asked her about her new perfume—there was a slightly herby, and a slightly charred, smell that continued to cling to her—she couldn't help but laugh out loud. The lady, who had been trying to make conversation, smiled a stiff smile and moved away, for she resented being laughed at by someone she was supposed to pity and be kind to.

Aerin sighed, for she understood the stiff smile, and wondered if she were going to smell of herbs and burning—and slightly of clean floors—forever.

There was an unnatural activity at her father's court at present; Thorped had been only the precursor of a swelling profusion of official visitors, each more nervous than the last, and a few inclined to be belligerent. The increasing activity on Damar's northern Border worried everyone who knew enough, or cared to pay attention; there was more traveling among the villages and towns and the king's City than there had been for as long as Aerin could remember, and the court dinners, always tense with protocol, were now stretched to breaking point with something like fear.

Aerin, after the morning her father had given her permission to take Talat out alone, had begun to visit the king at his breakfast now and then, and always he looked glad to see her. Sometimes Tor ate with the king as well, and if Arlbeth noticed that Tor joined him at breakfast more often now that there was a chance he would see Aerin as well, he said nothing. Tor was home most of the time now, for Arlbeth had need of him near.

Aerin persisted in being unaware of the way Tor watched her, but was acutely aware that conversation between them was awkward at best these days; a new constraint seemed to have come between them since the night Tor had told his cousin of the Hero's Crown. Aerin decided the new awkwardness probably had something to do with his having finally begged off crossing swords with her. She had perfectly understood that with the current workload he had had to, so she tried to be polite to show she didn't mind. When this didn't seem to help, she ignored him and talked to her father. It did seem odd that Tor should take it so seriously—surely he gave her credit for some understanding of what the first sola's life was like?—but if he wanted to be stiff and formal, that was his problem.

So it was the three of them lingering over third cups of malak one morning when the first petitioner of the day came to speak to the king.

The petitioner reported a dragon, destroying crops and killing chickens. It had also badly burned a child who had accidentally discovered its lair, although the child had been rescued in time to save its life.

Arlbeth sighed and rubbed his face with his hand. "Very well. We will send someone to deal with it."

The man bowed and left.

"There will be more of them now, with the trouble at the Border," said Tor. "That sort of vermin seems to breed faster when the North wind blows."

"I fear you are right," Arlbeth replied. "And we can ill spare anyone just now."

"I'll go," said Tor.

"Don't be a fool," snapped the king, and then immediately

said, "I'm sorry. I can spare you least of all—as you know.
Dragons don't kill people very often any more, but dragon-
slayers rarely come back without a few uncomfortable
burns."

"Someday," said Tor with a wry smile, "when we have
nothing better to do, we must think up a more efficient way to
cope with dragons. It's hard to take them seriously—but they
are a serious nuisance."

Aerin sat very still.

"Yes." Arlbeth frowned into his malak. "I'll ask tomorrow
for half a dozen volunteers to go take care of this. And pray
it's an old slow one."

Aerin also prayed it was an old slow one as she slipped off.
She had only a day's grace, so she needed to leave at once; fortunately she had visited the village in question once on a state
journey with her father, so she knew more or less how to get
there. It was only a few hours' ride.

Her hands shook as she saddled Talat and tied the bundles
of dragon-proof suit, kenet, sword, and a spear—which she
wasn't at all sure she could use, since, barring a few lessons
from Tor when she was eight or nine years old, she was entirely self-taught—to the saddle. Then she had to negotiate her
way past the stable, the castle, and down the king's way and
out of the City without anyone trying to stop her; and the
sword and spear, in spite of the long cloak she had casually
laid over them, were a bit difficult to disguise.

Her luck—or something—was good. She was worrying so
anxiously about what she would say if stopped that she gave
herself a headache; but as she rode, everyone seemed to be
looking not quite in her direction—almost as if they couldn't
quite *see* her, she thought. It made her feel a little creepy. But
she got out of the City unchallenged.

The eerie feeling, and the headache, lifted at once when she
and Talat set off through the forest below the City. The sun
was shining, and the birds seemed to be singing just for her.
Talat lifted into a canter, and she let him run for a while, the
wind slipping through her hair, the shank of the spear tapping
discreetly at her leg, reminding her that she was on her way to
accomplish something useful.

She stopped at a little distance from the dragon-infested
village to put on her suit—which was no longer quite so
greasy; it had reached its saturation point, perhaps, and then

adapted, as well-oiled boots adapt to the feet that wear them. Her suit still quenched torches, but it had grown as soft and supple as cloth, and almost as easy to wear. She rubbed ointment on her face and her horse, and pulled on her long gloves. Shining rather in the sunlight then and reeking of pungent herbs, Aerin rode into the village.

Talat was unmistakably a war-horse, even to anyone who had never seen one before, and her red hair immediately identified her as the first sol. A little boy stood up from his doorstep and shouted: "They're here for the dragon!" and then there were a dozen, two dozen folk in the street, looking at her, and then looking in puzzlement for the five or six others that should have been riding with her.

"I am alone," said Aerin; she would have liked to explain, not that she was here without her father's knowledge but that she was alone because she was dragon-proof (she hoped) and didn't need any help. But her courage rather failed her, and she didn't. In fact what the villagers saw as royal pride worked very well, and they fell over themselves to stop appearing to believe that a first sol (even a half-foreign one) couldn't handle a dragon by herself (and if her mother really was a witch, maybe there was some good in her being half a foreigner after all), and several spoke at once, offering to show the way to where the dragon had made its lair, all of them careful not to look again down the road behind her.

She was wondering how she could tell them delicately that she didn't want them hanging around to watch, since she wasn't at all sure how graceful (or effective) her first encounter with a real dragon was likely to be. But the villagers who accompanied her to show her the way had no intention of getting anywhere near the scene of the battle; a cornered dragon was not going to care what non-combatant bystanders it happened to catch with an ill-aimed lash of fire. They pointed the way, and then returned to their village to wait on events.

Aerin hung her sword round her waist, settled the spear into the crook of her arm. Talat walked with his ears sharply forward, and when he snorted she smelled it too: fire, and something else. It was a new smell, and it was the smell of a creature that did not care if the meat it ate was fresh or not, and was not tidy with the bones afterward. It was the smell of dragon. Talat, after his warning snort, paced onward carefully.

They came soon to a little clearing with a hummock of rock at its edge. The hummock had a hole in it, the upper edge of which was rimed with greasy smoke. The litter of past dragon meals was scattered across the once green meadow, and it occurred to Aerin that the footing would be worse for a horse's hard hoofs than a dragon's sinewy claws.

Talat halted, and they stood, Aerin gazing into the black hole in the hill. A minute or two went by and she wondered, suddenly, how one got the dragon to pay attention to one in the first place. Did she have to wake it up? Yell? Throw water into the cave at it?

Just as her spearpoint sagged with doubt, the dragon hurtled out of its den and straight at them: and it opened its mouth and blasted them with its fire—except that Talat had never doubted, and was ready to step nimbly out of its way as Aerin scrabbled with her spear and grabbed at Talat's mane to keep from falling off onto the dragon's back. It spun round—it was about the height of Talat's knees, big for a dragon, and dreadfully quick on its yellow-clawed feet—and sprayed fire at them again. This time, although Talat got them out of the worst of it, it licked over her arm. She saw the fire wash over the spear handle and glance off her elbow, but she did not feel it; and the knowledge that her ointment did accomplish what it was meant to do gave her strength and cleared her mind. She steadied the spear-butt and nudged Talat with one ankle; as he sidestepped and as the dragon whirled round at them again, she threw her spear.

It wouldn't have been a very good cast for a member of the thotor, or for a seasoned dragon-hunter, but it served her purpose. It stuck in the dragon's neck, in the soft place between neck and shoulder where the scales were thin, and it slowed the dragon down. It twitched and lashed its tail and roared at her, but she knew she hadn't given it a mortal wound; if she let it skulk off to its lair, it would eventually heal and re-emerge nastier than ever.

It bent itself around the wounded shoulder and tried to grip the spear in its teeth, which were long and thin and sharp and not well suited for catching hold of anything so smooth and hard and narrow as a spearshaft. Aerin dismounted and pulled out her sword, and approached it warily. It ignored her, or appeared to, till she was quite close; and then it snapped its long narrow head around at her again and spat fire.

It caught her squarely; and dragonfire had none of the friendliness of a woodfire burning by the side of a river. The dragonfire pulled at her, seeking her life; it clawed at her pale shining skin, and at the supple leather she wore; and while the heat of it did not distress her, the heat of its malice did; and as the fire passed over her and disappeared she stood still in shock, and stared straight ahead of her, and did not move.

The dragon knew it had killed her. It was an old dragon, and had killed one or two human beings, and knew that it had caught this one well and thoroughly. It had been a bit puzzled that she did not scream when it burned her arm, and that she did not scream now and fall down writhing on the earth; but this did not matter. She would not trouble it further, and it could attend to its sore shoulder.

Aerin took half a dozen stiff steps forward, grasped the end of the spear and forced the dragon to the ground, swung her sword up and down, and cut off the dragon's head.

Then there was an angry scream from Talat, and she whirled, the heat of the dead dragon's fresh-spilled blood rising as steam and clouding her vision: but she saw dragonfire, and she saw Talat rear and strike with his forefeet.

She ran toward them and thought, Gods, help me, it had a mate; I forgot, often there are two of them; and she chopped at the second dragon's tail, and missed. It swung around, breathing fire, and she felt the heat of it across her throat, and then Talat struck at it again. It lashed her with its tail when it whirled to face the horse again, and Aerin tripped and fell, and the dragon was on top of her at once, the claws scrabbling at her leather tunic and the long teeth fumbling for her throat. The smoke from its nostrils hurt her eyes. She yelled, frantically, and squirmed under the dragon's weight; and she heard something tear, and she knew if she was caught in dragonfire again she would be burned.

Then Talat thumped into the dragon's side with both hind feet, and the force of the blow lifted them both—for the dragon's claws were tangled in leather laces—and dropped them heavily. The dragon coughed, but there was no fire; and Aerin had fallen half on top of the thing. It raked her with its spiked tail, and something else tore; and its teeth snapped together inches from her face. Her sword was too long; she could not get it close enough for stabbing, and her shoulder was tiring. She dropped the sword and struggled to reach her right boottop, where she had a short dagger, but the dragon rolled, and she could not reach it.

Then Talat was there again, and he bit the dragon above its small red eye, where the ear hole was; and the dragon twisted its neck to spout fire at him, but it was still dazed by its fall, and only a little fire came out of its mouth. Talat plunged his own face into the trickle of smoke and seized the dragon by the nostrils and dragged its head back; and still farther back. Its forefeet and breast came clear of the ground, and as the dragon thrashed, Aerin's leg came free, and she pulled the dagger from her boot and thrust it into the dragon's scaleless breast. The dragon shrieked, the noise muffled by Talat's grip on its nose, and Aerin stumbled away to pick up her sword.

Talat swung the dying dragon back and forth, and slashed at its body with one forefoot, and the muscles of his heavy stallion's neck ran with sweat and smudges of ash. Aerin lifted up the sword and sliced the dragon's belly open, and it convulsed once, shuddered, and died. Talat dropped the body and stood with his head down, shivering, and Aerin realized what she had done, and how little she had known about what it would involve, and how near she had come to failure; and her stomach rebelled, and she lost what remained of her breakfast over the smoking mutilated corpse of the second dragon.

She walked a few steps away till she came to a tree, and with her hands on its bole she felt her way to the ground, and sat with her knees drawn up and her head between them for a few minutes. Her head began to clear, and her breathing slowed, and as she looked up and blinked vaguely at the leaves overhead, she heard Talat's hoofbeats behind her. She put out a hand, and he put his bloody nose into it, and so they remained for several heartbeats more, and then Aerin sighed and stood up. "Even dragons need water. Let's look for a stream."

Again they were lucky, for there was one close at hand. Aerin carefully washed Talat's face, and discovered that most of the blood was dragon's, although his forelock was singed half away. "And to think I almost didn't bother to put any kenet on your head," she murmured. "I thought it was going to be so easy." She pulled Talat's saddle off to give him a proper bath, after which he climbed the bank and found a nice scratchy bit of dirt and rolled vigorously, and stood up again mud-colored. "Oh dear," said Aerin. She splashed water on her face and hands and then abruptly pulled off all her dragon-tainted clothing and submerged. She came up again when she needed to breathe, chased Talat back into the water to wash the mud off, and then brushed and rubbed him hard till she was warm and dry with the work and he was at least no more than damp.

She dressed slowly and with reluctance, and they returned to the battlefield. She tried to remember what else she ought to have thought of about dragons. Eggs? Well, if there were eggs, they'd die, for new-hatched dragons depended on their parents for several months. And if there were young dragons, surely we'd have seen them—?

With much greater reluctance she tied together some dry brush and set fire to it from her tinder box, and approached the dark foul-smelling hole in the rock. She had to stoop to get inside the cave at all, and her torch guttered and tried to go out. She had an impression of a shallow cave with irregular walls of rock and dirt, and a pebbly floor; but she could not bear the smell, or the knowledge that the grisly creatures she had just killed had lived here, and she jerked back outside into the sunlight again, and dropped her torch, and stamped out the fire. She didn't think there were any eggs, or dragon kits. She'd have to hope there weren't.

She thought: I have to take the heads with me. The hunters always bring the heads—and it does prove it without a lot of talking about it. I don't think I can talk about it. So she picked up her sword again and whacked off the second dragon's head, and then washed her sword and dagger in the stream, re-sheathed them, and tied her spear behind the saddle. The dragons looked small now, motionless and headless, little bigger and no more dangerous than rabbits; and the ugly heads, with the long noses and sharp teeth, looked false, like masks in a monster-play for the children during one of the City holidays, where part of the fun is to be frightened—but not very much. Who could be frightened of a dragon?

I could, she thought.

She tied the heads in the heavy cloth she'd carried her leather suit in, and mounted Talat, and they went slowly back to the village.

The villagers were all waiting, over a hundred of them, gathered at the edge of town; the fields beyond the village were empty, and men and women in their working clothes, looking odd in their idleness, all stood watching the path Aerin and

Talat had disappeared down only an hour ago. A murmur arose as the front rank caught sight of them, and Talat raised his head and arched his neck, for he remembered how it should be, coming home from battle and bearing news of victory. The people pressed forward, and as Talat came out of the trees they surrounded him, looking up at Aerin: Just the one girl and her fine horse, surely they have not faced the dragon, for they are uninjured; and they were embarrassed to hope for a sol's burns, but they wished so sorely for the end of the dragon.

"Lady?" one man said hesitantly. "Did you meet the dragon?"

Aerin realized that their silence was uncertainty; she had suddenly feared that they would not accept even the gift of dragon-slaying from the daughter of a witchwoman, and she smiled in relief, and the villagers smiled back at her, wonderingly. "Yes, I met your dragon; and its mate." She reached behind her and pulled at the cloth that held the heads, and the heads fell to the ground; one rolled, and the villagers scattered before it as if it still had some power to do them harm. Then they laughed a little sheepishly at themselves; and then everyone turned as the boy who had announced Aerin's arrival said, "Look!"

Seven horsemen were riding into the village as Aerin had ridden in. "You weren't supposed to get here till tomorrow," she murmured, for she recognized Gebeth and Mik and Orin, who were cousins of hers a few times removed and members of her father's court, and four of their men. Gebeth and Orin had been on many dragon hunts before; they were loyal and reliable, and did not consider dragon-hunting beneath them, for it was a thing that needed to be done, and a service they could do for their king.

"Aerin-sol," said Gebeth; his voice was surprised, respectful—for her father's sake, not hers and disapproving. He would not scold her in front of the villagers, but he would certainly give Arlbeth a highly colored tale later on.

"Gebeth," she said. She watched with a certain ironic pleasure as he tried to think of a way to ask her what she was doing here; and then Orin, behind him, said something, and pointed to the ground where the small dragons' heads lay in the dust. Gebeth dropped his gaze from the unwelcome sight of his sovereign's young daughter rigged out like a soldier boy who has seen better days, realized what he was looking at, and yanked his eyes up again to stare disbelievingly at red-haired Aerin in her torn leather suit.

"I—er—I've gotten rid of the dragons already, if that's what you mean," said Aerin.

Gebeth dismounted, slowly, and slowly stooped down to stare at her trophies. The jaws of one were open, and the sharp teeth showed. Gebeth was not a rapid nor an original thinker, and he remained squatting on his heels and staring at the grisly heads long after he needed only to verify the dragonness of them. As slowly as he had stooped he straightened up again and bowed, stiffly, to Aerin, saying, "Lady, I salute you." His fingers flicked out in some ritual recognition or other, but Aerin couldn't tell which salute he was offering her, and rather doubted he knew which one he wanted to give. "Thank you," she said gravely.

Gebeth turned and caught the eye of one of his men, who dismounted and wrapped the heads up again; and then, as Gebeth gave no further hint, hesitated, and finally approached Talat to tie the bundle behind Aerin's saddle.

"May we escort you home, lady?" Gebeth said, raising his eyes to stare at Talat's pricked and bridleless ears, but carefully avoiding Aerin's face.

"Thank you," she said again, and Gebeth mounted his horse, and turned it back toward the City, and waited, that Aerin might lead; and Talat, who knew about the heads of columns, strode out without any hint from his rider.

The villagers, not entirely sure what they had witnessed, tried a faint cheer as Talat stepped off; and the boy who announced arrivals suddenly ran forward to pat Talat's shoulder, and Talat dropped his nose in acknowledgment and permitted the familiarity. A girl only a few years older than the boy stepped up to catch Aerin's eye, and said clearly, "We thank you." Aerin smiled and said, "The honor is mine." The girl grew to adulthood remembering the first sol's smile, and her seat on her proud white horse.

❧ CHAPTER 11 ❧

IT WAS A SILENT journey back, and seemed to take forever. When they finally entered the City gates it was still daylight, although Aerin was sure it was the daylight of a week since hearing the villagers' petition to her father for dragon-slaying. The City streets were thronged, and while the sight of seven of the king's men in war gear and carrying dragon spears was not strange, the sight of the first sol riding among them and looking rather the worse for wear was, and their little company was the subject of many long curious looks. They can see me just fine coming home again, Aerin thought grimly. Whatever shadow it was that I rode away in, I wish I knew where it had gone.

Hornmar himself appeared at her elbow to take Talat off to the stables when they arrived in the royal courtyard. Her escort seemed to her to dismount awkwardly, with a great banging of stirrups and creak of girths. She pulled down the bundles from behind Talat's saddle and squared her shoulders. She couldn't help looking wistfully after the untroubled Talat, who readily followed Hornmar in the direction he was sure meant oats; but she jerked her attention back to herself and found Gebeth staring at her, frozen-faced, so she led the way into the castle.

Even Arlbeth looked startled when they all appeared before him. He was in one of the antechambers of the main receiving-hall, and sat surrounded by papers, scrolls, sealing wax, and emissaries. He looked tired. Not a word had passed between Aerin and her unwilling escort since they had left the village, but Aerin felt that she was being herded and had not tried to escape. Gebeth would have reported to the king immediately upon his return, and so she must; it was perhaps just as well that she had so many sheepdogs to her one self-conscious sheep, because she might have been tempted to put off the reckoning had she ridden back alone.

"Sir," she said.

Arlbeth looked at Aerin, then at Gebeth and Gebeth's frozen face, then back at Aerin.

"Have you something to report?" he said, and the kindness in his voice was for both his daughter and his loyal, if scandalized, servant.

Gebeth remained bristling with silence, so Aerin said: "I rode out alone this morning, and went to the village of Ktha, to . . . engage their dragon. Or—um—dragons." What was the proper form for a dragon-killing report? She might have paid a little more attention to such things if she'd thought a little further ahead. She'd never particularly considered the *after* of killing dragons; the fact that she'd done it was supposed to be enough. But now she felt like a child caught out in misbehavior. Which at least in Gebeth's eyes she was.

She unwrapped the bundle she carried under her arm, and laid the battered dragon heads on the floor before her father's table. Arlbeth stood up and came round the edge of the table and stood staring down at them with a look on his face not unlike Gebeth's when he first recognized what was lying in the dust at his horse's feet.

"We arrived at the village . . . after," said Gebeth, who chose not to look at Aerin's ugly tokens of victory again, "and I offered our escort for Aerin-sol's return."

At "offered our escort" a flicker of a smile crossed Arlbeth's face, but he said very seriously, "I would speak to Aerin-sol alone." Everyone disappeared like mice into the walls, except they closed the doors behind them. Gebeth, his dignity still outraged, would say nothing, but no one else who had been in the room when Aerin told the king she had just slain two dragons could wait to start spreading the tale.

Arlbeth said, "Well?" in so colorless a tone that Aerin was afraid that, despite the smile, he must be terribly angry with her. She did not know where to begin her story, and as she looked back over the last years and reminded herself that he had set no barriers to her work with Talat, had trusted her judgment, she was ashamed of her secret; but the first words that came to her were: "I thought if I told you first, you would not let me go."

Arlbeth was silent for a long time. "This is probably so," he said at last. "And can you tell me why I should not have prevented you?"

Aerin exhaled a long breath. "Have you read Astythet's *History?*"

Arlbeth frowned a moment in recollection. "I . . . believe I did, when I was a boy. I do not remember it well." He fixed her with a king's glare, which is much fiercer than an ordinary mortal's. "I seem to remember that the author devotes a good deal of time and space to dragon lore, much of it more legendary than practical."

"Yes," said Aerin. "I read it, a while ago, when I was . . . ill. There's a recipe of sorts for an ointment called kenet, proof against dragonfire, in the back of it—"

Arlbeth's frown returned and settled. "A bit of superstitious nonsense."

"No," Aerin said firmly. "It is not nonsense; it is merely unspecific." She permitted herself a grimace at her choice of understatement. "I've spent much of the last three years experimenting with that half a recipe. A few months ago I finally found out . . . what works." Arlbeth's frown had lightened, but it was still visible. "Look." Aerin unslung the heavy cloth roll she'd hung over her shoulder and pulled out the soft pouch of her ointment. She smeared it on one hand, then the other, noticing as she did so that both hands were trembling. Quickly, that he might not stop her, she went to the fireplace and seized a burning branch from it, held it at arm's length in one greasy yellow hand, and thrust her other hand directly into the flame that billowed out around it.

Arlbeth's frown had disappeared. "You've made your point; now put the fire back into the hearth, for that is not a comfortable thing to watch." He went back behind his table and sat down; the weary lines showed again in his face.

Aerin came to the other side of his table, wiping her ashy hands on her leather leggings. "Sit," said her father, looking up at her; and leaving charcoal fingerprints on a scroll she tried delicately to move, she cleared the nearest chair and sat down. Her father eyed her, and then looked at the ragged gashes in her tunic. "Was it easy, then, killing dragons when they could not burn you?"

She spread her dirty fingers on her knees and stared at them. "No," she said quietly. "I did not think beyond the fire. It was not easy."

Arlbeth sighed. "You have learned something, then."

"I have learned something." She looked up at her father with sudden hope.

Arlbeth snorted, or chuckled. "Don't look at me like that. You have the beseeching look of a puppy that thinks it may yet get out of a deserved thrashing. Think you that you deserve your thrashing?"

Aerin said nothing.

"That's not meant solely as a rhetorical question. What sort of thrashing are you eligible for? You're a bit old to be sent to your room without any supper, and I believe I rather gave you your autonomy from Teka's dictates when I let you and Talat ride out alone." He paused. "I suppose you needed to get far enough away from the City to build a fire big enough to test your discovery thoroughly." Aerin still said nothing. "I can't forbid you Talat, for he's your horse now, and I love him too well to deny him his master."

He paused again. "You seem to be rather a military problem, but as you have no rank I cannot strip you of it, and as you do not bear a sword from the king's hands he can't take it away from you and hit you with the flat of it." His eyes lingered for a moment on Aerin's eighteenth-birthday present hanging by her side, but he did not mention it.

This time the pause was a long one. "Will you teach the making of the fire ointment if I ask it?"

Aerin raised her head. He could command her to explain it, and knew that she knew he could so command her. "I would gladly teach any who . . . gladly would learn it," and as she recognized that he did not command her, he recognized that she said gladly would learn from *me*, the witchwoman's daughter; for he knew, for all that it had never been spoken in his ears, what his second wife had been called.

"*I* would learn." He reached for the sack of ointment that Aerin had left lying on his table, took a little of the yellow grease on his fingertips, and rubbed thumb and forefinger together. He sniffed. "I suppose this explains the tales of the first sol's suddenly frequent visits to the apothecaries."

Aerin gulped and nodded. "I would—would be honored to show you the making of the kenet, sir."

Arlbeth stood up and came over to hug his daughter, and left his arm around her shoulders, mindless of the sleek fur of his sleeve and the condition of her leather tunic. "Look, you silly young fool. I understand why you have behaved as you have done, and I sympathize, and I am also tremendously proud of you. But kindly don't go around risking your life to prove any more points, will you? Come talk to me about it first at least.

"Now go away, and let me get back to what I was doing. I had a long afternoon's work still ahead of me before you interrupted."

Aerin fled.

A week later, when she finally dared face her father at breakfast again, which meant sitting down at the table and risking such conversational gambits as he might choose to begin, Arlbeth said, "I was beginning to feel ogreish. I'm glad you've crept out of hiding." Tor, who was there too, laughed, and so Aerin learned that Tor knew the dragon story as well. She blushed hotly; but as the first rush of embarrassment subsided she had to admit to herself that there was probably no one in the City who did not know the story by now.

Breakfast was got through without any further uncomfortable moments, but as Aerin rose to slink away—she still wasn't recovered quite enough for the receiving-hall, and had been spending her days mending her gear and riding Talat—Arlbeth said, "Wait just a moment. I have some things for you, but I gave up bringing them to breakfast several days ago."

Tor got up and disappeared from the room, and Arlbeth deliberately poured himself another cup of malak. Tor returned swiftly, although the moments were long for Aerin, and he was carrying two spears and her small plain sword, which he must have gone to her room to fetch from its peg on the wall by her bed. Tor formally offered them to the king, kneeling, his body bowed so that the outstretched arms that held the weapons were as high as his head; and Aerin shivered, for the first sola should give such honor to nobody. Arlbeth seemed to agree, for he said, "Enough, Tor, we already know how you feel about it," and Tor straightened up with a trace of a smile on his face.

Arlbeth stood up and turned to Aerin, who stood up too, wide-eyed. "First, I give you your sword," and he held it out to her with his hands one just below the hilt and one two-thirds down the scabbarded blade, and she cupped her hands around his. He dropped the sword into her hands, and then cupped his fingers around her closed fingers. "Thus you receive your first sword from your king," he said, and let go; and Aerin dropped her arms slowly to her sides, the sword pressing against her thighs. She carried the sword of the king now; and so the king could call upon it and her whenever he had need—to do, or not to do, at his bidding. The color came and went in her face, and she swallowed.

"And now," Arlbeth said cheerfully, "as you have received your sword officially by my hand I can officially reprimand you with it." He reached for the hilt as Aerin stood dumbly holding it by the scabbard, and pulled the blade clear. He whipped it through the air, and it looked small in his hands; then he brought the blade to a halt just before Aerin's nose. "Thus," he said, and slapped her cheek hard with the flat of it, "and thus," and he slapped her other cheek with the opposite flat, and Aerin blinked, for the blows brought tears to her eyes. Arlbeth stood looking at her till her vision cleared, and said gravely, "I am taking this very seriously, my dear, and if I catch you riding off again without speaking to me first, I may treat you as a traitor."

Aerin nodded.

"But since you are officially a sword-bearer and since we take pride in officially praising your recently demonstrated dragon-slaying skills," he said, and turned and picked up the spears Tor still held, "these are yours," Aerin held out her arms, the scabbard strap hitched up hastily to dangle from one shoulder. "These are from my days as a dragon-hunter," Arlbeth said. Aerin looked up sharply. "Yes; I hunted dragons when I was barely older than you are now, and I have a few scars to prove it." He smiled reminiscently. "But heirs to the throne are quickly discouraged from doing anything so dangerous and unadmirable as dragon-hunting, so I only used these a few times before I had to lay them aside for good. It's sheer stubbornness that I've kept them so long."

Aerin smiled down at her armful.

"I can tell you at least that they are tough and strong and fly straight from the hand.

"I can also tell you that there's another report of a dragon come in—yesterday morning it was. I told the man I'd have his answer by this morning; he's coming to the morning court. Will you go back with him?"

Aerin and her father looked at each other. For the first time she had official position in his court; she had not merely been permitted her place, as she had grudgingly been permitted her undeniable place at his side as his daughter, but she had won it. She carried the king's sword, and thus was, however irregularly, a member of his armies and his loyal sworn servant as well as his daughter. She had a place of her own—both taken and granted. Aerin clutched the spears to her breast, painfully banging her knee with the sword scabbard in the process. She nodded.

"Good. If you had remained hidden, I would have sent Gebeth again—and think of the honor you would have lost."

Aerin, who seemed to have lost her voice instead, nodded again.

"Another lesson for you, my dear. Royalty isn't allowed to hide—at least not once it has declared itself."

A little of her power of speech came back to her, and she croaked, "I have hidden all my life."

Something like a smile glimmered in Arlbeth's eyes. "Do I not know this? I have thought more and more often of what I must do if you did not stand forth of your own accord. But you have—if not quite in the manner I might have wished—and I shall take every advantage of it."

The second dragon-slaying went better than had the first. Perhaps it was her father's spears, which flew truer to their marks than she thought her aim and arm deserved; perhaps it was Talat's eagerness, and the quickness with which he caught on to what he was to do. There was also only one dragon.

This second village was farther from the City than the first had been, so she stayed the night. She washed dragon blood from her clothing and skin—it left little red rashy spots where it had touched her—in the communal bathhouse, from which everyone had been debarred that the sol might have her privacy, and sleeping in the headman's house while he and his wife slept in the second headman's house. She wondered if the second headman then slept in the third's, and if this meant eventually that someone slept in the stable or in a back garden, but she thought that to ask would only embarrass them further. They had been embarrassed enough when she had protested driving the headman out of his own home. "We do you the honor fitting your father's daughter and the slayer of our demon," he said.

She did not like the use of the word *demon*; she remembered Tor saying that the increase of the North's mischief would increase the incidence of small but nasty problems like dragons. She also wondered if the headman did not wish himself or his pregnant wife to spend a night under the same roof as the witchwoman's daughter, or if they would get a priest in—the village was too small to have its own priest—to bless the house after she left. But she did not ask, and she slept alone in the headman's house.

The fifth dragon was the first one that marked her. She was careless, and it was her own fault. It was the smallest dragon she had yet faced, and the quickest, and perhaps the brightest; for when she had pinned it to the ground with one of her good spears and came up to it to chop off its head, it did not flame at her, as dragons usually did. It had flamed at her before, with depressingly little result, from the dragon's point of view. When she approached it, it spun around despite the spear that held it, and buried its teeth in her arm.

Her sword fell from her hand, and she hissed her indrawn breath, for she discovered that she was too proud to scream. But not screaming took nearly all her strength, and she looked, appalled, into the dragon's small red eye as she knelt weakly beside it. Awkwardly she picked up her sword with her other hand, and awkwardly swung it; but the dragon was dying already, the small eye glazing over, its last fury spent in closing its jaws on her arm. It had no strength to avoid even a slow and clumsy blow, and as the sword edge struck its neck it gave a last gasp, and its jaws loosened, and it died, and the blood poured out of Aerin's arm and mixed on the ground with the darker, thicker blood of the dragon.

Fortunately that village was large enough to have a healer, and he bound her arm, and offered her a sleeping draught which she did not swallow, for she could smell a little real magic on him and was afraid of what he might mix in his draughts. At least the poultice on her arm did her good and no harm, even if she got no sleep that night for the sharp ache of the wound.

At home, pride of place and Arlbeth's encouragement brought her to attend more of the courts and councils that administered the country that Arlbeth ruled. "Don't let the title mislead you," Arlbeth told her. "The king is simply the visible one. I'm so visible, in fact, that most of the important work has to be done by other people."

"Nonsense," said Tor.

Arlbeth chuckled. "Your loyalty does you honor, but you're in the process of becoming too visible to be effective yourself, so what do you know about it?"

The most important thing that Aerin learned was that a king needed people he could trust, and who trusted him. And so she learned all over again that she lacked the most important aspect of her heritage, for she could not trust her father's people, because they would not trust her. It was not a lesson she learned gratefully. But she had come out of hiding, and just as she could not scream when the dragon bit her, so she could not go back to her former life.

And the reports of dragons did increase, and thus she was oftener not at home, and so her excuse for eluding royal appearances was often the excellent one of absence, or of exhaustion upon too recent return. And she grew swifter and defter in dispatching the small dangerous vermin, and lost no more than a lock of hair that escaped her kenet-treated helmet to the viciousness of the creatures she faced. And the small villages came to love her, and they called her Aerin Fire-hair, and were kind to her, and not only respectful; and even she, wary as she was of all kindness, stopped believing that the headmen asked priests to drive out the aura of the witch-woman's daughter after she left them.

But killing dragons did her no good with her father's court; the soft-skinned ministers who worked in words and traveled by litter and could not hold a sword still mistrusted her, and privately felt that there was something rather shameful about a sol killing dragons at all, even a halfblood sol. Their increasing fear of the North only increased their mistrust of her, whose mother had come from the North; and her dragon-slaying, especially when the only wound she bore from a task that often killed horses and crippled men was a simple flesh wound, began to make them fear her; and the story of the first sola's infatuation, which had begun to fade as nothing more came of it, was brought up again, and those who wished to said that the king's daughter played a waiting game. They knew the story of the kenet, knew that anyone might learn the making of the stuff who wished to learn it; but why was it Aerin-sol who had found it out?

No one but Arlbeth and Tor asked her to teach them.

Perlith one night, after a great deal of wine had been drunk, amused the company by singing a new ballad that, he said, he had recently heard from a minstrel singing in one of the smaller dingier marketplaces in the City. She had been a rather small and dingy minstrel as well, he added, smiling, and she had been traveling through some of the smaller dingier villages of the Hills of late, which is where the ballad came from.

The ballad told of Aerin Fire-hair, whose hair blazed brighter than dragonfire, and thus she slew them without hurt to herself, for the dragons were ashamed when they saw her, and could not resist her. Perlith had a sweet light tenor voice, and the ballad was not so very badly composed, and the tune was an old and venerable one that many generations had enjoyed. But Perlith mocked her with it by the most delicate inflections, the gentlest ironies, and her knuckles were white around her wine goblet as she listened.

When Perlith finished, Galanna gave one of her bright little laughs. "How charming," she said. "To think—we are living with a legend. Do you suppose that anyone will make up songs about any of the rest of us, at least while we are alive to enjoy them?"

"Let us hope that at least any songs made in our honor do not expose us so terribly," Perlith said silkily, "as this one explains why our Aerin kills her dragons so easily."

Aerin knew she must sit still but she could not, and she left the hall, and heard Galanna's laugh again, drifting down the corridor after her.

It was a week after Perlith sang his song that the news of Nyrlol came in. Aerin had been out killing another dragon the day the messenger arrived, and had not returned to the City till the afternoon of the next day. She had had not only a pair of adult dragons this time, but a litter of four kits; and the fourth one had been nearly impossible to catch, for it was small enough still to hide easily, and enough brighter than its siblings to do so. But the kits were old enough that they might forage for themselves, and so she did not dare leave the last one unslain. She would not have found it at all but for its dragon pride that made it send out a small thread of flame at her. It was grim thankless work to kill something so small; the kit wasn't even old enough to scorch human skin with its tiny pale fires. But Aerin concentrated on the fact that it would grow up into a nasty creature capable of eating children, and dug it out of its hole, and killed it.

The town the dragons had been preying upon was large enough to put on a feast with jugglers and minstrels in her honor, and so she had spent the evening, and the next morning had slept late. She could feel the nervous excitement in the City as she rode through it that day, and it made Talat fidgety.

"What has happened?" she asked Hornmar.

He shook his head. "Trouble—Nyrlol is making trouble."

"Nyrlol," Aerin said. She knew of Nyrlol, and of Nyrlol's temperament, from her council meetings.

Six days later Aerin faced her father in the great hall with the sword she had received at his hands hanging at her side, to ask him to let her ride with him; and watched his face as he came back a long long way to be kind to her; and discovered what the place she had earned in his court was worth. Aerin Dragon-Killer. King's daughter.

PART TWO

❧CHAPTER 12❧

TEKA BROUGHT HER THE MESSAGE from Tor three days later. He had tried to see her several times, but she had refused to talk to him, and Teka could not sway her; and from the glitter in her eye Teka did not dare suggest to Tor that he simply announce himself. His note read: "We ride out tomorrow at dawn. Will you see us off?"

She wanted to burn the note, or rip it to bits, or eat it, or burst into tears. She spent the night sitting in her window alcove, wrapped in a fur rug; she dozed occasionally, but mostly she watched the stars moving across the sky. She did not want to stand in the cold grey dawn and watch the army ride away, but she would do it, for she knew it had hurt her father to deny her what she asked—because she was too young; too inexperienced; because he could not afford even the smallest uncertainty in his company's faith when they went to face Nyrlol, and because her presence would cause that uncertainty. Because she was the daughter of a woman who came from the North.

They could at least part with love. It was like Tor to make the gesture; her father, for all his kindness, was too proud—or too much a king; and she was too proud, or too bitter, or too young.

And so she stood heavy-eyed in the castle courtyard as the cavalry officers and courtiers mounted their horses and

awaited the king and the first sola. The army waited in the
wide clearing hewn out of the forest beyond the gates of the
City; Aerin imagined that she could hear the stamp of hoofs,
the jingle of bits, see the long shadows of the trees lying across
the horses' flanks and the men's faces.

Hornmar emerged round the looming bulk of the castle,
leading Kethtaz, who tiptoed delicately, ears hard forward and
tail high. Hornmar saw her and wordlessly brought Kethtaz to
her, and gave his bridle into her hand. The first sola's equerry
waited impassively, holding Dgeth. Hornmar turned away to
mount his own horse, for he was riding with the army; but
meanwhile he was giving the king's daughter the honor of
holding the king's stirrup. This was not a small thing: holding
the king's stirrup conferred luck upon the holder, and often in
times past the queen had demanded the honor herself. But
often too the king ordered one who was considered lucky—a
victorious general, or a first son, or even a first sola—to hold
his stirrup for him, especially when the king rode to war, or to
a tricky diplomatic campaign that might suddenly turn to war.

No one said anything, but Aerin could feel a mental chill
pass across the courtyard as some of the mounted men
wondered if the witchwoman's daughter began their mission
with a bad omen, and she wondered if Hornmar had done her
a favor. If the army rode out expecting the worst, they were
likely to find it.

Aerin held Kethtaz's reins grimly, but Kethtaz did not like
grimness, and prodded her with his nose till she smiled involuntarily and petted him. She looked up when she heard the
king's footsteps, and when she met her father's eyes she was
glad she had yielded to Tor's request. Arlbeth kissed her forehead, and cupped her chin in his hands, and looked at her for
a long moment; then he turned to Kethtaz, and Aerin grasped
the stirrup and turned it for Arlbeth's foot.

At that moment there was a small commotion at the courtyard gate, and a man on a tired horse stepped onto the glassy
stone. The horse stopped, swaying on wide-spaced legs, for it
was too weary to walk trustingly on the smooth surface; and
the man dismounted and dropped the reins, and ran to where
the king stood. Arlbeth turned, his hand still on Aerin's shoulder, as the man came up to them.

"Majesty," he said.

Arlbeth inclined his head as if he were in his great hall and this man only the first of a long morning's supplicants. "Majesty," the man said again, as if he could not remember his message, or dared not give it. The man's gaze flicked to Aerin's face as she stood, her hand still holding the stirrup for mounting, and she was startled to see the gleam of hope in the man's eyes as he looked at her.

"The Black Dragon has come," he said at last. "Maur, who has not been seen for generations, the last of the great dragons, great as a mountain. Maur has awakened."

Sweat ran down the man's face, and his horse gave a gasping shuddering breath that meant its wind was broken, so hard had it been ridden. "I beg you for . . . help. My village even now may be no more. Other villages will soon follow." The man's voice rose in panic. "In a year—in a season Damar may all be black with the dragon's breath."

"This is mischief from across the Border," Tor said, and Arlbeth nodded. There was silence for a long, sad, grim moment, and when Arlbeth spoke again, his voice was heavy. "As Tor says, the Black Dragon's awakening is mischief sent us, and sent us crucially at just this moment when we dare not heed it." The messenger's shoulders slumped, and he put his hands over his face.

Arlbeth went on, so quietly that none but Aerin and Tor and the man might hear. "We go now to meet a trouble that may be even deadlier than dragons, for it is human and Damarian and spurred by mischief. Damar may yet face the dragon; a Damar broken to bits would be nothing, even though the dragon lay dead." He turned to Kethtaz again, set his foot in the stirrup, and mounted. Aerin stepped back as Kethtaz pranced, for he cared nothing for dragons and much for bearing the king at the head of a procession.

"We shall return as soon as we may, and go to meet your Black Dragon. Rest, and take a fresh horse, and go back to your village. All those who wish it may come to our City and await us in its shelter." He raised his arm, and his company rustled like leaves, waiting the order to march; and one of the sofor led the messenger's wind-broken horse to one side, and the king's procession passed the courtyard gate, and went down the king's way and beyond the City walls to where the army awaited them.

Aerin had meant to climb to the top of the castle and watch the glitter of their going till it disappeared into the trees beyond the City; but instead she waited, standing beside the messenger, whose hands were still over his face. When the last sound of the king's company's going faded he dropped his hands, as if till then he had been hoping for some reprieve; and he sighed. "Almost I missed them entirely," he murmured, staring into the empty air. "And it was to no purpose. Better I had missed them, and not used my poor Lmoth so ill," and his eyes turned to the horse he had ridden.

"Lmoth will be cared for well in our stables," said Aerin, "and I will take you now to find food and a bed for yourself."

The man's eyes turned slowly toward her, and again she saw the dim flicker of hope. "I must return as soon as I may, at least with the message of the king's charity for those of my folk left homeless or fearful."

Aerin said, "Food first. It's a long weary way you have come."

He nodded, but his eyes did not leave her face.

Aerin said softly: "I will come with you when you ride home; but you know that already, don't you?"

The hopeful gleam was now reflected in a smile, but a smile so faint that she would not have seen it at all if she had not, in her turn, hoped for it.

"Thank you, Aerin-sol, Dragon-Killer," he said.

They rode out together that afternoon. Talat was fresh, and inclined to bounce; he did not heed the dragon spears attached to his saddle because he believed he knew everything he needed to know about dragons. It was a silent journey. They went as quickly as they dared push the horses—a little less quickly than the messenger liked, but Aerin knew she and Talat had a dragon before them, and Talat was old; and if he did not wish to remember it, then it was all the more important that Aerin remember it for him.

Their course was almost due north, but the mountains were steepest in that direction, so they went out of their way to take the easier path, and moved the swifter for it. At dawn on the third day a black cloud hung before them, near the horizon that the mountains made, although the sky overhead was clear; and by afternoon they were breathing air that had an acrid edge to it. The messenger's head had sunk between his shoulders, and he did not raise his eyes from the path after they first saw the black cloud.

Talat picked his way carefully in the other horse's wake. He was better-mannered now than he had been when he was young and the king's war-horse; then the idea of following any other horse would have made him fret and sulk. Aerin left it to him, for she looked only at the cloud. When the messenger turned off to the left, while the cloud still hung before them, she said, "Wait."

The man paused and looked back. His expression was dazed, as if hearing the word "Wait" had called him back a long distance.

"The dragon lies ahead; it is his signature we see in the sky. I go that way."

The man opened his mouth, and the dazed expression cleared a little; but he closed his mouth again without saying anything.

"Go to your people and give them the king's message," Aerin said gently. "I will come to you later, as I can—or not."

The man nodded, but still he sat, turned in his saddle to look at the king's daughter, till Aerin edged Talat past him and down the path the man had left, straight toward the cloud.

She made camp that night by a stream black with ash; to boil water for malak she had first to strain it, and strain it again, through a corner of her blanket, for this was not a contingency she had planned for. "Although I suppose I should have," she said to Talat, hanging the soggy bedding over a frame of branches by the fire in the hope that it might dry before she had to wrap herself in it. She'd had to strain water for Talat too, for he'd refused to drink the ashy stuff in the running stream, snorting and pawing at it, and tossing an offended head with flattened ears.

The campfire was less comfort than it should have been; the light glared, and hurt the eyes, and it seemed to smoke more than a small campfire should, and the smoke hung low to the ground and would not drift away, but clung to the throat and lungs. Aerin rolled herself in the still damp blanket and tried to sleep; but her dreams woke her, for she heard the dragon breathing, and it seemed to her that the earth beneath her thudded with the dragon's heartbeat. Talat was restless too, and turned his head often to stare into the darkness, and shivered his skin as if he felt ash flakes brushing him.

Dawn came, and Aerin lay wide awake, watching the light

broaden, and still she felt the earth tremble with the dragon's pulse; and the light did not grow as bright as it should, but remained grey as twilight. She rolled her blanket, and left it and her cooking gear in the lee of a rock; and she rubbed Talat all over with kenet, and herself as well, and donned her greasy leather suit; and then she rubbed herself and her horse with kenet all over again, and even Talat was subdued by the grey light and the trembling ground and did not protest this deviation from the proper schedule. Aerin rubbed her spears with kenet, and checked that the rough suede grips were looped firmly in place; and she checked the clasp of her swordbelt and the lie of the short knife she carried in her right boot. Lastly she pulled on her gauntlets; the fingers felt as stiff as daggers.

Maur was waiting for them. They had spent the night separated from the dragon by no more than a knob of rock a little taller than Talat; and it was in the direction the dragon lay that Talat had so often looked during the dark hours. Or perhaps Maur had approached them from where it had lain yesterday and it was the weight of its footsteps Aerin had felt as its heartbeat as she lay awake by the smoky campfire.

Perhaps the dragon was not so large as a mountain; but the heavy black cloud that clung around it made it larger than a mountain, and when it first caught sight of them it lifted its wings, briefly, and the sun disappeared, and a wind like a storm wind howled around them. Then it bowed its long neck to the ground, its nose pointed toward them, and its half-lidded red eyes stared straight at them.

Talat stopped as they rounded the protective stone shoulder, and threw up his head. Aerin was ready to dismount hastily if Maur was too much even for Talat's courage, for he had not had the warning she had had, and at least till the night before he must have believed that they went to fight a dragon like other dragons. But he stood, feet planted, and stared back at the dragon, and Maur's red eyes opened a little wider, and it began to grin a bit, and smoke seeped out between its teeth, which were as long as Talat's legs. The smoke crawled along the ground toward them, and curled around Talat's white ankles, and Talat stamped and shivered but did not move, and the dragon grinned a little more.

They were in a small cup of valley; or what remained of the valley with the dragon in it was small. There had been trees in the valley, and on the steep slopes around them, but there were no trees now. It was hard to see anything. The smoke was rising around them, and the valley was blackened; when a low rocky hillock moved toward them, Aerin realized suddenly that it was some of the dragon's tail. Dragons sometimes stunned their prey with their tails when they did not care to expend the energy that breathing fire required, or didn't feel the prey was worth it.

She loosened a dragon spear in its place, and drove Talat forward with her legs. He was only a little slow to respond. She lifted the spear and hurled it with all her strength at the dragon's nearer eye.

Maur raised its head with a snap, and the spear bounced harmlessly off the horny ridge beneath its eye; and Talat lurched out of the way of the striking tail. The dragon's head snaked around as Talat evaded the tail, and Talat dodged again, and fire sang past Aerin's ear, fire like nothing either Talat or Aerin had ever seen before, any more than this dragon was like any other dragon they had seen. The fire was nearly white, like lightning, and it smelled hard and metallic; it smelled like the desert at noon, it smelled like a forest fire; and the blast of air that sheathed it was hotter than any Damarian forge.

Talat's eye showed white as he glared back over his shoulder at the dragon; Maur was sitting half crouched now, but it was grinning again, and it made no further move toward them.

Aerin was shivering in the saddle, the long convulsive shudders of panic. She loosened the second spear, and reluctantly she turned Talat to face the dragon once more; she wanted desperately to run away and hide, and had her throat not been dry with terror she would have sobbed. Her shoulder creaked as she lifted the spear. She urged Talat forward, and he moved stiff-legged, tail lashing anxiously; she put him into a trot as if they were going to pass the dragon by on their left side; all the time she was horribly aware of Maur's slitted eyes watching them. She coughed on the rising smoke, and almost lost her grip on the spear; and as they were almost past the dragon's farther shoulder she kneed Talat abruptly around, swerving in under the dragon's breast as it crouched, and flung the spear at the soft spot under the jaw.

Maur swung away from them faster than anything so large should have been able to move; the wind of its movement knocked Talat off his stride, and he stumbled. Maur threw up its head with a roar that sounded like mountains falling, and yellow-white fire spouted into the sky. Aerin clung weakly to Talat's mane as he swerved away from the dragon's raking foreclaw, and saw that her spear had found its mark; it dangled under the dragon's chin, looking as frail as a blade of grass, and Aerin knew it was no good. Had her throw been true, Maur would have fallen at once in its death agonies, not lashed its head down toward them again and spat another long white-hot gout of fire at them.

Talat swerved again, and the fire only nicked them in passing. Maur shook its head violently and Aerin's spear came free and whipped away like a leaf on a gale; the dragon's eyes were wide open now, and they heard the hiss of its breath, and it sent more fire at them, and Talat spun desperately aside once again. There was sweat on his neck, and sweat ringing his dark eyes; and Aerin could do nothing but cling dumbly to the saddle; her brain refused to function. Her spears were gone, and there was nothing useful to be done with her sword. Talat leaped aside once more, nearly unseating her; she cowered miserably and wondered why Talat did not turn tail and run, but continued to face the monster, waiting for her to do . . . something.

Another blast of fire, and this time, as Talat reared back on his hocks and spun frantically to the right, the weak hind leg gave way. He screamed, with fear or shame, as the leg buckled and he fell; and Aerin fell with him, for her reflexes were too numb to pitch her free. And so she was a little above him as they fell together, and the dragonfire caught her, briefly, and she fell through it.

One arm was flung up, or left behind, as she fell, and the fire burned the kenet-rich leather to ash instantly, and scorched the arm within; and the helmet on her head blackened and fell away, and most of her hair vanished, and her kenet-smeared face was on fire. She opened her mouth to scream, and she was almost past the band of fire then, or she would have died at once; but still a little of the outermost edge of the dragonfire, no hotter, perhaps, than the fire used to temper the king's swords, slid between her lips and down her throat and into her lungs, and then she had nothing left to scream with.

Then she was below the fire lash, and lying on the ground,

and one foot was caught under Talat's body, and Talat lay still. The pain of her scorched throat and lungs was so great she almost forgot the pain of her arm and her head; but she found, somewhere, enough consciousness left to be surprised, when she saw a great shadow shifting toward them and looming over them, that she could still see, and out of both her eyes. I'm still alive, she thought, and blinked; her unburnt cheek was pressed against the ground, which felt as cold as ice. That's the dragon leaning over us, she thought; it will kill us for sure this time. There was a red haze hanging before her eyes, or maybe her eyes were only sore from the smoke and ash; but she could not see clearly. She must have imagined that she saw the dragon's jaws opening, for had she seen it, there would have been no time left. As it was she had time to think, calmly and clearly, I've killed Talat because he wouldn't turn and run; he's a war-horse. Well, perhaps I can run forward, not back too, now that it's too late.

She hadn't had time to figure out how seriously hurt she was, so she picked herself up and flung herself at the dragon's nose as it bowed its head to nuzzle them, or swallow them, or whatever it had planned; and she found out too late that the ankle that had been caught under Talat was broken, and her left arm so withered by the fire that it could not obey her; but somehow still she had grabbed Maur's nostrils, and as it yanked its head up she held on grimly with one hand and one foot, and perhaps with her teeth. This is for Talat, she thought, but dimly now. There's still a knife in my boot, but I have only one hand; I can't hold on and pull it out both.

But Maur reared up as it raised its head, and the weight of the air held her flat upon its nose for a moment, and almost she laughed, and worked her good hand down to her boottop and pulled the knife free. The dragon finished rearing, and clawed at its nose with one front leg; but its eyes were set too low and far back on its head to see her where she lay, and its skin was too thick for it to feel her location accurately, and the swipe missed. She thought, A few steps, only a few, it doesn't matter that my ankle's broken; and she half stood up and ran the length of the dragon's head, flung herself down flat again, and plunged her knife into Maur's right eye.

The force of the blow had all her weight behind it, for all that she had little strength left, and her weight carried the knife deep into the dragon's eye, and on into its brain, and as her gauntleted fingers were clutched convulsively around the knife's hilt, her arm followed, its passage shoulder deep. The dragon's fiery blood fountained out and covered her, and she fainted.

❧ CHAPTER 13 ❧

WHEN SHE CAME to herself she was screaming, or she would have been screaming had her ravaged throat been capable of it. It hurt to breathe. She lay on the ground, a little distance from where the dragon lay crumpled up against the mountain-side, its head and tail outflung and motionless. She thought, I must have killed it after all; but the thought did not please her particularly. She hurt too much. Water was her next thought. There was a stream. . . . The thought of water made her wounds burn the more fiercely, and she fainted again.

Somehow during that long afternoon she crawled to the stream; it was not until twilight that she finally put out her hand—her right hand, caked with dragon gore—and felt water running over it. She had been afraid that she had, in her desperate need, imagined the sound and smell of running water, and her periods of unconsciousness were full of dreams that told her she was crawling in the wrong direction. Two or three tears crept down her blackened face, and she pulled herself up on her right elbow again, and dragged herself forward, and fell full length into the water. It was shallow where she lay, and she feebly propped herself against a moderate-sized boulder where the water could run freely over her left arm and the left side of her face and yet let her breathe.

She spent at least that night in the cool stream, moving only to drink, and then turning her face up again against the rock that she might go on breathing; although she wondered, occasionally, as she wandered in and out of consciousness, why she cared. Dawn came; or perhaps it was the second dawn since she had pulled herself into the water; or the twelfth. She watched the sun rise and it occurred to her that she seemed to be spending more time conscious, and she was sorry for this. It would have been simpler if sometime during the night when she had wandered off, leaving her crippled body in the cold running water, she had not returned. But instead she found herself blinking at the light of morning, and then staring at a vaguely familiar pale hulk at the shore of the stream. Talat.

"Talat," she croaked, and discovered that her voice was not entirely gone after all. Talat raised his drooping head and looked at her; he had not recognized the thing in the stream as his beloved Aerin, and he whinnied eagerly but uncertainly.

"If you're still around," Aerin whispered, "then perhaps I'd better stay too," and she hunched herself painfully into a sitting position.

Talat backed a step or two away from the thing in the stream as it rose up at him, but it croaked "Talat" at him again and he paused. The voice did not sound the way Aerin's voice should sound, but he was quite sure it had something to do with his Aerin, and so he waited. Aerin found out that sitting up was as far as she could go in that direction, so she lay down again, rolled over on her belly, and hitched her way slowly up onto the shore of the stream. Talat lowered his head anxiously and blew, and the touch of his breath on her face made her grunt with pain. She worked her right hand out of its sodden gauntlet, and raised her good hand to her horse, and he lipped her fingers and then gave a great sigh—of relief, she thought; but she turned her face away from his warm breath. "A lot you know," she whispered, but for the first time since they had fallen together before the dragon it occurred to her that she might not die.

Her burns and her broken ankle throbbed more harshly once she was out of the water, and she thought, I could spend the rest of my life lying in streams. A very small thought added, That may be no very long time anyway. Then she thought: I have to find a way at least to stand up and get Talat's saddle off before it galls him. Well, I still have one arm and one leg.

It was very awkward, and Talat was unhappy at the way she

pulled herself up his left foreleg till she could grab the girth and pitch her shoulders across the saddle and prop herself up that way; but he stood as still as the dead dragon, and only the stiffness of his neck and back told her he was worried. "I'm worried too, my friend," she murmured. She managed to unbuckle the girth and let the saddle slide to the ground; there was a pink, almost raw spot behind his elbow where the sweaty girth had rubbed him for too long. There were also two long angry red weals, one across his croup and one other down his flank. Dragonfire.

She slithered back to the ground again, landing on the saddle. She found herself staring at the buckles that had held the saddlebags. Food. Where did I leave my gear? It was near the stream here somewhere. Behind a rock. She looked around, but her sight was blurry, and she could not tell which smaller humps were rocks and which might be saddlebags. Her mouth and throat throbbed. I probably can't eat anything but mush, she thought, and grimaced, but wrinkling her face for the grimace was so painful that she could think of nothing for a few minutes.

It was Talat who found her saddlebags. He ambled away from her, snuffling along the ground by the edge of the stream; and he paused by one particular group of small dim hummocks and bumped them with his nose; and Aerin knew by the noise that they were not rocks. He moved away from them again, and one hoof in passing glanced off them, and again the noise was a faint rustle instead of the tunk of hoof against stone.

It was another long afternoon before she dragged herself within reach of her saddlebags, for she had often to climb back into the water and soothe her burns and her throbbing ankle. She lay with one hand on their smooth leather, and then thought: A fire. If I could boil something to a pulp till I could swallow it. . . . She fumbled one of the flaps open; there was still bread, and she put it in her hand and held her hand in the water till she felt it begin to disintegrate, and then lapped it up slowly.

She did build a fire; she found a way to wedge her tinder between stones so that she could strike it with her good hand; and fortunately there was plenty of fuel by the shores of the stream. Trees still grew here, for they were a little protected from the dragon's valley by the long stone shoulder that had

hidden Maur from Aerin's campsite. She found the remains of
her campfire, and it looked old and weathered; and she
thought to notice that the stream was running clear again, and
she wondered again how long she had lain in the stream. She
found a flat rock for a lid, and began the long process of boil-
ing dried meat in her tin till it was soft enough for her to eat.
She didn't dare make the fire very large, for she could not go
far to fetch wood for it; nor could she bear the heat of it.

She slept, or fainted again, often, drifting back and forth
across the boundary of selfhood; it was no longer only obliv-
ion that those periods of blankness brought her, but the beginning of healing. She pried the boot off her right foot, gingerly
felt the ankle, wrapped it in strips made from spare clothing,
tying knots with one hand and her teeth; and hoped she was
doing something useful. The wrappings reminded her, if they
did no other good, to keep the foot quiet, and the ache of it
ebbed away to a dull mutter.

She had looked only once at her left arm, and had felt so
sick at the sight that she did not look again. But not looking
reminded her the same way as bandaging her foot reminded
her; and the pain of the burns had subsided but little, and she
had often to crawl back to the stream and soak herself in it.
And how long before I get sick from the cold? she thought,
shivering; for now that her body was trying to fight back it
recognized that lying in cold water for long periods of time is
not generally a good thing to do, and the unhurt bits of it
shivered. She sneezed, and sneezed again. Great, she thought
dully, and her eyes fell again on the saddlebags. It was hard to
think because of the pain.

Kenet, she thought. Kenet. It can't hurt to try.

Hope rose up and blocked her aching throat. She crept to
the saddlebags and unrolled the long wallet that held the
kenet; and twitched her left arm forward and let it lie in the
thick yellow ointment. She closed her eyes, trying not to hope
so desperately; she feared the pain might drive her mad soon,
and she could not spare the strength to withstand too great a
disappointment. But as she grappled with herself the pain in
her arm dwindled and ebbed and finally died away to a vague
queasy discomfort. I'm imagining this, she thought, holding
perfectly still so as not to disrupt the beautiful unexpected
dream of peace. She opened her eyes. Her arm was still black
and horrible-looking. She lay down, very, very slowly, till her

left cheek was cradled as well in the dragonfire ointment; and slowly her face, too, hurt less and less till it did not hurt at all. She fell into sleep, real sleep, the first real sleep she had had since the evening she had read Tor's note.

She dreamed that she woke up, lying with her left arm curled around her head, and her left cheek pressed to the ground. She rose up on both elbows and noticed without finding it remarkable that both arms were whole and strong. She sat up, hands falling easily and languorously into her lap. She rubbed her palms together and thought uncomfortably that she had had a most unpleasant dream about a very large dragon. . . . As she bent her head forward her hair fell forward too, and she noticed two things: first, that her hair was short, barely chin length. This disturbed her, for she knew that she would never cut her hair; Teka was adamant about this, and Aerin was secretly a little proud of the fact that her hair was even longer than Galanna's, falling unbound almost to her ankles, the weight of it stretching the curls into long ripples. It was also nearly straight now; and when she was younger and her hair shorter, it had been mercilessly curly. But, worst of all, it was the wrong color. It was still red, but it was the darker color of flaring embers, not the paler shade of the leaping flames. Panic seized her; she was not herself; she had died; or, worse, she, Aerin still existed, but the dream of the dragon had not been a dream at all, but real, and the real Aerin still lay somewhere with a burned face and a blackened arm and a broken ankle, and this healthy painless body she presently inhabited belonged to someone else; she would not be permitted to stay.

"I will help you if I can," said a voice; but she was dreaming, and could not be sure if the words were spoken aloud. She looked up from where she sat huddled on the ground; a tall blond man stood near her. He knelt beside her; his eyes were blue, and kind, and anxious. "Aerin-sol," he said. "Remember me; you have need of me, and I will help you if I can." A flicker came and went in the blue eyes. "And you shall again aid Damar, for I will tell you how."

"No," she said, for she remembered Maur, and knew Maur was real, whether or not she was dreaming now; "no, I cannot. I cannot. Let me stay here," she begged. "Don't send me back."

A line formed between the blue eyes; he reached one hand

toward her, but hesitated and did not touch her. "I cannot
help it. I can barely keep you here for the space of a dream;
you are being pulled back even now."

It was true. The smell of kenet was in her nostrils again, and
the sound of running water in her ears. "But how will I find
you?" she asked desperately; and then she was awake. Slowly
she opened her eyes; but she lay where she was for a long time.

Eventually she began walking again, leaning heavily on a thick
branch she had found and laboriously trimmed to the proper
length. She had to walk very slowly, not only for the sake of
her ankle, but that her left arm not be shaken too gravely; and
she still had trouble breathing. Even when she breathed in tiny
shallow gasps it hurt, and when she forgot and sucked in too
much air she coughed; and when she coughed, she coughed
blood. But her face and arm were healing.

She had also discovered that the hair on the left side of her
head was gone, burnt by the same blast of dragonfire that had
scarred her cheek. So she took her hunting knife, the same ill-
used blade that had been forced to chop her a cane, and sawed
off the rest of her hair till none of it was longer than hand's
width. Her neck felt rubbery with the sudden weightlessness,
and the wind seemed to whistle in her ears and down her collar
more than it used to. She might have wept a little for her hair,
but she felt too old and grim and worn.

She avoided wondering what her face looked like under her
chopped-off hair. She thought fixedly of other things when
she rubbed kenet into her cheek, and when she dressed and re-
bound her arm. She did not think at all about being willing to
face other people again, except to cringe mentally away from
the idea. She was not vain as Galanna was vain, but she who
had always disliked being noticed was automatically con-
spicuous as the only pale-skinned redhead in a country of
cinnamon-skinned brunettes; she could not bear that her
wounds now should make her grotesque as well. It took
strength to deal with people, strength to acknowledge herself
as first sol, strength to be the public figure she could not help
being; and she had no strength to spare. She tried to tell
herself that her hurts were honorably won; even that she
should be proud of them, that she had successfully done
something heroic; but it did no good. Her instinct was to hide.

She had briefly thought with terror that the villagers who

had sent the messenger to the king that morning so long ago might send another messenger to find out what had become of either sol or dragon; but then she realized that they would do no such thing. If the sol had killed the dragon (unlikely), she would doubtless come and tell them about it. If she didn't, the dragon could be presumed to have killed her, and they would stay as far away as possible.

At last she grew restless. "Perhaps we should go home," she said to Talat. She wondered how it had gone with Arlbeth and Tor and the army; it could all be over now, or Damar could be at war, or—almost anything. She didn't know how long she'd been in the dragon's valley, and she began to want urgently to know what was happening outside. But she did not yet have the courage to venture out of Maur's black grave— out where she would have to face people again.

Meanwhile she walked a little farther and a little farther each day: and one day she finally left the steam bank, and hobbled around the high rock that separated the stream from the black valley where Maur lay. As the sound of the stream receded she kept her eyes on her feet; one booted and one wrapped in heavy tattered and grimy rags; and one of them stepping farther than the other. She watched their uneven progress till she passed the rock wall by, and a little gust of burnt-smelling breeze pressed her cheek, and the sound of her footsteps became the slide-crunch, slide-crunch of walking on ash and cinders. She looked up.

Carrion beasts had not gotten far with the dead dragon. Its eyes were gone, but the heavy hide of the creature was too much for ordinary teeth and claws. Maur looked smaller to her, though; withered and shrunken, the thick skin more crumpled. Slowly she limped nearer, and the small breeze whipped around and stroked her other cheek. There was no smell of rotting flesh in the small valley, although the sun beat down overhead and made her cheek, despite the kenet on it, throb with the heat. The valley reeked, but of smoke and ash; small black flakes still hung in the air, and when the breeze struck her full in the face the cinders caught in her throat and she coughed. She coughed, and bent over her walking stick, and gasped, and coughed again; and then Talat, who had not wanted to follow her into the dragon's valley but didn't want to let her out of his sight either, blew down the back of her bare neck and touched his nose to her shoulder. She turned toward him and threw her right arm over his withers and pressed the side of her face into his neck, breathing through the fine hairs of his mane till the coughing eased and she could stand by herself again.

The dragon's snaky neck lay stretched out along the ground, the long black snout looking like a ridge of black rock. Ash lay more heavily around the dragon than in the rest of the small valley, in spite of the breeze; but around the dragon the breeze lifted a cloud that eddied and lifted and swelled and diminished so that it was hard to tell—as it had been when she and Talat had first ridden to confront the monster—where Maur ended and the earth began. As she watched, another small brisk vagrant breeze swept down the body of the dragon, scouring its length from shoulder hump to the heavy tail; a great black wave of ash reared up in the breeze's wake and crested, and misted out to drift over the rest of the valley. Aerin hid her face in Talat's mane again.

When she looked up she stared at Maur, waiting to think something, feel something at the sight of the thing that she had killed, that had so nearly killed her; but her mind was blank, and she had no hatred or bitterness nor any sense of victory left in her heart; it had all been burned away by the pain. Maur was only a great ugly black lump. As she stared, another small breeze kicked up a windspout, a small ashy cyclone, just beyond the end of the dragon's nose. Something glittered there on the ground. Something red.

She blinked. The wind-spout died away, and the ash fell into new ribs and whorls; but Aerin thought she could still see a small hummock in the ash, a small hummock that dimly gleamed red. She limped toward it, and Talat, his ears half back to show his disapproval, followed.

She stood on one foot and dug with her stick; and she struck the small red thing, which with the impulsion of the blow sprang free of the black cinders, made a small fiery arc through the air, and fell to the earth again, and the ash spun upward in the air draught it made and fell in ripples around it, like a stone thrown into a pond.

Aerin had some trouble kneeling down, but Talat, who had adjusted to his lady's new slow ways, came and stood beside her and let her clutch her way one-handed down a foreleg. She picked the red thing up; it was hard and glittering and a deep translucent red, like a jewel. "Well," she whispered. "I can't take the head away as a trophy this time; so I will take this. Whatever it is."

She tucked it into the front of her tunic, where her bound arm made a cradle for it, and pulled herself back up Talat's foreleg again. He had gotten so good at being an invalid's assistant that she could lean her stick against him and he would not move till she took it back in her hand, that she need not have to pick it up from the ground.

A few days after she found the red dragon stone she looked around for something high enough to let her climb up onto Talat's back, and low enough that she could climb up onto it in the first place. This took some doing. She finally persuaded him—he was willing to be persuaded once he could figure out what strange thing she next wanted of him—to stand in the stream while she edged out, balanced precariously on her buttocks and one hand, down a long heavy overhanging branch from a tree growing near the shallow bank; and lowered herself as slowly as possible onto his bare back. He gave a little whicker of pleasure to have her there again, and took steps as smooth as silk when he carried her; and she sat up a little straighter than she could stand on her own feet, and felt a tiny bit more like a king's daughter than she had for a long time. She rode him up and down the bank of the stream that day, just for the pleasure of a motion that didn't hurt her right ankle; and the next day she saddled him and tried it again, and the day after that she saddled him and tied the remains of her belongings clumsily behind the saddle, and they left the stream and Maur's valley forever. The red stone knocked gently against her ribs as her body swung back and forth in rhythm to Talat's long gentle stride.

❧ CHAPTER 14 ❧

IT TOOK THEM three days of Talat's careful walking to come to the crossroads where they had parted with their guide to go on and face the dragon; three days complicated by the fact that Aerin didn't dare dismount till she found something near a campsite that would let her remount in the morning.

She was deadly tired each evening; her ankle throbbed from hanging vertical so long; and she realized how much weaker she was even than she had thought. It was hard to make herself eat; she was never hungry, and eating hurt, and she ate dutifully because eating was something one did; but she got more pleasure out of watching Talat graze. He had eaten everything edible along the banks of their stream, including some of the bark off the trees, and he tore with great enthusiasm into the fresh grass they now camped beside.

Not infrequently during the day she would come to herself again and look around and realize that she had drifted away. Sometimes it would take her a minute or two just to recognize the trees around her, common Damarian trees whose shapes and leaf patterns had been familiar to her since childhood. Occasionally she woke up and found herself collapsed forward on Talat's neck. But he would not let her fall off, and she didn't. He carried her steadily, his ears pricked and cautious; and he seemed to feel no hesitation about their direction.

"Well, my friend, you know what you are doing," she whispered to Talat, his ears cocked back to listen, when at last they reached the crossroads. "It wasn't I that got us here."

When they set out from the crossroads again the next morning, the way opened up. She had not remembered that the narrow path became a small roadway so soon; but that had been when she still had her hair and the use of all her limbs, and open spaces had held no terrors for her. The mountains climbed steeply to their left, but on their right she looked through hedgerows to planted fields, crops waving green and gold in the sunlight. She tried to make herself feel better by thinking that had she not killed Maur—whatever it may have cost her personally—the crops would have been black by now, and the farmers, dragon's meat. But the comfort was cold, and she could not feel it; she was too deep in dread for what was to come.

She was drifting in and out of awareness again that afternoon, her good hand wrapped in Talat's mane that she might not fall forward and hurt her burnt arm, when Talat suddenly came to a halt and stiffened—and neighed. Aerin shook herself awake with the sound; and he neighed again, and trembled, and she knew he would have reared to cry greeting and challenge as the Damarian warhorses were taught, but he did not for her sake, and she closed her eyes briefly on tears of exhaustion and self-pity.

She could not see who approached; Talat told her that it was not merely someone, but someone that he knew, and thus it was necessarily someone from the City. But her vision had never quite cleared since she had fallen through the dragonfire, and her left eye burned and leaked tears as she squinted and tried to look down the road. The effort made her dizzy, and the road leaped and heaved under her eyes. But she then saw that it was not the road that heaved, but riders on the road who galloped toward her; and when Talat neighed again, someone answered, and she saw the lead horse's head toss upward as he neighed, and finally she recognized him: Kethtaz. And Tor's mare, Dgeth, galloped beside.

Aerin threw her own head up in panic, and the scabs on her face pulled and protested. Her right hand scrabbled at the collar of her tunic, and pulled a fold of her cloak up over her head for a hood; and her fingers briefly touched the left side of her head where a determined stubble grew.

Her father and her cousin and the riders with them were

upon her almost at once, and Arlbeth called out to her, but she did not answer, for her croaking voice could not have been heard above the sound of the hoofbeats; and then Tor rode up beside her and said anxiously, "Aerin, it *is* you?" but she delayed answering him till he reached over and seized her—by her left forearm. She screamed, except that she could not scream, but she made a hoarse awful sound, and Tor dropped his hand and said something she did not hear, for her scream made her cough, and she coughed and could not stop, and the bleeding began, and flecks of her blood dripped down Talat's neck, and her body shook, and the cloak fell away from her and onto the ground, and Tor and Arlbeth sat frozen on their horses, helplessly watching.

She remembered little of the rest of the journey. They tried to rig a sling for her, that she might travel lying down, but while she lay down obediently there was no comfort in it, and at the first stop she struggled out of her litter and went grimly to Talat, who had been hovering nearby wondering what he had done that his lady had been taken away from him. She hung an arm over his neck and hid her face in his mane, ignoring the feel of it wisping against her left cheek. Tor followed her at once. "Aerin—" His voice was full of unshed tears, and her fingers tightened in Talat's mane, dear cheerful Talat who felt that so long as she was riding him there was nothing too serious wrong. She spoke into his neck: "There's no ease in being carried. I would rather ride." And so she rode, and the company all went at Talat's gentlest walking pace, and it was a long time before they reached the City.

When at last the stone City rose up before them from the forest, she felt for her cloak, and pulled it forward to shadow her face again, and her father, who rode at her side, watched her. She looked at him, and let the cloak slip back where it had lain, and straightened herself in the saddle; and she remembered the description of Gorthold's death in Astythet's *History*, and how he was carried, bleeding from many mortal wounds, into the City, where all folk saluted him as their savior; and he died in the castle of the king, who was his cousin; and all Damar grieved for his death.

A grim sort of smile touched Arlbeth's mouth. "You're riding into the City a hero, you know; word of your victory has gone before you, and the messenger who first brought the tale of the Black Dragon's awakening is there with most of his village, and they are all vying among themselves to describe how great and wicked Maur was.''

"How did they know?''

Arlbeth sighed. "I didn't ask. Several of them met us as we rode east toward the City, and we didn't wait for details. Look between Talat's ears; he knows all about this sort of thing; all you have to do is sit up. We're just your honor guard.''

"But—'' she began, but Arlbeth turned away and, indeed, as they neared the great gates, he and Tor dropped back, and Talat pretended to prance, but only pretended, so as not to joggle his rider. She did as her father told her, sitting straight and still in the saddle, and looking not quite between Talat's ears where she might see something, but at them, and at his poll, where his forelock grew and lifted in the breeze when he tossed his head. The streets were quiet, but many people watched them as they rode by; and from the corners of her eyes she could see many of their audience touching the backs of their hands to their foreheads and flicking out the fingers in the Damarian salute to their sovereign but Arlbeth rode at his daughter's heel. A breeze wandered among them and riffled Aerin's ruined hair, and the sunlight shone pitilessly on her scarred face; but the audience was still silent, and motionless but for the right hands and the flicking fingers.

When they came to the courtyard of the castle, rows and rows of the king's army stood in a three-sided square, leaving a space large enough for the honor guard to file in behind the king's daughter when Talat came to a halt. Before them on the ground lay Maur's head, and around the head more ash fell and collected in little pools. She blinked at the trophy someone else had brought home for her. The skull around the empty eyesockets was now burnished bare and clean; and the bone was black. Her eyes trailed slowly down the long nasal bones and the ridged jaw, and she realized that much of the bone was showing; shreds only of the tough skin remained, and as the wind sidled along the head and flicked bits of it loose, they fell to the ground as ash. The parted jaws with their black grin leered at her.

She held to Talat's mane with her right hand, and slipped slowly down his side, her left foot touching the ground first. Then Arlbeth was beside her, and he led her past Maur's grinning skull, and the soldiers parted in a silent whiplash, a drill

maneuver, and they came to the castle door; and then he
turned to her and picked her up in his arms and carried her
down the long corridors and up the stairs to her room, and to
Teka.

There were healers in plenty who visited her after that; but
none of them could do better for her burns than the kenet, and
her ankle was healing of its own, and they could do nothing
for her cough, nor for her trouble breathing. She spent her
time in bed, or in the deep windowseat that overlooked the
rear of the courtyard, toward the stables. Hornmar led Talat
under her window occasionally, and while she could not call
down to him, it comforted her to see him. She tried to eat for
Teka's sake; she hadn't realized before that there was no flavor to her food since she had tasted dragonfire, but she learned
it now. And she took the dragon stone from the pocket she
had made from a knot of cloth, and laid it on the table near
her bed; it seemed as though when she stared at it, it grew
brighter, and red fire shivered deep inside it.

At last she grew restless, as she had in the dragon's valley,
and she began to creep about the castle, and visit Talat in the
stables. He had his old stall back, and Arlbeth's young Kethtaz had actually been moved one stall down to give his predecessor pride of place. Talat was very conscious of eminence
regained. She investigated his croup carefully with her fingers;
the weals from the dragonfire had disappeared, although she
could still see them, for the hair had grown back lying in the
opposite direction from the hair around them.

Her own hair was growing in vigorously if unevenly, and
Teka one day combed it out from a center spot at the top of
her skull and cut in a neat arch around her face, for it was
no longer curly. Aerin looked at herself in the mirror and
laughed. "I look like a boy."

"No," said Teka, sweeping up the trimmings. "You look
like a girl with a boy's haircut."

Aerin stared at herself. She had avoided mirrors as she had
avoided everyone but Tor and Teka and her father, and the
healers they sent, who could not be got rid of; and now that
she finally dared herself to look in a mirror she was surprised
at what she saw. The shiny scars across her left cheek—and a
few flecks, like freckles, on the other side of her face, where
the hot dragon blood had splashed her—were visible but not

disfiguring. Her scalp was still tender on the left, and she had to use her hairbrush tentatively; but her hair was coming back as thick as before, although it was several shades darker and almost straight. But her face was drawn and pale, except for two spots of red high on her cheekbones; and there were lines on her face that had not been there before, and her eyes looked as old as Arlbeth's. "I look a lot more like my mother now, don't I?" she said.

Teka paused with the cloth she'd used to gather the hair clippings dangling from her hand. "Yes," she said.

The first morning she came to breakfast with her father again, Tor was there too, and was not able to stop himself from jumping out of his chair and hugging her. He was so glad to see her walking, and with her hair grown out and combed smoothly around her face, that he almost managed not to think about how little there was of her to hug, how frail she felt; how each breath she took seemed to shake her, like a wind through a sapling. She smiled up at him, and he saw the red spots on her cheekbones, but he looked only at her smile.

She asked about Nyrlol, and Arlbeth said that he had been humble—no, craven—in a way Arlbeth had disliked even more than Nyrlol's usual overbearing bluster; it was as if the threat of secession had never happened. Nyrlol had seemed nervous, looking behind himself too frequently, starting at sounds no one else heard. He apologized, and claimed that he was not sleeping well; that there was too much raiding on his borders and he seemed able to do too little about it. Arlbeth, with the army at his back, had made the correct noises, and after a visit of the shortest possible length consistent with courtesy, headed for home, leaving a division of his army behind to help watch the Border near Nyrlol's land for him. Nyrlol had seemed honestly grateful, and that made Arlbeth even more uneasy; but there was nothing more he could do.

"I have no doubt that we were lured away from the City just then for a purpose," said Arlbeth, "and the best I could do then was return as quickly as the horses could run. I had almost forgotten Maur."

"I hadn't," murmured Tor, and his eyes flicked up to Aerin's face and away again, and she knew that he had guessed she would ride back with the messenger and face the Black Dragon alone.

Arlbeth frowned into his cup. "But if the only purpose was

to set the Black Dragon upon us, why then does the feeling of a dark fate still cling around us? For it does."

"Yes," said Tor.

There was a silence, and Arlbeth said at last: "We can only hope that Aerin-sol has so disturbed their plans"—and by *their* his auditors knew he meant the Northerners—"that we will have time enough to prepare, and strength enough in reserve."

Neither Arlbeth nor Tor ever told her what they had thought when they first saw her, bent and burnt and coughing blood onto Talat's white neck; and Aerin did not ask. All else that was said on the subject occurred that same morning: "I owe you a punishment for carrying the king's sword without the king's wishes, Aerin-sol," her father said gravely.

She had been thinking much of this herself lately, and she nodded. "I await your command."

Tor made a noise, and Arlbeth waved him to silence. "The punishment is that you remain prisoned in the City and not carry your sword for two seasons, half a year, and not less. Maur has taken care of that for me."

She bowed her head; and then a woman of the hafor brought fresh malak and hot rolls, and they busied themselves with passing and pouring, and that was the end of it. She put milk in her malak now, to cool it before she drank it, so that she would not have to wait so obviously for it to grow tepid by itself—a long process at the king's castle, where it was served in huge heavy earthenware cups with wide thick bases and narrow tapered rims. She didn't like the flavor so well—malak was supposed to bite, and the milk gentled it—but there were worse compromises she had to make.

Arlbeth asked her when they might hold the banquet in her honor, and she blinked stupidly at him, thinking, My birthday isn't till—?

"Maur," he said gently. "We wish to honor you for your slaying of Maur."

Tor and Arlbeth both knew she wanted nothing of the sort, but she said grimly, "I thank you. Name the day."

The hush that fell on the great hall that evening when she entered it was worse even than what she had imagined. It should have been little different than it ever had been, for her father's court had never been easy in the presence of his daughter; but it was different nonetheless. Her head buzzed with the silence, and her dim vision dimmed further, till the people around her were no more than vague hulks draped in the bright colors of their court clothing. She wore a long brown dress, high in the collar, and with sleeves that fell past her wrists; and while there was much embroidery on it, the threads were black and darker brown, and she went bareheaded, and wore only one ring, on her right hand. She looked around, and the hulks turned slowly away from her, and she took her place at her father's side. The talk started up again, but she did not hear the words of it; she heard the broken flickering fear beneath it, and calmly she thought: It is I that they are afraid of.

Maur's ugly black skull had been hung high on one wall of the great hall, whose ceilings were three stories tall. It had been placed there by some other direction, for she had had nothing to do with it, nor would have wanted it there had she been asked. Even in the great hall it was huge; she looked at it, and it she could see clearly, and it leered at her. I am the shape of their fear, it said, for you dared to slay me.

I am the shape of their fear, the thing said.

But I am lame and crippled from our meeting, she replied; I am human like them, for I was sorely wounded.

The thing laughed; the laugh came as a ripple of heavy silence that muffled the uncertain conversation in the hall; but only Aerin heard. Ah, but you lived, and you slew me; that is enough, and more than enough, for I was as big as a mountain and might have swallowed all of Damar at last. The villagers who saw me before you came—the man who guided you to me —all say that when I reared up, my head touched the stars; that nothing human could have stood against me. They say it who saw me, with awe and gratitude for their deliverance; but that is not how the story travels.

She heard the rhythm of the voices around her; the broken rhythm of syllables under the words they said aloud. Witch, they said. Witchwoman's daughter.

But I saved them, she said desperately. I saved them.

The head howled: Better you had not! Better that they lay now in my belly's pit!

See how the first sola still looks at the witchwoman's daughter, for all that her face is haggard and scarred; see how he looks at her, as if he does not wish to look at anything else.

As if he cannot look at anything else.

The old ones among them said: Remember how the king looked at the witch, how she spelled him to sire her a child that she might be born again with greater strength, for the blood of Damar would run in the child's veins with her own witch's wickedness!

Witchwoman's daughter. Nothing human could have killed Maur. She will swallow Damar as the Black Dragon never could have; for we could have hidden in deep caves till it slept again.

Shall we let her spell the first sola?

We remember the old tales of Maur. We remember.

Witchwoman's daughter.

And the words spoken aloud: The North. The raiders from the North, they come oftener, stronger. Why is Nyrlol afraid of his own shadow? He, who was never known for wisdom, was never known either for lack of courage. Mischief.

Witchwoman's daughter.

You had done better to let me eat you! the thing on the wall shrieked.

It was only luck that I slew you! she cried. I only dared because I knew I was already dead!

The thing laughed.

Witchwoman's daughter.

It was only luck!

Was it? said Maur's head. Was it?

Aerin stood up abruptly and said, "You must excuse me." She turned and walked, slowly, for she still limped a little, toward the gaping door that would let her out of the hall. Tor was at her elbow. "Aerin?"

"Let me be!" she cried. "Go talk to your guests! Don't come near me!" She began to cough, and still she ran from him, staggering, not caring that she limped in the sight of the entire hall, through the door and away.

❧ CHAPTER 15 ❧

SHE COULD NOT SLEEP, and she coughed, and blood spotted her pillow; and the fever that came and went, and would not leave her alone even as her burns healed and her hair grew, came again that night, and light-headedly she relived the scene in the hall; and she heard the thing laugh, and heard the court say, Witchwoman's daughter.

Near dawn she dreamed of the tall blond man she had seen once before, while she slept in the dragon's valley. He did not speak to her, nor did he seem to know she watched him. Perhaps he is only a dream, her dreaming self thought; but she looked at the way his blond eyelashes caught the sunlight, at the freckles on the backs of his hands, at the way the little fingers curled under the base of the cup he held, at the steam that rose from the cup. He blinked when it wafted into his eyes.

Where? her dreaming self thought. If he exists, where?

She woke, coughing.

He had said he would help her. How could he help her? He had said he would tell her how she could aid Damar. Damar didn't seem to like her aiding it. She turned onto her back and stretched till her throat and chest lay flat and straight; sometimes that eased the coughing. She listened to the gurgling rasp of her breathing; no matter how shallowly she breathed, still the air rustled in her lungs. She thought dispassionately, This cough will kill me before too long, and Maur will have slain me after all.

Perhaps the man in my dream could cure my cough.

If she could find him. If he existed. She was so tired; she could not imagine what it was like not to be tired. She fell asleep again, listening to her breath rattle in her chest like dead leaves, and woke tired. She stared into the canopy over her head for several minutes, her eyes tracing the graceful embroidered forms of the galloping horses and their supernaturally long manes and tails, the manes almost like wings, the grass underfoot almost like clouds.

The fever would not let her go. She could not get out of bed that day, nor the next. Tor came to see her, and she would not speak to him; but he came again, and she remembered she had one thing she needed to say to him. "What happened?" he asked her over and over again.

At last she said, "I grew dizzy," but would not say more; and Tor fell silent, holding her hand in a hand almost as feverish as hers.

It was only luck, she had pleaded with Maur. Was it? Maur's head had answered her.

"Aerin." Tor's voice. What was it she needed to say to him?

"Will you . . . take Maur's head off the wall . . . and put it . . . somewhere far away . . . that no one may see it?"

"Of course," he said anxiously. "Of course. It shall be done today."

She remembered little clearly after that; she saw Teka's face bent over hers, and Tor's, and her father's, and others' whom she dimly remembered as the healers who had done her so little good before. She did not know how many days or weeks she spent this way; and then one night she woke again from an especially vivid dream of the blond man.

"You stupid woman—climb off your deathbed while you still can, and come to me."

The words still rang in her ears. She sat up slowly. She drew on her boots, and her leggings and tunic; she picked up the red stone on the table by her bed, and thrust it into the breast of her shirt. She looked at her sword—the king's sword—hanging over her bed, and did not touch it, she fumbled for a cloak, and drew it over her shoulders. She had to sit down on the edge of her bed again and catch her breath.

I must tell them where I am going, she thought. But I don't *know* where I am going.

She stood up again, and made her way slowly into her sitting-room, to the desk there. The ink was dry; she had to carry a glass from her bed table, filled with water from the pitcher there, into her sitting-room, to wet it; her hand shook, and she spilled most of it on the desk, and the ink would not mix, but stayed pale and uneven. It would have to do. There was nothing to write on. She sat at the desk, staring at its blank top, as if paper or parchment would appear if she waited for it. She did not seem able to collect her thoughts, but her hand reached out of its own accord, and groped in the rear of the small desk cabinet, and drew something out. It was the note Tor had written her, long ago, asking her to see the king's army off the next morning.

She turned it over, and took up a pen; the ink dripped and ran on the page. "Tor," she wrote. "I have dreamed of someone who might help me, and I go to look for him. I will come back as I may."

Stealthily she made her way to the ground floor and outside. The inner corridors were pitch dark, but she found she could see her way; there was a soft silvery light around her—*she* was glowing, she realized suddenly; and for the first time since Maur's head had spoken to her she felt a glimmer of hope, and the hope warmed her a little, and steadied her footsteps.

Someone should have seen her as she crossed the open courtyard, particularly as she persisted in glowing like foxfire in a rotting tree; but no one came. She dragged Talat's small light saddle from its peg opposite his stall, but left the trappings of the king's breastplate as she had left her sword. Talat's pale head thrust over the stall half-door at her. His nostrils moved in a silent whicker of welcome, but from his campaigning days he could recognize secrecy when he saw it. She had to wrestle the saddle onto his back, for she was too weak to lift it; but it was on at last, and Talat stepped after his lady as softly and carefully as a lover going to his beloved's bed.

She was surprised to find that it was high summer, for she had lost all sense of the passing of time within the walls of her illness. "Although lucky for me," she whispered into Talat's pointed ears. She ate the fruit from the trees, when she remembered to eat, and at night she slept leaning against Talat's side, as he rested his nose on the earth near his folded knees. Sometimes he flicked his tail in his sleep, after flies, real or imaginary, and Aerin would come half awake—she was never profoundly asleep in the first place—and feel the silky hairs slip down her face like raindrops.

They traveled west at first, then north, with the mountains on their right and the heavy Airdthmar forests on their left, forests that had never been completely explored, that held creatures no one had ever named. When times were peaceful the kings of Damar had set up expeditions to drive deeper into the forest, for it stood in the way of their kingdom's free trade and concourse from one town to the next; but the Airdthmar was not kind to the folk who tried to chart it and lay roads through it. Arlbeth claimed to be fond of it. "It is quiet, it causes no courteous passer-by any trouble, it keeps its own counsel," he said. "Would that all the quarters of the Damarian compass were so civilized."

Aerin gazed into the trees as she rode, but she saw only blackness looking back at her. She had thought to go west originally because the Airdthmar seemed like the obvious place to look for a mysterious mage who visited dreams; but as they cleared the foothills Talat shied away and veered north, and Aerin half permitted, half agreed with him.

There was no trail for them to follow; they wove their way back into the foothills again, away from the smooth way that Arlbeth and his army had gone to meet with Nyrlol, or that any folk with legitimate business took around the eastern edge of the Airdthmar; Aerin did not want to meet anyone who might take word of her back to the City, nor be overtaken by any party sent in pursuit.

They came at last to a pocket valley in the hills, a small undistinguished valley like many others, well furnished by the thick purple color grass, which did not grow in the City, and with a few trees. The sun was setting as they paused, and Aerin, seeing a rock that would do for a mounting block, thought that this would be a good place to stop for the night; but she made no move to dismount, and Talat remained standing, ears pricked, uninterested in the lush lolor, which generally he preferred to anything else. As the sun disappeared it seemed to Aerin that the light never quite faded; but that might have been the glitter of her fever.

Talat looked back over his shoulder at her, and Aerin's knee as if of its own volition bent him toward the mountains behind the foothills—east again; and Talat at once found the hidden trail that began at the edge of the pocket valley.

The way was soon so steep that Aerin worried about Talat's weak leg; but when she tried to slip off his back and walk beside him for a while he sidled all around and rubbed her against the trees that grew close around them, and she at last gave it up. He was right; climbing uphill would make her cough. He went slowly, and all four feet hit the ground evenly, and Aerin concentrated on hanging on to the front of the saddle with both hands. And breathing. It had seemed to her lately that she had to remember to breathe, that her lungs would prefer to be still.

By dawn she was light-headed with fever and altitude and exhaustion, for even though she slept little, lying quietly on the earth was an easier way to pass the time than clinging to a heaving saddle. Still Talat toiled on, the sweat running down his shoulders, though the air was cool. Aerin let go the saddle and wound her cold fingers in his mane to warm them.

The ground leveled abruptly. Talat paused disbelievingly, all four feet braced; then he went on again, and the trees gave way before them, and the secret track Talat had followed so trustingly was a plain trail before them, and at the end of a short way was a small bare courtyard, set round with pillars, and a great grey stone building. Talat walked into the courtyard and stopped. Aerin unwound her hands from his mane and stared down past his wet shoulder to the ground, and thought about dismounting; and then a tall blond man was standing beside her. She wished to feel alarm, for she had not seen or heard his approach; but Talat was not disturbed, and she recognized the man's face from her dreams. He lifted her bodily from the saddle, and as his arms took her weight, fear crossed his face: "May all the gods listen—there's nothing left of you."

He carried her into the stone hall, and she leaned her head against his chest, and thought of nothing. His boots were soft-soled and his footsteps silent; but the rustle of her breathing echoed through the hall like the wings of a flock of small birds. He set her in a high-backed chair at the far end of the hall, and picked up a goblet from a small table, glared at it, muttered over it, said, "This will have to do," and gave it to her.

She held it, dreamily, but even with both hands around it, it swayed and began to sag, and the man, with a muffled exclamation, leaned over her and grasped the stem of the goblet around her two hands. His hand was warm, like Talat's mane, and the goblet was cool. "Who are you?" she asked, looking into the frowning face bending over her.

"I am Luthe," he said. "Drink."

She took the first sip, obediently, as she had drunk Teka's draughts when she was young and had fevers. She did not remember a second sip.

She awoke, pressed down with blankets, in a narrow curtainless bed. The bed was one of many, set side by side down a long narrow corridor; the heads were pushed up against one wall where slit windows high above shed sunlight on their feet; and beyond the beds was a narrow passage and then the far wall, taller than the window wall, the roof slanting up sharply from the one to the other. She blinked drowsily at the far wall; it was blank grey stone, like the rest of Luthe's hall. Or not blank: Aerin sat up, shedding blankets, and frowned; etched into the grey stone were faint relief pictures, but she could not quite decide what they depicted: men with antlers, women with wings, trees with eyes that watched. She blinked again; her vision hadn't been trustworthy in a long time.

Her fever was gone. She felt as weak as when she had first dragged herself to the stream after Maur's death, but she felt happy, with a senseless transparent happiness like that of a very young child. She wrestled cheerfully with the enshrouding blankets, got feebly to her feet, and began to make her way down the row of beds by clinging to the foot of each in turn—all of them empty, and all but hers neatly made up with coarse dark blankets, and pillows wrapped in smooth dark cloth. She came to an arch of doorway and looked through; the thickness of the wall it pierced made the entrance dark, but beyond it the great hall was bright with daylight. There were windows cut high into the two lengthwise walls of the great chamber, the walls themselves high enough that the windows looked out over the roofs of the sleeping corridors; and yet far above them still the ceiling was invisible in darkness.

Luthe saw her and frowned. "You should have slept longer."

"No, I shouldn't. I have slept just the right amount; I feel dazzlingly"—she ran out of breath, and leaned against the threshold—"hungry. I haven't felt hungry in a long time."

"I will claim that as my consolation; but evidently I still have not learned to get simple sleeping draughts right. Lily would be ashamed of me. Come eat, then." He watched her drift toward him; it seemed to be a long way from the sleeping-chamber door to the table before the hearth, where he was. His hands closed over the high back of the chair he stood behind as he watched her, but he did not offer to help her. She fetched up against the table at last; it was a small delicate table, but she was little more than a wraith, and when she flattened both hands on the top of it to steady herself it held her slight weight easily.

She looked up at him and smiled: a lover's smile, sweet and brilliant, but it was not directed at him; her eyes looked at something invisible that she herself did not recognize, and yet his heart stirred in a way he did not like. He returned her smile with a deeper frown, and she chuckled—a little tapping sound, like mouse feet on a stone floor. "I am not blind, sir, though I do seem to see light where there is only darkness and strange pictures on a blank wall; and I am quite sure that I see you scowling furiously at me, like a tutor at a student who persists in misbehaving. Pray tell me what I have done."

"You have waited too long to come here."

Her smile ebbed away. "I have not been thinking clearly for long . . . I had so many strange dreams." She thought of Maur's head speaking to her from a wall in her father's castle, and a spasm crossed her face, and she raised one hand from the table to cover it. "It was easy," she said through her fingers, "not to believe there was any use in them."

There was silence between them; Aerin stirred, and dropped her hand, but her face was still sad. "Talat?" she asked.

". . . is eating his head off in a meadow among my cattle. You need have no fear for him."

"I have none." Abruptly she asked: "Am I dying?"

"Yes."

"Can you cure me?"

Luthe sighed. "I'm not sure. I think so. Had not . . ."

"Had I not listened to Maur's head, I would have come here long since," Aerin said dreamily. "Had it not told me that I could not win against the Black Dragon, for no one could, I might have believed that there was enough left of my life to be

worth healing; but I am Dragon-Killer, the least of my family,
and if I have done a great thing, then I must die of it." Her
words floated on the air, half visible, like spider silk.

"You are not the least of your family," Luthe said violently; "your mother was worth seven of her husband, and
you've the courage she had, or she'd not have borne you, and
you would not be standing here now after what Maur has done
to you—and does to you yet."

Aerin stared at him. "Does to me yet? . . . They hung its
skull in the great hall, and it spoke to me. I was stronger for a
while, till I saw it there, and it spoke to me."

"Spoke—? How could anyone, even a hundred generations
later, be so stupid as to bring back the Black Dragon's head as
a trophy and hang it on a wall for folk to gape at? Surely—"

"I asked them to take it away—where no one might look at
it again."

Luthe paced twice around the table before he said anything.
"Dragon-Killer indeed. They do not know how lucky they
are to have had you. To have had you at all. And I am fool
enough to want to give you back to them."

Witchwoman's daughter, Aerin thought. But I told Tor I
would come back if I could.

Luthe sat wearily down. "I have sat up here too long; it is so
pleasant, not meddling. Perhaps after a hundred generations it
is possible to forget."

"You knew my mother?"

"Yes."

It was not an answer, nor a tone of voice, to encourage further questions. She looked down, and noticed that there was
bread and fruit on the table she leaned on, and she picked up a
handful of cora berries and began to eat them one at a time.

"She was like you, but smaller," Luthe said after she finished the last berry and had begun on a piece of bread. "The
burden she carried was different from yours, and it had worn
on her for many years. When I knew her she had forgotten
joy, although I believe Arlbeth gave her a little back again."

Aerin's low rough voice seemed to come from the high grey
walls and not from the thin figure bowed over the table before
him: "It is said in the City that she died of despair when she
found she had had a daughter and not a son."

"It is probably true," Luthe said, his voice level. "She had
courage enough, but little imagination; or she would not have

forgotten joy, whatever the weight on her, and heavy enough it truly was.''

"Is it a weight a son might have lifted from her?"

"It is a weight any of her blood and courage may lift. Damn you," he said, his voice rising. "Couldn't you tell the difference between a true dream and dragon poison?"

"Evidently not," she replied, and looked straight at him, although she still leaned on the table. "If it was so important, and the Black Dragon, even in death, so insidious, why did you not come and fetch me?"

There was a little pause, and Luthe smiled faintly. "I shan't try to bully you again."

"You have not answered my question."

"I don't wish to answer it."

She could not help herself, and she laughed: he sounded so much like a sulky child. And her laugh rang out, clear and free, as it had not done since she had first heard the name of Maur.

Luthe looked at her in wonder. "Yes, I believe I can cure you. I cannot believe that I will be let fail."

"I am glad to hear that," she said, and found herself surprised that she spoke the truth, and her mouth curled in a wry smile. "I am glad."

Luthe, watching her, knew both the truth of her words and the surprise they had caused her. She wandered around the little table till she came to another chair, and settled lightly into it; and with the smile still on her lips, her eyelids drooped, and she fell into the light doze of the chronic invalid, and sagged against the side of her chair, and Luthe watched over her sleep as Tor often had, and their thoughts were very similar. But Luthe had a choice to make, and a choice that he did not like; and it was a choice that must be made soon. Even as he thought of this choice, he knew the decision had already been made. But he was in no hurry that Aerin wake again, and he do what he must.

❧ CHAPTER 16 ❧

SHE COULD NOT THINK where she was when she awoke. She was sitting in a tall wooden chair, and a fire burned in a hearth not far from her outstretched feet; and she was in a hall so vast she could not see the ceiling. It was not until Luthe walked between her and the hearth, to lay another log on the fire, that she remembered all that had passed; and she sighed.

He turned to her at once, his face still solemn and frowning. "Talat?" she said, as if he was always the first thing on her mind. Luthe, exasperated, said: "If you have so little faith in my ability to look after one fat, elderly, self-centered stallion, then I will show you proof." He leaned over her again and picked her up, and strode out of the great grey hall.

"I can walk," said Aerin, with dignity.

"No, you can't," said Luthe over the top of her head, "although at some date in the near future you will have the opportunity to relearn."

He set her down, finally, on her own feet, at the edge of a wide unfenced meadow; several brown cows grazed in it, and at its farthest edge she saw one or two deer raise their heads and look toward her; but they did not seem alarmed.

Then she heard Talat's great ringing neigh, and he galloped up to them, coming to a sliding halt at the last minute (Luthe muttered something that sounded like "Show-off"), and slobbered green and purple down her shirt. "Horses," said Luthe with disgust; but she took a step away from his steadying hand

138

to wrap an arm over Talat's non-existent withers.

"Here, then," said Luthe. "You can be of some use." He boosted her onto Talat's well-rounded back and walked off. "This way," he said over his shoulder, and Talat pricked his ears and followed docilely. But Luthe's long legs covered the ground at a good pace, and Talat had to stretch himself to keep up, for he would lose his dignity if he broke into a trot; and so his ears eased half back in disapproval of so rude a speed. Aerin laughed her small half-laugh, that she would not cough.

They came soon to the edge of a wide silver lake. Aerin blinked her dim eyes, for it was hard to determine where the land ended and the water began; the stones of the shore were a barely flatter, duller grey than the water's gleaming surface. Talat stopped when his hoofs crunched on pebbles; it was the worst sort of footing for a horse with an unreliable leg. Luthe continued to the very edge of the water, and as he stopped just before he got his feet wet, the water gave a sudden little *gloop* and ripple, and a small outthrust finger of water reached out and splashed his toes. Luthe muttered something under his breath and the water replied by hunching itself up into ridges, and several tiny wave-edges crept humbly up the shoreline, but none quite touched his feet. "Here." called Luthe.

She slid off Talat's back, but found within two steps that Luthe had been right, she really couldn't walk. She sank down where she had been standing, and Talat crunched up beside her and lowered his nose for her hand, his ears saying anxiously, "It's all my fault—I don't really mind these wretched small stones—do please stand up again and I'll carry you."

Then Luthe was kneeling beside her, and he lifted her in his arms again; his hands were wet to the elbows. He set her down, carefully, by the lake's edge, and the water shouldered up in small ripples again, and flung itself up the stones toward her as if curious; but it did not quite touch her. Luthe dipped his hands into the water again, and held the leaky cup to her lips.

"Drink," he said.

"Is this another sleeping draught?" she said, trying to smile; but he only looked sad and grim.

"No," he said. The water dripped on her leg, and its touch through the cloth was somehow personal, soothing like the hand of a friend.

She drank awkwardly, over his thumb, and the water was

silver, almost white, even against Luthe's pale skin; and it was faintly sweet, and cold, and wild, somehow, wild with a wildness she could not put a name to beyond just that: *wild*. It seemed to course down her throat of its own volition, and foam up in her stomach. She looked up and met Luthe's blue frowning gaze as he bowed over her and his cupped hands. She said, "What is—? Not water," and then he and the lake and the taste of the water on her tongue disappeared; but just before her mind spiraled away after them she felt hands clamp on her shoulders, wet hands, for she could feel the damp through her sleeves, and these hands dragged her to her feet. "Aerin," came a voice from very far away, and then she no longer had feet, or ears either.

Aerin.

Her lungs were on fire like a swimmer's too far underwater, and she clawed her way toward the surface, and toward the voice that still called her name; and it seemed that her face broke the surface of the water which held her, and for a moment she lay gasping. The voice again.

Aerin.

She opened her eyes, and she was not on the shores of a silver lake, though a tall man stood before her, calling her name, and offering her a goblet. Drink, he said.

She reached to take the goblet; reached out to take it with her left hand, and noticed with mild surprise that the arm was unscarred and strong. Ah, she thought wisely, I am dreaming again; but she paused before she took the goblet, and looked around her. She stood in a wide chamber that at first she thought was round, till she realized the walls were straight, but that there were five of them. She looked up, and there was a heavy weight of bound hair on her head, and this preoccupied her, so she did not examine the strange clawed creatures that writhed, black and red and yellow, against that ceiling. She lowered her head again, puzzled, for she had never been in this room before, and yet its red walls seemed familiar to her.

Drink, said the man again, and his voice was impatient. *Drink*. The goblet in his outstretched hand trembled very slightly, and she wondered why he was so eager for her to take the cup.

She tried to look up into his face, but he wore a cloak with a hood, a red cloak, so bright that it hurt the eyes, and the hood was so deep she could not see the face within it. Drink, he said, half mad with impatience, and it occurred to her at last that this was not Luthe she stood before.

Drink.

Then she looked again at her left hand and arm, and she thought calmly. That is not my hand; this one is smaller, and the fingers are more delicate than ever mine were. She withdrew the hand, and put it to her head, and pulled a wisp of her hair free, and held it before her eyes. It was the color it had used to be, before Maur burned it; but the hairs of it were finer.

Aerin, said the red man; you shall take this, and drink it.

In a voice not hers she replied: No. But the voice despaired and the red man heard the despair, and thrust the goblet at her the more eagerly, knowing that he would succeed. *Drink*.

Slowly, hopelessly, her left hand reached out again, and took the goblet, and held it to her lips; but she did not taste what was within it, for she heard her name again, and paused. *Aerin*.

This was not the red man's voice, but another one, familiar to her. *Aerin*. The voice was Luthe's voice, and frantic.

The red man heard it too, and whirled around; the cloak spun on his shoulders, but still she saw nothing of his face. Luthe! he cried. You shall not have her!

Luthe's voice laughed weakly. No, I won't; but I shall have the other one; you shall not have them both.

Then there was a roaring around her, and it seemed that the red walls of the five-sided chamber were angry red mouths; but then the red faded to greyness, and yet still the roaring went on; and suddenly the greyness was the greyness of stone walls, not the pale stone of Luthe's hall, but the grey and darker grey and dull red and black of her City; but before its walls lay a desert plain, empty and barren, and three of the four monoliths that marked the City gates lay on their sides, and she saw no folk anywhere. She opened her mouth to scream, but her mouth filled with silver water, and she choked, and struck out with her hands; and felt sunlight on her face. Next she realized that she had a stiff neck; and then found she was stiff all over, from lying on . . . rocks.

No wonder she hurt. The dreams faded under the onslaught of the physical discomfort. She bent an elbow to prop herself up on, and then thought to open her eyes first. Trees, blue sky. Stones. She pulled herself up on the elbow. Stones, trees, blue sky. Lake. Luthe.

He sat up beside her. "Ack," he said, and stretched cau-

tiously. He was soaking wet; it occurred to her then that she
was too, although they were some distance from the water's
edge—nearer, in fact, to the trees. Then there was a familiar
stomp and whiffle behind her, and she reached up without
looking to encounter Talat's silky cheek.

Luthe was getting to his feet; he looked as stiff as she felt.
He watched her inscrutably as she staggered to her feet and
stood beside him. The lake's surface was smooth as glass. It
was strangely silent where they stood; she heard nothing but
the distant chirp of a bird and the occasional whisk of Talat's
tail.

Nothing.

"I can breathe," she whispered.

"Ah," said Luthe. "Yes, I hoped for that."

Then the cacophony of her dreams rushed back. The red
man she discarded, but—"My City—"

Luthe's inscrutable look settled over his face as if it was
there for life. "Later."

"Later? The end of my land, my City, my people? Later?"
My land, a far-off thought said to her mockingly. *My* City.
My people.

"Yes, later," he said gruffly. "It hasn't happened yet, and
your destiny lies elsewhere."

She stood rooted to the ground, staring at him. "My destiny
lies elsewhere," she said in a high voice. "My destiny has
always lain . . . elsewhere."

His face softened. "Yes, that's true, but not quite the way
you think. Come. I'll tell you what I can—of what you need to
know. We'll have to hope it's enough."

"It will have to be enough," she said fiercely, and as he
looked into her eyes they were golden from the flames of her
dreams; and he feared then for what he had done. "I had no
choice," he murmured to himself, but Aerin, still fierce in her
fear, said, "I can't hear you. What are you saying?"

Luthe shook his head. "Nothing that will do you any service
to hear. Come, then. What has happened to you is not all
bad."

❧ CHAPTER 17 ❧

HER VISION HAD CLEARED with her lungs, and just as she smiled involuntarily every time she took a deep breath, she was also fascinated by the sight of things like leaves on trees, or the way the muscles moved under Talat's skin when he went tearing across his meadow, bucking and kicking like a colt. She went for long directionless walks through the forests of Luthe's high valley, or strolled along the edge of the silver lake, watching tiny rainbows reflect off the water. If she was absent too long, Luthe came to fetch her; he always seemed able to find her without trouble, however far she'd wandered. Occasionally he came with her when she set out.

She had paused, staring at a tree like many other trees, but the leaves of it were waving at her; each tiny, delicate, sharp-edged green oval shivered just for her when the breeze touched it; turned that she might admire its either side, the miniature tracery of green veins, the graceful way the stem fitted to the twig, and the twig to the branch, and the branch set so splendidly into the bole. A green vine clung round the tree, and its leaves too stirred in the wind.

Luthe idly snapped a small twig from the vine and handed it to her. She took it without thinking and then saw what it was —surka—and all her pleasure was gone, and her breath caught in her throat; her fingers were too numb even to drop what they held.

"Hold it," snapped Luthe. "Clutch it as if it were a nettle."

Her frantic fingers squeezed together till the stem broke, and the pale green sap crept across her palm. Its touch was faintly warm and tickly, and she opened her hand in surprise, and a large furry spider walked onto her wrist and paused, waving its front pair of legs at her.

"Ugh," she said, and her wrist shook, and the spider fell to the ground and ambled slowly away. There was no sign of the broken surka twig.

Luthe snorted with laughter, tried to turn it into a cough, inhaled at the wrong moment, and then really did cough. "Truly," he said at least, "the poor surka can be a useful tool. You cannot blame it for the misfortunes of your childhood. If you try to breathe water, you will not turn into a fish, you will drown; but water is still good to drink."

"Ha," said Aerin, still shaken and waiting for the nausea or the dizziness, or something; she hadn't held it long, but long enough for something nasty to result. "The taste of water doesn't kill people who aren't royal."

"Mmm. If the truth be known, the touch of the sap of the surka doesn't kill people who aren't royal either, although eating it will certainly make them very sick, and the royal plant makes a good story. It's the *kelar* in your blood that brings the surka's more curious properties out—although poor old Merth killed himself just as surely with it. As you would have killed yourself were it not for your mother's blood in your veins—and serve you right for being so stupid about that Galooney woman. Anything powerful is also dangerous, and worth more respect than a silly child's trick like that."

"Galanna."

"Whatever. All she uses her Gift for is self-aggrandizement, with a little unguided malice thrown in. Tor doesn't realize how narrowly he escaped; a flicker more of the Gift in her and less in him and he'd have married her, willy-nilly, and wondered for the rest of his life why he was so miserable." Luthe did not sound as though the prospect caused him any sorrow. "But you have no excuse for falling into her snares."

"What is *kelar*?"

Luthe pulled a handful of leaves off the surka and began to weave them together. "It's what your family calls the Gift. They haven't much of it left to call anything. You're stiff with it—be quiet. I'm not finished—for all you tried to choke it off by an overdose of surka." He eyed her. "Probably you will always be a little sensitive to it, because of that; but I still believe you can learn to control it."

"I was fifteen when I ate the surka and—"

"The stronger the Gift, the later it shows up, only your purblind family has forgotten all that, not having had a strong Gift to deal with in a very long time. Your mother's was late. And your uncle's." He frowned at the wreath in his hands.

"My mother."

"Most of your *kelar* is her legacy."

"My mother was from the North," Aerin said slowly. "Was she then a witch—a demon—as they say?"

"She was no demon," Luthe said firmly. "A witch? Mmph. Your village elders, who sell poultices to take off warts, are witches."

"Was she human?"

Luthe didn't answer immediately. "That depends on what you mean by human."

Aerin stared at him, all the tales of her childhood filling her eyes with shadows.

Luthe was wearing his inscrutable look again, although he bent it only on the surka wreath. "Time was, you know, there were a goodly number of folk not human who walked this earth. Time was—not so long ago. Those who were human, however, never liked the idea, and ignored those not human when they met them, and now they . . ." The inscrutable look faded, and he looked up from his hands and into the trees, and Aerin remembered the creatures on the walls of her sleeping-hall.

"I'm not," he said carefully, "the best one to ask questions about things like humanity. I'm not entirely human myself." He glanced at her. "Time I fed you again."

She shook her head, but her stomach roared at her; it had been almost ceaselessly hungry since she had swum in the silver lake. Luthe seemed to take a curious ironic pleasure in pouring food into her; he was an excellent cook, but it didn't seem to have much to do with culinary pride. It was more as if a mage's business did not often extend to the overseeing of convalescents, and the interest he took in his humble role of provider ought to be beneath his dignity, and he was a little sheepish to discover that it wasn't.

"Aerin."

She looked up, but the shadows of her childhood were still in her eyes. He smiled as if it hurt him and said, "Never mind." And threw the surka wreath over her head. It settled around her shoulders and then rippled into long silver folds that fell to her feet, and shivered like starlight when she moved.

"You look like a queen," Luthe said.

"Don't," she said bitterly, trying to find a clasp to unfasten the bright cloak. "Please don't."

"I'm sorry," said Luthe, and the cloak fell away, and she held only silver ashes in her hands. She let her hands fall to her sides, and she felt ashamed. "I'm sorry too. Forgive me."

"It matters nothing," Luthe said, but she reached out and hesitantly put a hand on his arm, and he covered it with one of his. "There may have been a better way than the Meeldtar's to save your life," he said. "But it was the only way I knew; and you left me no time. . . . I was not trained as a healer." He shut his eyes, but his hand stayed on hers. "No mages are, usually. It's not glamorous enough, I suppose; and we're a pretty vain lot." He opened his eyes again and tried to smile.

"Meeldtar is the Water of Sight, and its spring runs into the lake here, the Lake of Dreams. We live—here—very near the Meeldtar stream, but the lake also touches other shores and drinks other springs—I do not know all their names. I told you I'm not a healer . . . and . . . when you got here, finally, I could almost see the sunlight through you. If it weren't for Talat, I might have thought you were a ghost. The Meeldtar suggested I give you a taste of the lake water—the Water of Sight itself would only have ripped your spirit from what was left of your body.

"But the lake—even I don't understand everything that happens in that lake." He fell silent, and dropped his hand from hers, but his breath stirred the hair that fell over her forehead. At last he said: "I'm afraid you are no longer quite . . . mortal."

She stared up at him, and the shadows of her childhood ebbed away to be replaced by the shadows of many unknown futures.

"If it's any comfort, I'm not quite mortal either. One does learn to cope; but within a fairly short span one finds oneself longing for an empty valley, or a mountaintop. I've been here . . ."

"Long enough to remember the Black Dragon."

"Yes. Long enough to remember the Black Dragon."

"Are you sure?" she whispered.

"One is never sure of anything," he snapped; but she had learned that his anger was not directed at her, but at his own fears, and she waited. He closed his eyes again, thinking. She's being patient with me. Gods, what has happened to me? I've been a master mage since old Goriolo put the mark on me, and he could almost remember when the moon was first hung in the sky. And this child with her red hair looks at me once with those smoky feverish eyes and I panic and dunk her in the lake. What is the matter with me?

He opened his eyes again and looked down at her. Her eyes were still smoky, green and hazel, still gleaming with the occasional amber flame, but they were no longer feverish, and their calm shook him now almost as badly as their dying glitter had done. "I followed you, you know, when you went under. I—I had to make a rather bad bargain to bring you back again. It was not a bargain I was expecting to have to make." He paused. "I'm pretty sure."

The eyes wavered and dropped. She looked at her one hand tucked over Luthe's arm, and brought the other up to join it; and gently, as if he might like his comfort no better than she had liked his gift, he put his other arm around her; and she leaned slowly forward and rested her head against his shoulder. "I'm sorry," he said.

She laughed the whisper of a laugh. "I was not ready to die yet; very well, I shall live longer than I wished."

She stirred, and moved away from him, and her arms dropped; but when he took one of her hands she did not try to withdraw it. The wind rustled lightly in the leaves. "You promised me food," she said lightly.

"I did. Come along, then."

The way back to Luthe's hall was narrow, and as they walked side by side, for Luthe would not relinquish her hand, they had to walk very near each other. Aerin was glad when she saw the grey stone of the hall rear up before her, and at the edge of the small courtyard she broke away from the man beside her, and ran up the low steps and into the huge high room; and by the time he rejoined her she was busily engaged in pretending to warm her hands at the hearth. But she had no need of the fire's warmth, for her blood was strangely stirred, and the flush on her face was from more than the fire's red light.

Over supper she said, "I have not heard anyone else call it *kelar*. Just the Gift, or the royal blood."

He was grateful that she chose to break the silence and answered quickly: "Yes, that's true enough, although your family made themselves royalty on the strength of it, not the other way round. It came from the North originally." He smiled at her stricken look. "Yes, it did; you and the demon-kind share an ancestor, and you have both lived to bear *kelar* through many generations. You need that common ancestor; without the unphysical strength the *kelar* grants you, you could not fight the demonkind, and Damar would not exist."

She laughed her whispered laugh again, and said, "One in the eye for those who like to throw up to me my status as a halfblood."

"Indeed," said Luthe, and the flicker of temper she had grown accustomed to seeing whenever they discussed her father's court flashed across his face. "Their ignorance is so great they are terrified by a hint of the truth; a hint such as you are in yourself."

"You overrate me," Aerin said. "I may be all you say of me now, but I have been nothing—nothing but an inconvenient nuisance; inconvenient particularly because I had the ill grace to get born to the king, where I could not be ignored as I deserved."

"Ignored," said Luthe. "You should be queen after your father. The sober responsible Tor is no better than a usurper."

"No," she replied, stung. "Tor is sober and responsible and he will make a far better king than I would a queen. Which is just as well, since he's for it and I'm not."

"Why not?" said Luthe. "It is you who is Arlbeth's child."

"By his second marriage," said Aerin. "If Queen Tatoria had borne a child, of course it would have ruled after Arlbeth —or it would certainly have ruled if it were a son. But she didn't. She died. Kings aren't supposed to remarry anyway, but they may under extreme duress, like childless widower-hood; but they can't marry unknown foreigners of question-able blood. I'm sure it was a great relief to all concerned when the unknown foreigner's pregnancy resulted in a girl—they usually manage not to let even firstborn girls of impeccable breeding inherit, so shunting me aside was as easy as swearing by the Seven Perfect Gods.

"Galanna prefers to think I'm a bastard, but I've seen the record book, and I am down as legitimate—but not as a legitimate heir. The priests chose to call my father's second marriage morganatic—my mother wasn't even permitted to be Honored Wife. Just in case she had a boy."

Aerin's sense of the passage of time had been uncertain since she met Maur; and as her health returned in Luthe's mountain valley, she yet had difficulty in believing that days and weeks had any meaning. When it occurred to her that one season had passed and another was passing, and that these were things she should take note of, she backed away from that knowledge again, for it was then that what Luthe had told her about the price she had paid to regain her life rose up and mocked her. Immortality was far more terrible a price than any she might have imagined.

As the air grew colder and the grass in the meadow turned brown and dull violet and as the flowers stopped blooming she pretended to notice these things only as isolated phenomena. Luthe watched her, and knew much of what she thinking, but had no comfort for her; all he could offer was his knowledge, of magic, of history, of Damar; of the worlds he had traveled, and the wonders he brought back. He taught her eagerly, and eagerly she learned, each of them distracting the other from something each could not yet face. Snow fell, and Talat and the cattle and sheep spent their days in the low open barn at the edge of their meadow; and sometimes a few deer joined them at their hay and oats; but the deer came mostly for the company—and the oats—because winter never fell harshly where Luthe was, nor did ice ever rime even the shores of the Lake of Dreams.

Sometimes what she learned frightened her, or perhaps it was that she could learn such things from a mage that frightened her; and one day, almost involuntarily she asked: "Why do you tell me . . . so much?"

Luthe considered her. "I tell you . . . some you need to know, and some you have earned the right to know, and some it won't hurt you to know—" He stopped.

"And some?"

He raised his hands and his eyebrows; smiled faintly. The pale winter sun gleamed on his yellow hair and glinted in his blue eyes. There were no lines in his face, and his narrow shoulders were straight and square; but still he looked old to her, old as the mountains, older than the great grey hall he inhabited, that looked as though it had stood there since the sun first found the silver lake. "Some things I tell you only because I wish to tell them to you."

Aerin's lessons grew longer and longer, for her brain's capacity seemed to increase as the strength of her body did; and she began to love the learning for its own sake, and not merely for the fact that there was *kelar* in her blood, and that the house of the king of Damar need not be ashamed to claim her; and then she could not learn enough.

"I shall have to give you the mage mark soon," Luthe said, smiling, one grey afternoon as the snow fell softly outside.

Aerin stood up and paced restlessly, twice the length of the hall to the open door and back to the hearth and the table where Luthe sat. It was a wonderful hall for pacing, for it took several minutes, even for the fidgetiest, to get from one end of it to the other and back again. The door stood open all year long, for the cold somehow stayed outside, and the only draughts were warm ones from the fire. Aerin stared at the glinting white courtyard for a moment before returning to Luthe and the table before the fire.

"I came here first for healing and second for knowledge—but by the gods and their hells I do not know if I can bear either. And yet I have no choice. And yet I do not know even what I wished to know."

Luthe stood up, but came only a few steps nearer the fireplace. "I tell you all that I may."

"May," said Aerin fiercely. "What can you tell me that you may not? What am I, now that I am neither human—which I understand I never was—nor mortal, which I used to be? Why did you heal me? Why did you call me here at all? Why do you teach me now so much that you threaten me with the mage mark, that all who look upon me may know to fear me? That will be splendid fun at home, you know; I'm so popular already. Why? Why don't you tell me to go away?" She stopped and looked down at her feet. "Why don't I just leave?"

Luthe sighed. "I'm sorry. Again. I thought that perhaps it

would be easier if you first had some idea of your own strength."

She was still staring at her shoes, and he stepped toward her, and hesitantly touched one shoulder. The shoulder hunched itself up and the face turned away from him. Her hair was almost shoulder length now, and it fell across her face like a curtain. Luthe wanted to tell her the reasons she ought to stay—good honest Damarian reasons, reasons she would understand and acknowledge; reasons that were born with her as the king's daughter, however outcast her people made her; reasons that he had to tell her soon anyway. But he wanted . . . "Do you wish so desperately to leave?" he said almost wistfully.

"It matters little," said a low voice from behind the hair. "I am not missed."

"Tor," said Luthe darkly.

"Oh, Tor," said the voice, and it unexpectedly gave a choke of laughter, and then she raised her hands and parted the curtain, rubbing her cheeks hastily with her palms as she did so. Her eyes were still a little too bright. "Yes, Tor, and Arlbeth too, and I do feel badly for Teka; but I would guess they live hopefully, and guess to see me again. I do not mind staying here . . . a little longer. I don't much care to travel in winter anyway."

"Thank you," Luthe said dryly. "By spring I shall be ready . . . to send you on your way again."

Aerin said lightly, "And what shall that way be?"

"To Agsded," Luthe said. "He who holds Damar's future in his hands."

"Agsded?" Aerin said. "I do not know the name."

"He it is who sends the mischief across your borders; he it is who stirred Nyrlol to rebellion just long enough to distract and disturb Arlbeth, and he who awoke your Maur, and who even now harries your City with his minions, whose army will march south in the spring. Agsded, although none know his name now, and the Northern generals believe they band together through no impulse but their mutual hatred of Damar.

"Agsded is a wizard—a master mage, a master of masters. The mark on him is so bright it could blind any simple folk who look upon it, though they knew not what they saw. Agsded I knew long ago—he was another of Goriolo's pupils; he was the best of all of us, and he knew it; but even Goriolo did not see how deep his pride went. . . . Goriolo had another pupil of Agsded's family: his sister. She feared her brother; she had always feared him; it was fear of what his pride might do that led her to Goriolo with him, but it was on her own merit that Goriolo took her.

"And I—I must send you into the dragon's den again, having barely healed you, and that at great cost, from your encounter with the Black Dragon. Maur is to your little dragons what Agsded is to Maur. I teach you what I may because it is the only shield I may—can—give you. I cannot face Agsded myself—I cannot. By the gods and hells you have never heard of," Luthe broke out, "do you think I like sending a child to a doom like this, one I know I cannot myself face? With nothing to guard her but half a year's study of the apprentice bits of magery?

"I know by my own blood that I cannot defeat him; though by some of that blood I have held him off these many years longer, that the chosen hero, the hero of his blood, might grow up to face him; for only one of his blood may defeat him." Luthe closed his eyes. "It is true your mother wanted a son; she believed that as only one of his blood might defeat him, so only one of his own sex might, for to such she ascribed her own failure. She felt that it was because she was a woman that she could not kill her own brother."

"Brother?" whispered Aerin.

Luthe opened his eyes. "Had she tried, she might yet have failed," he went on as though he had not heard her, "but she could not bear to try; until Agsded, who knew the prophecy even as she did, from long before there was apparent need to know it, sought to bring her under his will or to destroy her.

"He could not do the former; almost he did the latter, and in the end she died of the poison he gave her." Luthe looked at her, and she remembered the hand that was not her own holding a goblet, and a voice that was not Luthe's saying "Drink." "But she had meanwhile fled south, and found a man with *kelar* in his blood, and been got with child by him. She had only the strength left to bear that child before she died."

Luthe fell silent, and Aerin could think of nothing to say. Agsded beat in her brain; a moment ago she had told Luthe she did not know the name, and yet now she was ready to swear that it had haunted all the shadows since before her birth; that her mother had whispered it to her in the womb; that the despair she had died of was the taste of it on her tongue. Agsded, who was to Maur what Maur had been to her first dragon; and the first dragon might have killed her—and Maur *had* killed her, for the time she lived now was not her own. Agsded, of her own blood; her mother's brother.

She felt numb; even the new sensitivities that had awoken in her since her dive into the Lake of Dreams and Luthe's teaching—all were numb, and she hung suspended in a great nothingness, imprisoned there by the name of Agsded.

After a pause Luthe said, as if talking to himself: "I did not think your *kelar* would so hide itself from you. Perhaps it was the hurt you did yourself and your Gift by eating the surka. Perhaps your mother was not able entirely to protect the child she carried from the death so close to her. I believed that you had to know at least something of the truth—I believed it until I saw you face Maur with little more than simple human courage and a foolhardy faith in the efficacy of a third-rate healer's potion like kenet against the Black Dragon. And I knew then not only that I was wrong about you, but that I was too late to save you from the pain your simplicity would cause you; and I feared that without your *kelar* to draw upon, you would not survive that meeting. And I was terribly near right.

"I have been much occupied while you were growing up, and I do not mark the years as you do; and I have not watched over you as I should have. As I promised your mother I would. Again I am sorry. I have been often sorry, with you, and there is so little I can do about any of it.

"I believed that you would grow up knowing some destiny awaited you; I thought what ran in your veins could not help but tell you so much. I thought you would know the true dreams I sent you as such. I thought many things that were wrong."

"The *kelar* may have tried to tell me," Aerin said dully; "but the message did get a little confused somehow. Certainly I was left in no doubt that my destiny was different than Arlbeth's daughter's should have been, but that was a reading anyone could have done."

Luthe looked at her, and saw her uncle's name like a brand on her face. "If you wish," he said lightly, "I shall go personally to your City and knock together the heads of Perlith and Galooney."

Aerin tried to smile. "I shall remember that offer."

"Please do. And remember also that I never leave my mountain any more, so believe how apologetic I must be feeling to make it in the first place."

Aerin's smile disappeared. "Am I truly just as my mother was?" she asked, as she had asked Teka long ago.

Luthe looked at her again, and again many things crowded into his mind that he might say. "You are very like her," he said at last. "But you are to be preferred."

❧ CHAPTER 18 ❧

AFTER THIS, suddenly the winter was too short, despite the nightmares of a man with eyes brighter than a dragon's, who wore a red cloak. The snow melted too soon, and too soon the first tight buds knuckled out from the trees, and the first vivid purple shoots parted the last year's dry grass. There was a heavy rich smell in the air, and Aerin kept seeing things in the shadows just beyond the edge of sight, and hearing far high laughter she could not be sure she did not imagine. Sometimes when she saw or heard such somethings she would whip around to look at Luthe, who, as often as not, would be staring into the middle distance with a vague silly smile on his face.

"You aren't really alone up here at all, are you?" she said, and was surprised to feel something she suspected was jealousy.

Luthe refocused his eyes to look at her gravely. "No. But my . . . friends . . . are very shy. Worse than I am."

"I'll be leaving soon anyway," Aerin said. "They'll come back to you soon enough."

Luthe did not answer immediately. "Yes. Soon enough."

She got out Talat's saddle and gear and cleaned everything, and oiled the leather; and upon request Luthe provided her with some heavy canvas and narrow bits of leather, and she rigged a plain breastplate, for Talat had insufficient wither to carry a saddle reliably straight. She also made a little leather pouch to carry the red dragon stone, which had been living under a corner of her mattress, and hung it around her neck on a thong. Then she spent hours currying Talat while the winter hair rose in clouds around them and Talat made hideous faces of ecstasy and gratification.

She came dripping into the grey hall at twilight one evening, having shed a great deal of white hair and dust in the bathhouse, and found Luthe pulling the wrappings off a sword. The cloth was black and brittle, as if with great age, but the scabbard gleamed silver-white and the great blue gem set in the hilt was bright as fire. "Oh," breathed Aerin, coming up behind him.

He turned and smiled at her, and, holding the scabbard in a shred of ragged black cloth, offered her the hilt. She grasped it without hesitation, and the feel of it was as smooth as glass, and the grips seemed to mold to her hand. She pulled the blade free, and it flashed momentarily with a light that cut the farthest shadows of Luthe's ever shadowed hall, and there seemed to be an echo of some great clap of sound that deafened both the red-haired woman and the tall blond man; yet neither heard anything. And then it was merely a sword, glinting faintly in the firelight, with a great blue gem set at the peak of the hilt.

"Yes, I rather thought she was for you," Luthe said. "Goriolo said I would know when the time came. Funny I did not think of her sooner; there can be no better ally against Agsded."

"What—who is she?" Aerin said, holding the tip upright so the firelight would run like water down the length of the blade.

"She is Gonturan," Luthe said. "I—er—found her, long ago, on my travels in the—er—East. Before I settled here. Although I think it probable that she called me; there was no good reason for me to have been possessed of a desire to go haring off on a long journey East. I have never been a traveler by nature."

"Called you?" said Aerin, although she had no difficulty in believing that this particular sword could do anything—jump over the moon, turn herself into a juggernaut, speak riddles that might be prophecy.

"It's a long story," said Luthe.

Aerin took her eyes off the sword long enough to flash him an exasperated look.

"I'll tell you all of it someday," Luthe said, but his voice carried no conviction.

Aerin said quietly, "I leave at the next new moon."

"Yes," said Luthe, so softly she did not hear him but knew only that he must agree; and Gonturan slid like silk into her scabbard. They stood not looking at anything, and at last Aerin said lightly, "It is as well to have a sword; and I left mine in the City, for it is sworn to the king and the king's business; although if Arlbeth knew of Agsded he must admit that Agsded is king's business."

Luthe said, "He would; but he would never admit that it was your business, even if he knew all the story. Arlbeth is a worthy man but, um, traditional. But Gonturan goes with you, and Gonturan is better than a platoon of Damarian cavalry."

"And easier to feed," said Aerin.

"North you must go," said Luthe. "North and east, I think you will find the way."

Talat stood still while Aerin tied the last bundles behind his saddle, but his ears spoke of his impatience. It's been a pleasant sojourn, they said, and we would be happy to return someday; but it's high time we were off now.

Aerin gave a final tug on a strap and then turned to Luthe. He stood next to one of the pillars before his hall. She stared fixedly at the open neck of his tunic so she need not see how the young spring sunlight danced in his hair; but she found herself watching a rapid little pulse beating in the hollow of his throat, and so she shifted her attention to his left shoulder. "Good-bye," she said. "Thanks. Um."

The arm attached to the shoulder she was staring at reached out toward her, and she was so absorbed in not thinking about anything that its hand had seized her chin before she thought to flinch away. The hand exerted upward force and her neck reluctantly bent back, but her eyes stuck on his chin and stayed there.

"Hey," said Luthe. "This is me, remember? You aren't allowed to pretend I don't exist until after you leave my mountain."

She raised her eyes and met his; blue eyes smiled into veiled green ones. He dropped his hand and said lightly, "Very well, have it your way. I don't exist."

She had already turned away, but she turned back at that, and his arms closed around her, and so they stood, while the sun shone down on their two motionless figures and one impatient stallion.

Aerin broke free at last, and heaved herself belly down over the saddle, and swung her leg hastily behind, thumping a bundle with her boot in the process. Talat grunted.

"Come back to me," said Luthe behind her.

"I will," she said to Talat's ears, and then Talat was trotting briskly down the trail. The last Luthe saw of them was a stray blue gleam from the hilt of a sword.

Spring seemed to burst everywhere around them as they went, as though Talat's small round hoofs struck greenness from the earth; as if the last white hairs of his winter coat conveyed a charm to the earth they touched. When they slept, they slept in small glades of trees where leaves had just begun to show; but in the mornings, somehow, the leaves were uncurled and heavy with sap; even the grass Aerin lay on had thickened during the night hours. Talat seemed to grow younger with every day, his shining whiteness brilliant in the sunlight, tirelessly jogging mile after long mile; and the birds followed them, as the leaves opened for them, and the flowers cast their perfumes around them. Aerin saw, and wondered, and thought she was imagining things; and then thought again that perhaps she wasn't; but the sun told her that they went steadily north, and the hard feel of Gonturan in her hand reminded her of why they went.

They had first descended to the forest plain when they left Luthe, and turned right, or north, in the foothills; and here the grass grew to Talat's knees, and he had to wade through it, with a rushing sound like a ship's prow through the sea. Before them the grass was thinner; behind them, when she turned to look, the grass was deepest where their trail had been, and waves of grass rippled out from it in wide curving swells. Aerin laughed. "I believe we go in company after all, though the company chooses to be silent." Talat cocked his ears back to listen.

But soon they climbed into the mountains again, and there spring had more trouble following them, although she continued to try. Aerin was not conscious of guiding Talat, any more than she had been when they sought for Luthe; they both knew where they were going, and it drew them on; and behind them spring urged them forward. Higher they went, as the sun rose over them and set almost behind them, and the ground underfoot was no longer turf, but rock, and Talat's hoofs rang when they struck.

When they first came to the stony ground, his hoofbeats struck a hard warning sound; they seemed to thunder of doom and loss and failure, and Talat shied away from his own feet. "Nonsense," said Aerin, and dismounted, taking Gonturan with her; and she swung her up over her head and down, and thrust her into the trail before her, which was not rock at all, but earth; and as she drew the blade out again, there were some small crushed grass stems growing from the hole that she had made. Aerin knelt, and picked up a handful of dirt and pebbles from the tiny bit of broken earth before her; and threw her handful down the rocky way before them, as far as her arm could hurl; and as the handful disintegrated, the bits twinkled. She threw another handful after the first; and when she threw this into the air it smelled of the crushed leaves of the surka, and as she looked ahead she saw, as if her eyes had merely overlooked it the first time, a slender grey sapling bearing green leaves; and in its topmost branches there appeared a bird, and the bird sang; and around the tree's foot there grew a budding surka plant, which explained the heavy pungent smell in the air.

"What a pleasant place this is," said Aerin dryly, but it seemed that her words were sucked away from her, and echoed in some narrow place that was not the place where she stood. Her hand tightened a little on Gonturan's hilt, but she raised her chin, as if someone might be watching, and remounted Talat. Now his hoofs rang out merrily, like hoofbeats on the stony ways of the City; and there was grass growing in tufts among the stones, and a few wildflowers clinging to crevices over their heads.

The feeling of being watched increased as they went on, though she saw no one, except, perhaps, at night, when there seemed to be more rustlings than there had been when they were still below on the plain, and more quick glints that might have been eyes. The fifth night since she had plunged Gonturan into the earth, and the twelfth since she had left Luthe, she stood up from her fireside and said into the darkness, "Come, then, and tell me what you want." Her own voice frightened her, for it sounded as if it knew what it was doing, and she was quite sure she did not; and so she staggered and almost fell when after a few moments something did come, and pressed up against her, against the backs of her thighs. She did not move; and before her she saw the glints of many pairs of eyes, moving nearer, at about the right level for creatures the size of the thing that leaned against her legs. She had her arms crossed over her breast; now with infinite reluctance she unbent her right elbow and let the hand dangle down behind her leg, and she felt the creature's breath. She closed her eyes, and then opened them again with an involuntary yelp as a very rough tongue dragged over the back of her hand. The weight against her legs shifted a little, and then a round skull pressed into her palm.

She looked down over her shoulder with dread, and the great cat thing, one of the wild folstza of the mountains, which could carry off a whole sheep or bring down a horse, began to purr. "Pleased to make your acquaintance," Aerin said shakily. "I think."

Her eyes had grown more accustomed to the darkness, and in the shadows now she could see more of the folstza, ten, a dozen, sixteen, twenty; they roved restlessly through the undergrowth as they approached, for, like cats of any size, they did not wish to admit that they approached; all but the one who warmed Aerin's right thigh and shivered her with its purring. At last the folstza sat before her in a semicircle, blinking with green or gold or brown eyes, or looking off into space as if they couldn't imagine how they found themselves there. Some sat neatly, tails curled around four paws; some sprawled like kittens. One or two had their backs to her. They were all sizes, from younglings who hadn't grown into the length of their legs and the size of their feet, to some that were grey-muzzled with age.

"Well," said Aerin. "I'm sure I am—er—grateful for your companionship. If Agsded troubles you too, I'm sure you could be of use in our—er—meeting."

As if this were a signal, the cats stood up and wandered toward the small campfire, where Talat laid his ears back flat to his skull and rolled his eyes till the whites showed. "No," said Aerin bemusedly; "I rather think these are our friends," and she looked down at the thing that now twined itself between her legs (it had to scrunch down slightly to accomplish this) and rubbed its head affectionately against her hip.

It was the biggest of the lot of them. The rest were arranging themselves around the fire, some of them in heaps, some of them in individual curls and whorls. The one that now sat and stared up at Aerin was black, with yellow eyes, and short sharp ears with a fringe of fine long black hairs around each; and down his neck and back were cloudy grey splotches that dripped over his shoulders and haunches. She saw the flicker in his eyes and braced herself just in time as he sprang up on his hind legs and put his forepaws on her shoulders. His breath was soft against her face, and the ends of his whiskers tickled her cheeks. He looked faintly disappointed as she stood her ground and stared back at him; and he dropped to all fours again and padded silently over to her bedding, lying unrolled and ready near the fire. He batted it with a forepaw till he'd disarranged it to his liking, and then lay down full length upon it, and smiled at her.

Aerin looked at him. She looked around; the other cats were watching intently through slitted eyes, for all their languor; none of them had their backs to her now. She looked at Talat, who had backed up till his rump and flattened tail were pressed against a tree, and whose ears were still flat to his skull. She looked longingly at Gonturan, hanging from a tree on the far side of the fire, where she had set her when first making camp. Gonturan glittered in the firelight, but Aerin thought she mocked her even as the big cat did, and knew there was no help there.

"Even allies must know their place," Aerin said aloud, and was again startled at how decisive her voice sounded. She stalked over to her blanket and the cat on it, seized the hem of the blanket, and yanked. The cat rolled a complete circumference and came up again looking startled, but Aerin did not stop to watch. She wrapped her blanket around her shoulders, picked up the bundle she used as a pillow, and rearranged herself to sleep at the foot of the tree on the far side of the fire, with Gonturan's hilt in easy reach. She lay down with her back to the fire, and stared wide-eyed at the writhe of tree root before her.

Nothing happened.

The silence was broken only by the small snaps of the fire,

and even these, at last, subsided, and real darkness fell. I should keep the fire going. Aerin thought; who knows what else is out there waiting? Who knows . . . But her nightmares claimed her, and she fell asleep; and again she was suspended in nowhere, but nowhere was lit with a smoky red light, and a voice was calling her name; or she thought it was her name it called, but perhaps the word was "uncle."

She awoke at dawn with a cramp in her side, for a heavy blackfurred head was resting in the hollow between her last rib and her pelvis. As she stirred he began to purr. She sat up anyway, and glared at him. "You are horrible," she said, and he gave her the same sleepy smile as when he had attempted to usurp her bedding.

Talat was dozing uneasily, still leaning against his tree, and was inclined to be cross when she went to put his saddle on; but perhaps that was because of the four-footed grey-edged shadow she brought with her. She rode off without looking behind her; but she felt, if she could not hear, the fluid motion following, and the black cat trotted along beside them as he could, occasionally leaping into the rocks above them as the trail narrowed. Once he jumped over them, from a rockface on one hand to an evergreen tree on the other, showering them with small sharp needles and seedpods; and when he rejoined them Talat whirled and snapped at him, but he only glided out of the way. He was smiling again. "Don't let him tease you," Aerin murmured. Talat's ears stayed back all that day, and he was a little short on the weak leg, for he could not relax.

On the next day the yerigs joined them, the shaggy wild dogs with their great ruffs and silky feathery legs and long curling tails. They were a little less alarming than the folstza only because Aerin was accustomed to the king's hounds, which were only half the size of the yerigs. The royal barn cats who caught the mice that tried to invade the grain bins were barely a tenth the size of the foltsza.

The yerig leader had only one eye, and a torn ear. She touched Aerin's knee gently with her nose and then raised her head to stare fiercely into Aerin's face. "I welcome you," Aerin said to her; and the dogs with her ranged themselves on one side of the campfire while the cats, pretending that the dogs did not exist, still somehow all found themselves on the opposite side of the campfire; and that night Aerin slept very warm, for there was a cat to one side of her and a dog on the other.

Still they traveled north and east, and still the sun rose before them and sank behind them, but it seemed to Aerin, leading her quiet army, that it rose more sluggishly and sank sooner each day; and while the trees still shook out young leaves for her, there were fewer trees, and the solitary sound of Talat's shod hoofs rang duller and duller. Occasionally she thought wistfully of the Lake of Dreams, and of a grey stone hall that stood near it; but she struck these thoughts from her mind as soon as she recognized them.

And then the day came when dawn was barely a lessening of shadow, and the clouds hung so low it took an effort of will to stand up straight and not bow beneath their weight. "Soon," Aerin said to those that followed her; and *soon* came back to her in a rumble of many throats.

Talat stepped out that morning as if all his joints ached, and Aerin was willing enough to go slowly; she heard little gibbering voices snarling and sniveling at the edges of her mind, and there seemed to be a red fog over her eyes, as if the nothingness that haunted her nights would find her out in the days; and she murmured a word that Luthe had taught her, and the voices stopped, and the fog lifted. But she was not long allowed the pleasure of this small victory, for now a single voice murmured to her, and its murmurs reminded her of her Northern blood, her demon blood. . . . "No!" she cried, and bent forward to press her face in Talat's mane, and then she felt the pressure of a heavy paw on her shoulder, and whiskers tickled her cheek, and she opened her eyes to see two yellow eyes in a black face that did not smile; and Talat stood perfectly still, his head bowed, as the black cat's other forepaw pressed into his crest.

She sat up again, and the cat dropped to the ground, and Talat turned his head to look at the cat, and the cat turned his head to look back. Talat's ears, half back, eased a little, and one reluctantly came forward and pointed toward the cat, and the cat walked up to him and put up his nose. Talat's other ear came forward and pricked, and he lowered his nose, and the two breathed gently into each other's faces. Then they went on.

The mountains opened suddenly into an ugly uneven plain;

the footing was bad, crumbly and full of small hidden cre-
vasses, and there were no trees at all. Aerin's army stepped
and glided and shambled out of the shadows of the rocks and
the last leaves, and billowed up around her till she and Talat
were the hub of a wheel; and all looked around them. "We are
no longer in Damar," she said calmly, and Talat heaved a
great sigh. Aerin unslung Gonturan from her saddle, and carried the blade in her hand, for the comfort of her only, for
there was nothing for a sword to do in the wide bleak brooding
space before them, where no spring could come.

The silence hammered at her, and she heard the little gibbering voices again, but indifferently this time, as if she heard
them from behind a locked door whose strength she did not
doubt. "Come along, then," she said, and Talat walked forward, yerig and folstza making way for them and then falling
in beside them. There was nothing to see but the heavy grey
sky and the bleak grey landscape. Mountains again there must
be on the far side of this flat grey space; but the clouds ringed
them in, and there was no horizon. Her beasts followed her
because she led them, but they could not see what she led them
to.

Neither could she see aught that was useful; but the small
nasty voices in her mind seemed to push harder on one side of
her skull than another; and so she went toward them.

And before them suddenly was a black mountain, or crag,
or tower, or all three; for it was the size of a mountain, but of
the looming impossible shape of a crag that will be ripped into
an avalanche in the next great storm; and yet it was also a
worked shape, however improbable, as if a hand had built it—
surely in its peak was the glint of windows?—but the hand
must have belonged to a madman. Around it twined a vast
vine of the surka, and Aerin's stomach turned over and fell
back in her belly like a stone, and the gibbering voices could be
heard to laugh.

She dismounted and walked slowly forward. She raised
Gonturan, and Gonturan blazed blue, and the black tower
suddenly glowed red, fire red, and the peak of the tower lifted
and turned toward her, and the glint of windows was a dragon's red eyes, and the black shadow that bent toward her was a
dragon's black head, and it opened its mouth to breathe flame
at her. Her left arm went suddenly dead, and then the pain of
old burns bit deeply into it, new and fresh; and she smelled her

own flesh burning. "No!" she screamed, and dropped Gonturan, and threw up her right arm against the glare of flames, her left arm hanging limp beside her. She turned to run, but something was in her way; something sleek and black tripped her, and she fell against Talat's flank, and her mind cleared, and she no longer smelled scorched flesh. She turned back fearfully, for her left arm still throbbed with memory, but there was no fire, and no dragon; only the black monstrous shape twisted round with leaves.

She bent and picked up her sword; but the blue fire had gone out, and the blade was as dull as the grey plain around them. She looked again to the glint that might be windows, for she knew now that she had come to the place she looked for, knew that Agsded was here. And she knew also that there was no way in, for the way that Gonturan might have won her was lost to her now.

Slowly she circled the great tower, but there were no doors, and now it looked like a mountain after all, and nothing that should have had a door, it was foolish to have supposed otherwise; and her quest was a failure, for if not here then she knew not where. She crawled over the rocks below the surka that wrapped itself around the black crag, for she would not touch the surka if she could help it, this surka that the eye of Agsded must have touched, that his breath might have stirred; but she went alone, for Talat and the folstza and yerig waited where she had challenged the tower with Gonturan's flame and then lost it.

She came round the full circle and knew herself defeated, and she went up to Talat and put her arms around his neck and her face in his mane, as she had done so often before for little hurts and dismays; and now in this great hurt she had no other recourse. He tucked his chin against her arm, but it was no comfort, and she stepped away from him again—and he bolted forward, and reared, and neighed, a war-horse going to battle. She stared at him open-mouthed, the hilt of her dull sword prodding her elbow.

Talat scrambled up the rocks before them, and neighed again; and plunged into the twining surka, which slowed him little. Aerin watching felt that the leaves pulled at him and hindered his passage as best they might; but he surged through them and did not care. He neighed again as he reached the foot of the smoother walls of the tower itself; he was above the vines now, and Aerin could see streaks of their sap on him. He shook his head, and reared again, and struck the walls with his front feet; and sparks flew, and there was a smell as of burning, but of the burning of unclean things. He came to all fours, and then reared and struck again; and then the folstza and the yerig were flowing up over the rocks and through the clinging surka to join him, and the yerig queen flung herself at a high outthrust knob of rock, and scrabbled at it.

"It won't work," Aerin whispered, and Talat reared and struck again, and the smell of burning was stronger.

The folstza were clawing great ropes of vine from the base of the tower, and flinging them down, and the tower seemed to quiver in her sight. The sharp little elbow of rock that the yerig queen clung to gave way suddenly, dumping her at Talat's feet; but where it had been there was a crack in the black wall; and when Talat struck at the crack a fine rain of stone powder pattered down.

The torn vines thrashed like wild things when they touched the sandy grey ground. Aerin reached to touch one of the dark leaves, and it turned into a small banded snake with venomous eyes; but she picked it up anyway, and it was only a leaf. She stood staring as her army sought better purchase on the black rockface; distantly she heard the patter of stone chips, and she picked up another leaf, and wove it through the stem of the first; and another, and then another, and when, suddenly, there was a crash and a roar and she looked up, what she held in her hands was a thick heavy green wreath of surka; and her hands were sticky with the sap.

A great face of the crag had fallen, and within, Aerin saw stairs winding up into the black mountain, red with torchlight; and her army turned its eyes on her, and panted, and many of their mouths dripped pink foam, and many of their feet had torn and bleeding pads. Talat was grey with sweat. With the wreath in her hands, and Gonturan banging lifelessly at her side, she stepped carefully through the rubble, and through the ranks of her army, many of whom touched her lightly with their noses as she passed them, and set her foot on the first stair.

❧CHAPTER 19 ❧

THE STAIRS WENT UP and up in a long slow spiral, and Aerin followed, turning round and round till it seemed to her she must be climbing the well of the sky and at the end of the staircase she would step onto the moon's cold surface and look down, far away, upon the green earth. For a little while she could hear her friends, who waited restlessly at the foot of the stair; once she heard the thinnest thread of a whine, but that was all. None tried to follow her. Then she could no longer hear anything but the soft sound of her footsteps and the occasional slow stutter of a guttering flame. Her legs ached with climbing, and her back ached with tension, and her neck ached with keeping her head tipped up to look at the endless staircase; and her mind ached with thoughts she dared not think. Daylight had disappeared long since, had gone with the last sounds of her beasts; the light in her eyes was red. In the edges of her vision she saw gaping black doors that led into chambers she would not imagine, let alone turn her gaze to see; and sometimes the soft noise of her footsteps echoed strangely on a stair that opened into such a room.

The silence weighed her down; the air grew heavier with every step up. She recognized the weight, though she had never felt it thus before: evil. Maur's breath had stunk of evil, and its words had set evil tracks in her mind; but she had faced Maur on the earth and under the sky, not in a dark endless airless tower. She struggled on. With each step she felt her ankles and shinbones jar against the floor, and tendons grate across her kneecaps, the heavy thigh muscles twist and curl, her hips grind in their sockets. Her right ankle began to ache.

She was still carrying the surka wreath, and as she thought of Maur she remembered the red stone she had taken with her from its ashes, and remembered that she carried the stone even now. She had a moment's cold dread, wondering if she were carrying her own betrayal into Agsded's lair; but she put her hand into the breast of her tunic, and drew out the little soft pouch where the stone lay. The stone was hot to the touch when she let it fall into her palm from the pouch, and it seemed to writhe in her fingers; she almost dropped it, but she thought of spiders and surka leaves, and held on; then shook it back into its pouch, and curled her fingers around it.

Still she climbed, but she no longer felt alone. Evil was with her; red evil shone in her eyes, rode on her shoulders, harried her heels; waited in the dark doorways where she would not look, fell like ash and rose like smoke from the torches. Evil was all around her, and it watched her, eyelessly, watched for her first stumble. Still the stairs rose before her, and still her weary legs carried her up; she wondered how many days she had spent climbing stairs, and if her army had disbanded by now, and she worried about Talat, who was wearing his saddle and gear. She should have remembered to strip it off before she entered the dark tower.

The red light throbbed in time to her own pulse; she panted in a rhythm begun by its fluctuations; the sweat that ran into her eyes was red, and it burned. And now she had something else to worry about, for where she had touched the tender skin of her throat with her surka-sticky fingers when she pulled at the thong that held the dragon stone's pouch, it burned too. But its throb had nothing to do with the tower. It throbbed angrily and self-consciously, and her mind was distracted enough to think, This is typical. On my way to gods know what unspeakable doom, and I break out in a rash. But it lightened the evil a little; she did not notice this as such, only that she toiled on in a slightly better spirit. Idly she pulled one end of her collar loose and pressed it against the surka rash, which didn't help at all.

Up. And still up. Everything ached; it was impossible to tell the leg cramps from the headache any more; the only thing about her that still bore any individuality was the surka rash on her chest, which was spreading. Up. She had been climbing forever; she would be climbing forever. She would be a new god: the God That Climbs. It was no more improbable than some of the other gods: the God That Isn't There, for example (more often known as the God That Follows or the God That Goes Before), which was the shadow-god at midday. The rash had also begun to itch, and she had to curl her surka-stained fingers into fists to stop herself from scratching the too sensitive skin on her neck and chest. And still she climbed. The heat in the red stone now beat at one hand even through the pouch; and the crisp leaves of the surka pinched the fingers of the other hand.

When she came to the top she did not believe it. She stood dumbly, looking at the black hallway before her, opening from a black doorway like all the other doorways she had straitly passed on her long spiral ascent; but now the stairs were ended, and she must cross this threshold or turn around and go back. There were no torches lighting this hall; the last of them threw their shadows at her from half a dozen steps below. And suddenly those shadows flickered, though there was no draught, and she knew there was something on the stairs behind her, and she plunged forward into the darkness.

She would have said she had no strength left for running, but she did run, Gonturan banging painfully against her ankle, although her feet were numb with climbing. Then she saw that the hall was quite short, for the blackness before her was that of double doors, their frames edged with the thinnest line of red light; and she stopped abruptly a few strides from them, her muscles quivering and her knees threatening to dump her full length on the floor for the thing coming up the stairs to find.

She leaned against the outer edge of one door, her back to the narrow wall where it joined the corridor wall; her breath whined in her throat. Thank Luthe for the thoroughness of my cure, she thought as she felt the thick air surging into the bottom of her chest, being hurled out again, and a fresh lungful captured. The rash on her chest throbbed with extra enthusiasm as she panted, and the skin above her ribcage had to heave and subside more quickly. Well, thorough about the important thing, she amended.

Luthe. She had not thought of him, had not quite said his

name even in the dimmest, most private recesses of her mind, since she had left him. She had said she would come back to him. Her breathing eased; even the evil air seemed to taste less foul. Luthe. She looked down the hallway, but saw nothing coming toward her. Perhaps it is Nothing, she thought. Perhaps that is what follows here. She looked down at her hands. She could not open the doors behind her—supposing they opened in the usual fashion—with both hands full. She knelt down, kicking the tip of Gonturan to one side so it jammed up into a corner and gave Aerin's armpit a sharp poke with her hilt, and put the hidden stone and the green wreath on the stone floor. Slowly she upended the leather bag, and the hot red stone spilled out, burning in its own light, long red tongues of that light snaking down the corridor and up the walls. It made her dizzy. She prodded the wreath and made a small hollow in the twined stems, hastily picked up the stone as it tried to scorch her fingers, and dropped it in. It sizzled and hissed, but the surka seemed to quench it, and the red light subsided. Aerin pulled the leaves back over it again, shook the wreath to be sure it could not fall out, and stood up.

By the wings of the mother of all horses, her rash would drive her mad soon. She rubbed it helplessly, the hell of her hand chafing it against the inside of her shirt, and it responded gleefully by feeling as if it had caught fire; but as she dropped her hand again and then tried to bow her shoulders so that her shirt and tunic would fall away from the infected skin, she stopped thinking about what might be creeping up the stairs behind her. Bowing her shoulders did no good either. Irritably she turned to face the door, her free hand pressed flat against her chest again with shirt and tunic between; and pushed at the doors with the hand that held the surka. The leaves rasped against the inside edge of the doors, and the doors—

Exploded.

There was a roar like all the thunder gods came down off their mountain to howl simultaneously in her ears; and winds spun around her like endless spiral staircases, bruising her with their edges. There was torn redness before her eyes, rent with blackness, clawed with white and yellow; she felt that her eyes would be hammered out of their sockets. She staggered forward, still clutching the wreath, the hand that held it outstretched. She could not see floor nor walls nor ceiling, nor anything; only the shards of color, like mad rags of cloth streaming past. Her other hand fell to Gonturan's hilt, though she knew she hadn't a chance of drawing her in this vortex of storm; still it gave comfort to clutch at her.

The wind lifted her entirely off her feet for a moment and dropped her again and she stumbled and almost fell, and so the wind seized her yet again and threw her to one side, and only luck let her fall feet first the second time. This will not do, she thought, and braced herself as best she could. I'll probably lose her—and with a wild heave she pulled Gonturan free of her scabbard.

Blue fire blazed up and whirled around her, and the winds and thunders backed off. Aerin gave Gonturan an experimental swoop, and she sang, a shrill grim note, and the shards of red and black and claws of yellow and white disappeared into shadows and became a floor and five red walls and a ceiling overhead with things painted on it, fell things of red and black, with fangs and yellow claws.

And at the far end of the chamber stood a man dressed in white, with a red sword girt at his side, and she knew him at once, for she had seen his face often enough in her mirror.

She opened her mouth, but no words came out. He laughed, her own laugh, but greater, deeper, with terrible echoes that made tangled harmonies, and those harmonies found the places in her own mind that she had never looked into, that by their existence had long frightened her; that she had hoped always to be able to ignore. The air reeled over her in thick waves, and Gonturan's blue fire dimmed and flickered as her hand trembled.

"Well met, sister's daughter," he said. His voice was low and soft and courteous; a thoughtful, philosophical, wise, and kindly voice, a voice anyone might trust; a voice nothing like Aerin's own.

"Not well met," Aerin said at last in a strangled voice, which seemed to cut ugly holes in the air currents between them, which destroyed the harmonies that still hummed in her mind; but by the sound of her own voice she felt she had lost something treasured and beautiful that might have forever been hers. "Not well met. You killed my mother and you would kill my people and my country."

He raised his shoulders, and his white robe rippled and fell in long graceful folds that glinted softly, like the petals of spring flowers. His hazel eyes blinked gently at her; her own

eyes, but larger and set more deeply beneath a higher brow.
"And why, my dear, should you care? You never met your
mother, so you cannot miss her. I may have done you a favor;
many daughters would be glad to have escaped the tender min-
istrations of their mothers.

"And when has your land ever cared for you?" His voice
sank lower yet, purring, and he smiled Aerin's own smile.
"They call you witch's daughter—and so you are, and more,
for your mother might have been given the mage mark had she
not fled too soon—and they should revere you for it. But in
their small vicious way they choose to revile you.

"Your father is kind—why should he not be? You have
never been any trouble—you have never demanded your
rightful place as his daughter and his only child; and lately you
have been of some small use, slaying dragons, so that he need
not send out his valuable men on so inglorious a task. You
have kept to the shadows, and he has let you stay there, and
has done nothing to deny his people's voices when they
whisper, witchwoman's daughter.

"And Tor?" He chuckled. "Honest Tor. He loves you, you
know. You know that. So does everyone. They all say that you
are your mother's daughter—I think even the worthy Arlbeth
wonders just a little, sometimes—and your mother was a
witch; never forget that. Tor himself is, of course, not in a
position to do much thinking about this. And as you *are* your
mother's daughter, even when you do not remember it . . ."
He smiled her smile at her again, but it seemed very full of
teeth.

"No," said Aerin; it was almost a shriek. Gonturan wavered in her hand.

"But yes. And think of who accompanied you to this fateful
meeting. Do you come with your father's finest cavalry? Do
you come at least with a troop of well-meaning if inexperienced men? Why, no—you come without even the lowliest
Damarian foot soldier, without even a ragged village brat to
shine your boots. You come at all only because you escaped,
like a prisoner, from the City which ought to be yours to command. You come draggle-tailed, with wild beasts of the hills,
riding an old lame horse who should have been mercifully
killed years ago." He seemed to have some trouble saying the
word "mercifully": it was as if his teeth got in his way.

Aerin shook her head dumbly. His words buzzed in her ears

like insects waiting to sting her; and the terrible harmonies of his laugh bit deeper into her each time she moved. If only her chest didn't itch so; it was hard to concentrate on anything through the itching; it was worse even than the headache. He was talking about Talat, poor patient Talat, waiting for her while his saddle galled him; grey horses often had over-sensitive skin. If she had been born a horse she would undoubtedly have been grey. Her chest felt like it no longer had skin on it at all; perhaps it was being torn by those red-and-black creatures with the claws. The low murmuring buzzing voice went on.

"And Luthe." The voice paused a moment. "I knew Luthe very well once." Even through the gentle gracious melody of that voice she heard the malice behind it when it spoke Luthe's name; she was only too well aware of malice, for it was eating a hole in her breastbone now. Furthermore, it was her own voice she listened to, for all its beauty, and she knew, when it roughened, where the roughness came from. "Luthe, who doesn't dare leave his mountain any more. Little Luthe, never one of Goriolo's favorite pupils, for he was always a little slow—although he sometimes disguised this rather cleverly, I must admit, with his own unique style of obstinacy."

Do you think I like sending a child to a doom like this, one I know I cannot myself face? It was as though she were hearing the words for the first time, so loudly did they crash in her ears; Luthe's voice was not mellifluous, like her red-haired uncle's; Luthe's voice was raw and angry, like the spot on her chest.

"Luthe, and his games with children, for children's games were as much as he was capable—"

"Now that," Aerin said quite clearly and calmly, "is nonsense. If you can do no better than cheap insults, then the prophecy over-estimates you. I shall tell Luthe that he could have met you himself."

"The prophecy!" howled Agsded; and he seemed to grow till he towered over her, his robes billowing, his hair red as fire; and dimly Aerin thought, His hair is the color mine used to be before Maur burned most of it off. My hair isn't that color any more.

Agsded reached for his sword, and Aerin rasied Gonturan again and shook her, and blue fire ran down her edge and over Aerin's hand and wrist, and onto the floor; and where it touched, cracks appeared, and ran in tiny rays in all directions. "You may be right about Tor and my father," Aerin went on conversationally. "You may even be right about me. But you are wrong about Luthe."

The red sword whipped out of its scabbard and flew at her, but Gonturan flashed to stop it, and where the blades crashed together more blue fire dripped and splashed, and there was another series of small star-shaped cracks in the floor.

"Fool," boomed Agsded's voice, and it was velvety no longer. "Fool. The prophecy said that only one of my blood may face me, and so you have come this far; but your Damarian blood cannot stand against the one who wears the Hero's Crown."

Aerin raised her eyes to his forehead, and where she had not seen it before, the dull grey circlet that was Damar's dearest prize and treasure was bound closely to his brows. She could not help the shudder that ran through her, for what he said was true. Luthe, she thought, you should have come with me; you could have been the un-Damarian half.

The red sword bit at her again, and again Gonturan pulled her arm into place in time to deflect it. Yet even as death awaited her so near she could see its red jaws opening, her clearest thought was still a desperate desire to find a way to make her chest stop itching. I wonder if one can still itch if one is dead, she thought; and her arm jerked once more as Gonturan parried another slash. But the red sword almost broke through her guard, and her arm seemed suddenly weak; and she did not know if it was the fact of her opponent's wearing the Crown, or only her knowledge of the fact; and her eyes were drawn up again to his forehead. But she could not bear to look at that face for long, her own face, with wide mad green eyes, and hair red as fire. . . . My hair is not that color any more, she told herself, and my eyes are not those eyes, and I am not the man before me. I am not he, she thought; my mother fled him as I now face him, for what he is and we are not. And yet she was grateful that she could not look often into the face which was not hers, for she must watch the flicker of the red sword.

"Who taught you swordplay?" thundered Agsded. "No mortal can best me." And the red sword looked like seven swords as it swooped down on her again; and yet Gonturan was seven swords in return, and struck them all away.

I'm afraid you are no longer quite mortal. Mortal, Aerin thought. She laughed, and the red blade wavered when she laughed; perhaps the laugh of his sister's daughter echoed in Agsded's brain as horribly as his did in Aerin's. And as the red blade hesitated, Gonturan struck Agsded's shoulder. An inhuman scream went up, from the red mage or from the blue sword, Aerin could not tell; and then Agsded's sword came for her again, more swiftly than before, and Aerin could not even follow with her eyes as the two swords caught at each other, thrust and slammed and were hurled apart. "My Damarian blood," she panted, "uncle, is not so cursed as you think; for I have swum in the Lake of Dreams, and I—am—no—longer—quite—mortal."

"It will avail you naught," he cried, and leaped back, and threw up his hands; and fire leaped up all around him. Fire. Real fire; red and orange, with hot thick smoke, and bright terrible arms that reached out for her. Aerin quailed, and there was no black cat nor white horse to help her. This fire was no mage illusion; she could smell it, and the heat of it beat against her face; and again Gonturan's blue fire flickered and dulled in her hand.

Agsded laughed; and within the ring of fire he thrust his sword back into his belt and crossed his arms. "Well? Fire may still burn those who are—no—longer—quite—mortal." He laughed again, and Aerin flinched from his voice even as from the licking flames; and the grey Crown was red in the firelight.

Someday, she thought tiredly, I must learn to go forward of my own free will. If only my horrible chest would let me think clearly. She raised Gonturan, and the blue fire cascaded over her; it was cool against her face. She closed her eyes—closing my eyes is stupid, she thought—and jumped into the fire.

It hissed and roared around her, but she ran forward and opened her eyes, and her uncle was just a little late pulling his sword free again, and Gonturan rose for a slash at his neck, the cut she had missed the last time. This time the blade ran true, and struck him squarely.

And bounced off with a harsh ugly sound, and with a nick in her edge; and the recoil was such that she twisted out of Aerin's grasp and fell to the fiery floor, and Aerin fell with her.

"I am not precisely mortal either," said Agsded, and

grinned his grin again; and Aerin, looking up at the red sword
that was about to sink into her, thought, I imagine I'll be mortal enough when struck through the heart; I wonder what
mage trick it is he uses—or perhaps it's because he's wearing
the Crown. And because she had nothing else left to do, and
because she was still holding the wreath in her other hand, she
threw it at him.

He screamed. It was a scream that cut across all the senses,
sight and touch and taste and smell as well as hearing; it was a
scream sharper than any sword and as bitter as hatred, as
fierce as a hunting folstza and as implacable as winter. Aerin
had only the dimmest recollection, through the scream, of the
surka wreath touching his face, falling over his head to ring his
shoulders; of the dragon stone shining as brilliantly red as
Agsded's sword had been, but which now turned to the dull
rusted color of old blood; of a smaller fire, within the ring
of fire, rising around Agsded higher and higher till he disappeared from view, as the fire he had thrown between himself
and Aerin sank and darkened and died; and still the scream
went on. Aerin staggered to her feet, and found that she was
clutching Gonturan with both hands; and that the palm of one
was wet with her own blood where she had seized unwarily at
Gonturan's edge; and that her hands and arms glowed blue,
and as she bent her head the hair that fell forward around her
face was also blue, and when she looked down, her boots were
blue, and there was a pool of blue spreading around them, and
as the blue widened so did the tiny hairline cracks in the floor,
which spread and crackled and sputtered as she looked, with
Agsded's scream still beating at her. Then the scream and the
short sharp sounds the floor was making rose together in a tu-
multuous roar, and the stones on which Aerin stood gave way,
and she fell, and saw the walls toppling in on her. It would be
pleasant to faint at this point, she thought, but she didn't, and
she continued to clutch Gonturan, but she shifted the bloody
hand to join the other on the hilt. When I land, she thought, I
will fall over and cut myself in half on my own sword; but the
fall may already have killed me. The sound of the mountain
tower falling was so loud she could no longer make room for
her thoughts, and so she gave up thinking and blackness hurtled past her, and heavy fragments of that blackness fell with
her but did not touch her, and she wondered if she might fall
forever, as she had climbed, and thus perhaps become the God

That Falls, or perhaps the God That Climbs and Falls.

Then there was a shock, but to her feet or her skull or only her mind she did not know; whatever part of her was struck staggered, and she shook herself, and discovered that it was her head she was shaking, and then she blinked her eyes and looked up, and realized that she saw sunlight leaking through cracks as though through the ruined walls of an ancient building. At the same time that her confused eyes and brain figured out the sunlight she also realized that her feet were standing on something, that she hadn't chopped herself in two by landing on Gonturan, and that she was no longer falling.

She took a hesitant step, for she could see very little, and small pieces of rubble crunched and scattered under her feet. The pile of fragments teetered and threatened to spill her into the bottomless blackness again. There is no sense in taking my luck for granted, she told herself sternly, and resheathed Gonturan, gave an absent rub at her chest, and then stood still, blinking, till her eyes began to readjust to simple things like daylight, and stone walls with cracks in them.

❧ CHAPTER 20 ❧

SHE WAS ON THE FLAT TOP of a small mountain of rubble; and off to her right, at its foot, was a break in the surrounding circular wall wide enough that she thought she could probably squeeze herself through it. She made her way slowly and cautiously down the slope toward the broken place in the wall, but the stuff underfoot shifted and slithered, and she came to the bottom sitting back on her heels, with the unwounded hand holding Gonturan up by the scabbard so she wouldn't drag. She stood up and went toward the crack and, indeed, she could push through, although it was a tight fit; and then the sunlight dazzled her, and her abused legs turned abruptly to jelly, and she sat down quickly and put her head between her knees. Staring at the ground, she thought, I wonder how long it's been since I've eaten. Food might help. The mundane thought made her feel better at once, and hungry as well. She raised her head. She still felt shaky, and when she had clambered back to her feet—ungracefully using Gonturan as a prop—her knees were inclined to tremble, but she almost cheerfully put it down to lack of food.

She looked around. Where was she? The black tower had risen from a plain where nothing grew; now all around her she saw jungle, trees with vast climbing vines (though none of surka that she could see), and heavy brush between the trees. The sunlight fell on the ruined tower and the little rubble-covered clearing it made for itself, but the light could not make much headway through the thick leaves. Ugh. It would not be a pleasant journey out. And where might she find Talat? She set out to walk around what remained of the tower.

Nothing but tumbled rock and encroaching forest. Nothing else. No sign of anything else ever having been here either—but where was she? Was the ruined tower she was stumbling around now the same that she and Talat and her wild beasts had faced? She tipped her head back to look up at the remaining walls. They didn't look nearly big enough; the fallen rock was not enough to have been built into such vastness as she remembered. She sighed, and rubbed a hand over her face—and pulled it away again as she remembered that it was the wrong hand. But the cut had already healed; there was nothing on her palm but a narrow white scar. She stared at it, puzzled; but there were more important things to be puzzled about.

So what now? She was alone—somewhere—she was hungry, and the sun was getting low. She did not look forward to a night alone in this place—although it certainly didn't look as if anything big enough to trouble her much could get through that forest, there were always, well, spiders, for example. As she thought of spiders it occurred to her that her chest was only barely itching, almost idly, as if once it had gotten the way of it it didn't particularly want to stop, even though it didn't have much reason left. That's something, I guess, she thought; and glanced again at her scarred palm.

She sat down, closed her eyes, organized one or two of the simpler things Luthe had taught her, and thought about the air. She followed invisible eddies and tiny currents as they strayed over her and back among the trees again; and eventually she found one that felt damp, and she followed that until it sank to the ground, and there she found a spring. It looked all right; it felt like water.

She opened her eyes and stood up. The spring, when she reached it, still looked like water and smelled like water; and she sighed, because she had no choice. She ducked her head, and then threw her wet hair back, and then drank deep. She sat back on her heels and scowled into the underbrush. The tiny spring was only a few paces from the edge of the clearing, and yet it had taken her some expense of time and energy to hew her way even this far. How was she going to get out?

One thing at a time. Remembering something else Luthe

had taught her, she gathered a few dry twigs and a heap of dead leaves together, and set them on fire by glaring at them—though the effort gave her a fierce headache and she couldn't focus her eyes for a long time afterward, and the fire was sullen and inclined to smoke. She wandered around gathering more twigs, and saw at least two for each, and two hands reaching for them, and generally misjudged which hand and which twig were the real ones; but still she gathered enough at last to keep the fire going all night. She hoped. And the fire was beginning to burn a little better.

She had hot water for supper, by filling the pouch that had held the dragon stone with water and hanging it over the fire; it leaked very little. She'd try to figure out food tomorrow; she was weary enough with hunger, but weary too with everything else, and the sun had set, and twilight would soon be darkness. She lay down, making an uncomfortable pillow of a rock, with a piece of her tunic pulled up to protect her ear. She lay as still as the stones she rested against, without even the energy to try to scrabble for a more easy spot; but still her thoughts prowled at the ruin of the black mountain, picking at the rubble. Some of it, perhaps, Luthe could explain to her—but she shied away from the thought of seeing him again, of asking him. The forest troubled her, for she needed to find a way through it; its existence was far more than a philosophical dilemma—as was her solitude. Where was Talat? She could believe that her other allies had melted away as they had come; she had never understood why they joined her in the first place. But Talat would not have left. At least not of his own free will.

Then the worst thought of all hit her: Agsded is gone, or at least he seems to be gone; but I have yet failed, for the Hero's Crown is gone also.

She rolled over and stared at the sky. There was no moon, but the stars shone fiercely down on her. She realized suddenly that Agsded himself had never been quite real to her; her terror had been real enough, and her sick horror at the face he wore; and she had known that she went to a battle she had less chance of winning than she had had even when she faced Maur. But the thing that had held her, the dream that had drawn her on, was the Hero's Crown. It had nothing to do with her own blood and birthright as her mother's daughter, nothing of personal vengeance; it was the idea of bringing the

Crown back to her City, of presenting it to Arlbeth and Tor. She had been sure, for all that she had never consciously thought of it, that as Damar's doom lay with Agsded, so must the missing Crown. No one knew of Agsded; no one would believe her even if she told the story, and she could not tell it, for what could she say of the prophecy, of the kinship that made her the only possible champion? What would she say of her uncle?

But who Agsded was did not matter, or mattered only to her. The Crown mattered, and the story of it she might have told: that she had wrested it away from him who held it, to bring it back to her City, to lay it before her king. As it was, for all that she had done, she had done nothing. If she went to the City now—if she went home—it would be as a runaway dog might go home, tail between legs, its highest hope only for forgiveness.

Her eyes closed, and she slept the numbed sleep of failure; but soon after midnight even this was disturbed. The earth seemed to shiver under her, and she heard low rumblings like rocks falling far away; but perhaps she was only dreaming. Later she knew she dreamed, for she saw faces she had never met in her waking life.

A sad-faced girl sat by a pool. The white walls around her were so high there seemed to be clouds resting on their heads; low steps behind her led to an open door, and a room beyond it. There were no doors in the other walls, and the flat earth around the pool was covered with squares of white stone. The girl's long black hair fell forward as she stared into the calm water, and her look of sadness deepened. Then Aerin, in her dream, saw another walled garden, but the water here played in a fountain, and the walls were blue mosaic; and in the garden stood a tall young woman with yellow hair, taller by a hand's breadth than Aerin herself, and at her side a green-eyed folstza stood. And then she saw three men standing on the side of a mountain, on a little ridge of rock, facing a crack or a hole in the face of the mountain. A burly man with thinning black hair was staring at the crack with a set stubborn expression, and his fair-haired companion was saying, "Don't be a fool. *Tommy.* Listen to me." The third man was young and brown-skinned and slightly built, and he looked amused, but he said, "Leo, you should know better by now than to argue with him."

Their voices seemed to bring Aerin half awake, for her dreams became more confused, and she saw faces without being sure if she recognized them or not, and she felt the rocky bed beneath her again, and it seemed as if the ground pressed up unevenly, against a shoulder, a hip—then a lurch, and a stone she was sure had not been there before dug painfully into the small of her back. Still she could not awaken—and then, with a gasp, she opened her eyes and sat up; and it was morning, and her fire was out; not only out, but scattered, as if someone with fireproof hands had picked it up and tossed bits of it in all directions; or as if the earth had heaved up under it.

And the forest was gone.

She blinked, but it stayed gone. She was in the middle of the plateau she had crossed to come to the black tower, although the ground sloped gently but definitely from where she sat into the distance, toward the encircling mountains, and she had not gone uphill to reach Agsded's crag. It was a fine blue day, the sky high and cloudless, and she could see the width of the plateau in all directions; the Damarian Hills were a little farther away than the unnamed Northern mountains on the opposite side. In sudden fear she jolted to her feet, turned and looked over her shoulder—but the black mountain was still a ruin; she did not have to face all those stairs again, nor the meeting with a mage who bore her own face.

She had gone but a few steps in no particular direction when a long low black object slammed into her and knocked her flat. She had only just begun frantically to grope for Gonturan when she recognized him: it was the black king cat, and he, it would appear, was delighted to see her. His forepaws were tucked over her shoulders and he was rubbing her face with his own bristles-and-velvet face, and purring loudly enough, she thought, to bring what remained of the tower down on top of them.

He permitted her, eventually, to sit up, although he remained twined around her. She gingerly felt the places she had fallen on, and looked at him severely. "I had bruises enough before," she said aloud, and was rewarded by Talat's ear-shattering whinny, and Talat himself appeared around the edge of the tower. He trotted up and nosed her eagerly, and she stroked his chest and tumbled the cat off her lap that she might stand up, and Talat heaved a sigh of relief after she had done so. The last time he had rediscovered her after battle it had not been a merry meeting. He whiffled down her shirt and she pulled his ears, and the black cat twined among her legs and Talat's forelegs both, and Aerin said, "Something has come of my absence: you two have made friends." Whereupon the cat left off at once and stalked away. Aerin laughed.

She and Talat followed him and came shortly to where the rest of the great cats were, and the wild dogs were there as well, and while the two camps still held mostly to their own, Aerin had a strong sense that there was a reliable peace, if not exactly friendship, between them.

The folstza and yerig were curled up among mounds of rubble nearly under the shadow of the last standing walls; yet Aerin knew she had gone completely around the remains of the black mountain the day before, and had seen no sign of her friends. She ascended the slope toward them, and the dog queen came up to her, with the barest wave of her long tail. Aerin tentatively held out her hand and the dog queen tentatively took it between her jaws. Aerin stood quite still, and one narrow blue eye looked up at her, and she looked back. The tail waved again, and then she dropped Aerin's hand and trotted off, and some invisible command she gave to her folk, for they all followed her; and they rounded the edge of the mountain of rubble, going away from her, and disappeared.

Aerin felt a little forsaken. Had they only waited to—to see who won? Would they have known if Agsded had killed her, and run off then to spread the evil news to others of their kind, perhaps to all who lived wild in their forests and mountains? She had not known why the animals first came to her, but, knowing a little too much about the wrong kind of solitude, she had been glad of their company; and had been simply happy to find them here again after she fell asleep last night alone and comfortless, without thinking beyond the fact that they were her friends and she had missed them. But the cats showed no sign of leaving; and always there was Talat.

She pulled his saddle off, and was glad to see that he had no starting sores underneath; and then she eagerly opened the saddlebags and chewed a little of the end of the tough dried meat she had brought with her. Her stomach was grateful but it rumbled for more. She looked around her again, leaning into the solid reality of Talat's shoulder. The bare lands met her eye just as they had before. Her gaze dropped to the tumbled remains of her fire. Beyond just what she had laid her hands on last night there was no wood in sight nearer than the green verge of the boundary Hills of Damar. "Well," she said aloud to whoever was listening. "At least we can see where to go, to get back now."

As she spoke, a yerig trotted around the edge of the tower and into view again, and two or three others followed. She tried to suppress the little bubble of happiness that popped up in her throat when she saw them coming back to her; but then the yerig queen came into sight as well, and swung her head around at once to catch Aerin's eye, and Aerin couldn't help smiling. The queen held something in her mouth, and the young brown dog beside her also was carrying something. The queen dropped back a little, and her companion reached Aerin first; he had a fine fierce ruff and copper-colored eyes, and far less dignity than his leader, for he wagged his tail enthusiastically and flattened his ears as he came near. He dropped what he held on the ground at her feet: it was a charred circlet of surka leaves. So black and withered it was she would not have recognized it but for the red glint it showed: the dragon stone, still woven securely in its place. She stooped to pick it up as the one-eyed queen dropped what she held: it was the Hero's Crown.

❧ CHAPTER 21 ❧

THEY STARTED BACK toward the mountains before the sun had risen much higher. Aerin had buried the ashes of the fire, out of habit, for there was certainly nothing around that might burn; and she reverently wrapped the surka wreath and its stone, and the Crown, and stowed them in one of Talat's saddlebags. There was nothing else left to do.

Her entourage strung out behind her, cats on one flank, dogs on the other. Only once did she look back, when they were already well across the plain and the sun was beginning to drop toward evening. The way did slope down from the dark mountain, and she was sure that this one thing had changed, even if there had been a disappearing forest between. But if this was the worst of what remained, she thought, they were getting off very lightly.

The ruins of the black tower were small in the distance, and they seemed to leer at her, but it was a small nasty, useless leer, like a tyrant on the scaffold as the rope is placed around his neck. This plain would not be a healthy or attractive place for many years to come, but it would not be a dangerous one either. She went on with a lighter heart.

She was eager to reach the edge of her beloved Damarian Hills by nightfall, that she might camp in their shadow and drink from their clean waters, and so kept on into the beginning twilight. She wanted to sing when she caught the first breath of the evening breeze from the kindly trees; but her voice had never adapted itself to carrying a tune, so she didn't. Her army all seemed to be glad to be under familiar leaves again, and the dogs wagged their tails and made cheerful playful snaps at one another, and the cats knocked each other with clawless feet, and rolled on the ground. Talat pranced. And so they came merrily to a turn in the path they followed, paying attention to nothing but their own pleasure; and then Aerin caught a sudden whiff of smoke as from a small fire, and then the smell of cooking. She sat down hard, but Talat's ears flicked back at her. What do you mean stop here? and went on. And there was a small campfire, tucked in the curve of the trail where there was a little clearing and a stream curving around the other side of it.

"Good day to you," said Luthe.

Talat whickered a greeting, and Aerin slid off him and he went forward alone to nose Luthe's hands and browse in his hair. "I thought you never left your hall and your lake," said Aerin.

"Rarely," said Luthe. "In fact, increasingly exceedingly rarely. But I can be prodded by extraordinary circumstances."

Aerin smiled faintly. "You have had plenty to choose from here recently."

"Yes."

"May I ask which particular circumstance was sufficiently extraordinary in this case?"

"Aerin—" Luthe paused, and then his voice took on its bantering tone again. "I thought you might like to be dragged back to the present, that you might arrive in time to give Tor his Crown and end the siege; and of course now instead of a few hundred years hence there is no jungle to be compelled to claw your way through. I've no doubt you could have done it, but it would have put you in a foul temper, and you would have been in a fouler one by the time you came back to the Lake of Dreams—assuming you would have had the sense to make your way there, not in your case something one can count on. You would have needed my assistance to regain your own time—if lighting a little fire made you see double, charging about in time without assistance would have blinded you for good—and the longer you're out of it, the harder it would have been to get you back in. So I came to meet you."

Aerin stared at the fire, for she couldn't think at all when she looked at Luthe. "I really was a long time climbing, then," she said.

"Yes," said Luthe. "A very long time."

"And a very long time falling."

"And a very long time falling."

Aerin said nothing more while she pulled Talat's saddle off and dropped it by the fire, and rubbed his back dry, and checked his feet for small stones. "I suppose I should forgive you, then, for making me other than mortal," she said.

"You might. I would appreciate it if you did." He sighed. "It would be nice to claim that I knew this was going to happen all along, knew that your only chance of success in regaining your Crown was to do as I did. But I didn't. Sheer blind luck, I'm afraid."

He handed her a cup of malak, steaming hot, which she drank greedily; then stew on a thin metal plate, but she ate it so fast it had no time to burn her fingers, and then she had seconds and thirds. When she was finished at last, Luthe gave what remained to the king cat and queen dog, in carefully measured halves, on separate plates. Aerin heard his footsteps behind her as he returned from setting those two plates out, and she said, "Thank you."

The footsteps paused just behind her, and she felt him bend over her, and then his hands rested on her shoulders. She put her own hands up, and drew his down, till he was kneeling behind her, and he bowed his head to press his cheek to her face. She turned in his arms, and put her own arms around his neck and raised her face and kissed him.

They remained near the fire far into the night, feeding it with twigs so that it would keep burning; the animals were all long since asleep, and even Talat was relaxed enough to lie down and doze. Luthe sprawled on his back with his head in Aerin's lap, and she stroked his hair through her fingers, watching the thick curls wind around her fingers, stretch to their fullest length, and spring back again. "Is it so amusing?" said Luthe.

"Yes," said Aerin, "although I should like it just as well if it were straight and green, or if you were bald as an egg and painted your head silver."

She had not told him much of her meeting with her uncle, nor had she asked him any questions about him; but she could not say how much he guessed—or knew, in the same way he knew of her fire-starting—and she listened eagerly when he began to talk of Agsded, and of their school days together. The chill of hating someone with her own face eased as she listened, and eased still more at the sight of Luthe smiling up into her face as he talked; and at last she told him, haltingly, a little of what had passed between them.

Luthe looked wry, and was silent for a time, and they heard the soft contented moan of a dog stretching in its sleep. "Agsded was not entirely wrong about me," he said at last. "I was stubborn, and no, frankly, I was not one of Goriolo's most brilliant and promising pupils. But I survived on that stubbornness and stayed with my master long enough to learn more than most of the ones who had greater gifts to begin with and then went off and got themselves killed or became sheep farmers because a mage's life is such a grim and thankless one.

"I was also always at my worst when Agsded was around, for he was one of those glittering people whose every gesture looks like a miracle, whose every word sounds like a new philosophy. You've a bit of that yourself, valiantly as you seek to hide it.

"But I don't know that he and I are so unequal in the end; for as I made mistakes in ignorance, or obstinacy, he made mistakes in pride. . . ."

"You haven't asked me how I—how he lost and I won," said Aerin, after another pause.

"I have no intention of asking. You may tell me or not as you wish, now or later."

"There is something at least I wish to ask you."

"Ask away."

"It requires you move; I need to reach my saddlebags."

Luthe groaned. "Is it worth it?"

Aerin didn't mean to laugh, but she did anyway, and Luthe smiled languorously, but he did sit up and free her. "This," she said, and handed him the charred wreath and its red stone.

"The gods wept," said Luthe, and no longer looked sleepy. "I should have thought you might have this. I am the earth's most careless teacher and Goriolo would have my head if he were around to collect it." He parted the dry vines and spilled the red stone into his hand. It gleamed in the firelight; he rolled it gently from one hand to the other. "This makes your Hero's Crown look like a cheap family heirloom."

"What is it?" Aerin asked, nervously.

"Maur's bloodstone. The last drop of blood from its heart—the fatal one," Luthe replied. "All dragons who die by bloodletting spill one of these at the last; but you'd need a hawk's eyes to find that last curdled drop from a small dragon."

Aerin shuddered. "Then you keep it," she said. "I'm grateful for its wizard-defeating properties, and if I have the great misfortune ever to need to defeat another wizard, I shall borrow it from you. But I don't want it around."

Luthe looked at her thoughtfully, cradling it in his hand. "If you bound it into your Damarian Crown, it would make whoever wore it invincible."

Aerin shook her head violently. "And be forever indebted to the memory of Maur? Damar can do without."

"You don't know what you're saying. A dragon's bloodstone is not for good or wickedness; it just is. And it is a thing of great power, for it is its dragon's death—unlike its skull, which your folk treated like a harmless artifact. The bloodstone is the real trophy, the prize worth the winning; worth almost any winning. You're letting your own experience color your answer."

"Yes, I *am* letting my own experience color my answer, which is what experience is for. A dragon's heartstone may not be goodness or evil from your vantage point, but I was born a simple mortal not that long ago and I remember a lot more about the simple mortal viewpoint than maybe you ever knew. A bloodstone is not a safe sort of emblem to hand over to any of us—them—even to the royal family of Damar." She grimaced, thinking of Perlith. "Or even the sovereigns of Damar only. Even if it were used wisely, it cannot be well enough protected; for there will be others, like you, who know what it is—others with fewer mortal limits than Damarian kings. Look at the amount of harm Agsded did with the Crown alone."

She paused and then added slowly, "I'm not even sure I believe you about its being a power of neither good nor evil. Our stories say that the dragons first came from the North. Almost all the evil that has ever troubled our land has come from there, nor has it often happened that something from there was not evil. You said once that Damarian royalty—any of us with the Gift, with *kelar* have a common ancestor with the Northerners. So why have they and their land turned out their way and we ours?

"No. I'll not take the thing with me. You keep it, or I'll bury it here before we go."

Luthe blinked several times. "I've grown accustomed to being right—most of the time. Right all of the time in arguments with those who were born simple mortals not that long ago. I think—perhaps—in this case that you are right. How unexpected." He smiled bemusedly. "Very well. I shall keep it. And you will know where to find it if ever you have the need."

"I will know," said Aerin. "But gods preserve me from needing that knowledge ever again."

Luthe looked at her, a small frown beginning. "That's not a good sort of vow to make, at least not aloud, where things may be listening."

Aerin sighed. "You are indeed a terribly careless teacher. You never warned me about vow-making either." The frown cleared, and Luthe laughed, and it turned into a yawn halfway.

"Aerin," he said. "I'm wearied to death from dragging you backward through the centuries by the heel, and I must sleep, but it would comfort my rest to hold you in my arms and know I did succeed."

"Yes," said Aerin. "It was not a comfortable time I spent being so dragged, and I would be glad to know that I do not spend this night alone as I did that one."

In the morning Aerin said abruptly, as she fixed Talat's saddle in place. "Here—how do you travel? Do you float like a mist and waft upon the breeze?"

"Presumably I would then have to order myself a breeze to waft me in the right direction. No, dearheart, I walk. It's surprisingly effective."

"You walked here from your mountain?"

"I did indeed," he said, shouldering his pack. "And I will now walk back. I should, however, be grateful for your company as far as the foot of my mountain. Our ways lie together till then."

Aerin stared at him blankly.

"I can move quite as fast as that antiquated beast you prefer as transportation," he said irritably. "To begin with, my legs are longer, even if fewer, and, secondly, I carry a great deal less baggage. Stop staring at me like that."

"Mm," said Aerin, and mounted.

Luthe was right, however; they covered just as much ground as Aerin and Talat and their army would have on their own— although it could not be said they traveled together. Luthe walked somewhat less fast than Talat cantered, but a great deal faster than Talat walked, and they played a kind of leap-frog all day, Luthe calling directions as needed for the smoother and quicker route as Talat's heels passed him, and Talat pinning his ears back and snorting when Luthe had the temerity to pass them.

None of them saw much of the folstza and yerig that day, but at evening, when they camped, Aerin's four-legged army re-formed around them. "You know, my friends," she said to the rows of gleaming eyes, "I'm going south—far farther south than your homes and territories. You might want to think about that before you travel many more days with me."

The one-eyed queen's tail stirred by a quarter-inch; the black king ignored her words entirely.

"It never hurts to have a few more friends at your back," said Luthe, tending the pot over the fire.

"They're staying only for your cooking," said Aerin, who had gotten very tired of the usual Damarian trail fare on her way north.

Luthe looked at her from half-shut eyes. "I will take advantage wherever I can," he said mildly.

Aerin put her arms around him, and the arm that was not holding the spoon crept around her waist. "You may give up cooking at once, and paint your bald head silver," she said.

"Mm," he replied. "My love, I feel it only fair to warn you that I am feeling quite alert and strong tonight, and if you choose to sleep with me again, it is not sleep you will be getting."

"Then I look forward to no sleep whatsoever," Aerin said contentedly, and Luthe laughed and dropped his spoon.

The next few days went all too quickly; Aerin had to remind herself that it had been a fortnight she and Talat had spent on their way from the Lake of Dreams to Agsded's grey plain, for the way toward home seemed far shorter. On the fifth night Aerin drew Gonturan, and showed Luthe her edge, and the sharp knick broken out of it; the sight hurt her almost as much as the sight of the lamed Talat standing listlessly in his pasture once had.

It must have shown on her face, for Luthe said, "Don't

look so stricken. I can deal with this; and I don't have the worry about her mortality to get in my way either." Aerin smiled a small smile, and Luthe touched her cheek with his fingers. She aided him as he asked her, and the next morning Aerin resheathed a shining flawless blade; but she and Luthe slept heavily and long for the next two nights after.

Spring had come thoroughly to the lands they traveled through; the grass was lush everywhere, and the summer fruits were beginning to push through the last petals on the trees and bushes; and Luthe and Aerin saw everything as their friends, and the folstza and yerig were as polite to Luthe as they were to Aerin.

But Luthe and Aerin knew without speaking of it when their last night came, and Aerin was grateful for a moonless night, that she might weep and Luthe not see. He slept at last, curled up against her, her arm tucked under his and drawn over his ribs, her hand held to his breast and cradled with both of his. She stayed awake, listening to Luthe's breathing and the sound of the sky turning overhead; and when near dawn he sighed and stirred, she gently drew her hand from his and crept free of the blanket. She paced up and down some few minutes, and then stood by the ashes of last night's campfire to look at Luthe in the growing light.

The blanket had slipped down; his chest lay bare nearly to the waist, and one long hand was flung out. His skin where the sun never touched was as white as milk, almost blue, like skimmed milk, although his face was ruddied and roughened by sun and weather. She looked down at her own arms and hands; she was rose and gold next to him, although she looked as colorless as wax against full-blooded Damarians. She wondered where Luthe came from; wondered if she'd ever know; wondered what he would say if she asked. And knew that, on this morning, this last morning, she would not ask; and that in the last few days, when she might have, she had not thought to. And this gave her her first conscious pang of parting.

She knew too that it would be years before they met again, and so she stared at him, memorizing him, that she might draw out his likeness in her mind at any time during those years; and then she remembered with a little shiver that she was no longer quite mortal, and the shiver was not for the knowledge but for the pleasure it now gave her, the first pleasure it had ever given her, that she might look forward to seeing

Luthe again someday. And that pleasure frightened her, for she was the daughter of the king of Damar, and she was bringing the Hero's Crown home to the king and to the first sola, who would be king after, and whom she would marry.

She wondered if she had ever truly not known that Tor loved her, if it were only that she had always feared to love him in return. She was afraid no longer, and the irony of it was that Luthe had taught her not to be afraid, and that it was her love for Luthe that made her recognize her love for Tor. She had killed the Black Dragon, she carried an enchanted sword, and now she brought the Hero's Crown back to the land that had lost it, having won it in fair fight from him who had held it against her and against Damar. She could declare that she would no longer be afraid—of her heritage, of her place in the royal house of Damar, of her father's people; and so she could also, now, marry Tor, for such was her duty to her country, whether her country approved of the idea or not. And Tor would be glad to see her back; she had written a letter to him that night that she might have died; almost everything else had receded to fog and memory, but she had remembered Tor, and remembered to leave him word that she would come back to him.

She had once promised to return to Luthe also. She sat down near where he lay still sleeping and gazed at the white white skin and blue-tinted hollows. She thought, They say that everyone looks young when asleep, like the child each used to be. Luthe looks only like Luthe, sleeping; and her eyes filled with tears. She blinked, and when she could see clearly again, Luthe's eyes were open, and he reached up to draw her down to kiss her, and she saw, when she drew her head back a moment after the kiss, that when he closed his eyes again, two tears spilled from their corners and ran down his temples, glinting in the morning sunlight.

This morning they were careful, for the first time since they had met at the edge of Agsded's plain, that each should wrap only his or her own possessions in each bundle. They spoke little. Even Talat was subdued, looking anxiously over his shoulder at Aerin as she strapped the saddle in place, rather than doing his usual morning imitation of a war-horse scenting his enemy just over the next hill.

She did not mount at once but turned back to Luthe, and he held out his arms, and she rushed into them. He sighed, and her own breast rose and fell against his. "I have put you on a horse—that same horse—and watched you ride away from me before. I thought I should never get over it that first time. I think I followed you for that; not for any noble desire to help you save Damar; only to pick up whatever pieces Agsded might have left of you. . . . I know I shall never get over it this time. If you do it, someday, a third time, it will probably kill me." Aerin tried to smile, but Luthe stopped her with a kiss. "Go now. A quick death is the best I believe."

"You can't scare me," Aerin said, almost succeeding in keeping her voice level. "You told me long ago that you aren't mortal."

"I never said I can't be killed," replied Luthe. "If you wish to chop logic with me, my dearest love, you must make sure of your premises."

"I shall practice them—while—I shall practice, that I may dazzle you when next we meet."

There was a little silence, and Luthe said, "You need not try to dazzle me."

"I must go," Aerin said hopelessly, and flung herself at Talat just as she had done once before. "I will see you again."

Luthe nodded.

She almost could not say the words: "But it will be a long time—long and long."

Luthe nodded again.

"But we shall meet."

Luthe nodded a third time.

"Gods of all the worlds, say something," she cried, and Talat startled beneath her.

"I love you," said Luthe. "I will love you till the stars crumble, which is a less idle threat than is usual to lovers on parting. Go quickly, for truly I cannot bear this."

She closed her legs violently around the nervous Talat, and he leaped into a gallop. Long after Aerin was out of sight, Luthe lay full length upon the ground, and pressed his ear to it, and listened to Talat's hoofbeats carrying Aerin farther and farther away.

❧ CHAPTER 22 ❧

SHE RODE IN A DAZE of misery, unconscious of the yerig and folstza who pressed closely around Talat's legs and looked anxiously up into her face; and she stopped, numbly, at night-fall. She might have gone on till she dropped in her tracks, were she on foot; but she was not, and so at nightfall she stopped, and stripped her horse, and rubbed him down with a dry cloth. Talat was a little sore; that sudden gallop to begin a long day had done his weak leg no good, and so she unwrapped some ointment that would warm the stiffness, and massaged it in vigorously, and even smiled a little at the usual grimaces of pleasure Talat made.

When she lay down by the fire she sprang up again almost at once, and paced back and forth. She was dizzy with exhaustion and stupid with unhappiness, and she was riding to the gods knew what at the City; and as she remembered that, she remembered also flashes of what she had seen, deep in the Lake of Dreams. But that brought her back to Luthe again, and the tears ran down her face, and, standing before the campfire, she bowed her face in her hands and sobbed.

This would not do. She had the Crown, and she carried an enchanted sword; she was coming home a warrior victorious—and a first sol worthy of respect. She felt like dead leaves, dry and brown and brittle, although leaves were probably not miserable; they were just quietly buried by snow and burned by sun and harried by rain till they peacefully disintegrated into the 'eath. . . . She found herself staring at the earth under her feet. She had to get some sleep.

She turned despairingly back to her blanket and found two furry bodies already there. The dog queen smiled at her and moved her feathery tail an inch at least; the cat king flattened his ears and half-lidded his eyes. Neither paid the least attention to the other.

She laughed, a cracked laugh, half a choke. "Thank you," she said. "Perhaps I shall sleep after all." She pillowed her head on a cat flank, and a dog head lay in the curve between her ribs and pelvis, and a dog tail curled over her feet. She slept at once, and heavily; and she woke in the morning hugging the queen's neck with her face buried in her ruff, and the big yerig had a look of great patience and forbearance on her face that no doubt she wore when bearing with a new litter of puppies.

Aerin also woke with a sense of urgency; urgency so great that it broke through the numbness. "Soon," she said aloud to Talat, and he cocked his ear at her and grunted only a little at the indignity of having his girth tightened. "They need us soon."

He was stiff this morning as well, but Aerin paid attention and was careful, and he worked out of it. Before the darkness came upon them a second time they had nearly passed the Airdthmar on their right hand; and by the third evening Aerin could see the fault in the topline of the Hills that was the pass to the forested plain before the City, for her way home was short when she knew where she was going. Tomorrow, perhaps, they would stand in that pass.

Her friends slept with her again that night, but they had a less peaceful time of it, for her dreams were bad, full of battle and shouting, and the groans of the wounded, and the fell ghastly sound of the language of the folk of the North. She woke often and sweating, her fist clenched and her nerves jumping. In the last dream she had before dawn she heard Arlbeth's voice, weary and hopeless: "If only we had the Crown. We might yet . . ."

"If we had had the Crown," another voice, higher pitched: Perlith. "If we had had the Crown, we would not be so badly off in the first place."

"At least," said Galanna in a voice so low that Arlbeth

would not hear her, "we do not have our little bad-luck token with us. Thank the gods for that much."

Thank the gods . . . thank the gods she's not here . . . not here . . . the Crown, please the gods, we need the Crown, it is not here. . . .

She woke up. Dawn was just creeping above the mountains' crests. She did not want to be awake yet, for today she would come in sight of her City, and she was afraid of what she would find; afraid that she came too late; afraid that even the Crown was not enough. Afraid that they would not accept the Crown from her hands. Afraid that they would read in her face whom she had wrested the Crown from.

Afraid that they would read in her face that she knew, now, that she did not belong to Damar. She would love it all her life, and that life was likely to be a long one; and she had a duty to it that she might fulfill some part of, if she tried as hard as she could.

She told herself that she did not think of Luthe.

Her army flowed up on her either flank; a sea of furry backs, black and grey and brindled, golden and ruddy; there was no playfulness in them today. Their ears pointed in the direction they were going, and their tails were low. She had unwrapped the Crown, and at first she carried it before her balanced on the pommel, and then she thought of stowing it away again, but she wanted it close, where she could touch it and it touch her. She slung it at last up over her arm to her shoulder, and it warmed, riding there, till when she reached to touch it with her fingers it was the same temperature as her own skin.

As they rode into the morning the wind sang in her ears, but it carried strange sounds within it, and she smelled strange odors. It was Talat's restlessness, at last, that told her what was happening; for these were the sounds and smells of battle.

They wound their way up the smooth broad track that led between Vasth and Kar to the low forested hills before the City. As they reached the top of the pass Talat snorted and shied away, and Aerin clung to the saddle, not believing the glimpse she had had of the scene below them. Grimly she kneed Talat around, and reluctantly he obeyed her, but still he tried to sidle sideways, to turn and bolt. Even Maur had not been so bad as what lay before them.

The trees were gone; even, it seemed, the gentle hills were

flattened, and where there had been the greens and browns and deep blue shadows of leaves and trees there was the grisly heave and thrust of battle. The Northerners were there, between her and her City. She could see small human bands, the largest near the City gates, fighting desperately; but they were outnumbered, and they fought defensively, because their honor demanded it, and because fear of being captured alive by the Northerners drove them on; not because they had any hope left. And the Northerners knew this.

Aerin stared numbly at the ragged scarred landscape, and listened to the terrible cries and the heavy sound of blows, and the fumes of the fighting choked her, and made her eyes water. It was as though the forest she had daily seen from the highest towers of her father's castle had never been; it was as if, when Luthe dragged her back to her own time, he had miscalculated and she was some other Aerin on some other world. She waited for panic to take her. Talat quieted and stood, ears forward, tense, but awaiting her orders; and her army surrounded her, and made a huge pool behind her that splashed like surf up the rock sides of the pass.

"Well," she said aloud, and the calmness of her own voice frightened her. "Maybe not being quite mortal any more is going to count for less than I thought." She settled the Crown more firmly on her shoulder, and drew Gonturan, who gleamed blue along her edge; the blue rippled up, over the hilt and grip, and flowed over Aerin's hand. There was an odd subtle tingle at the touch of the blue shimmer, but it was not unpleasant; Aerin put it down to the twitching of her own nerves.

"I hope, my friends, that you will help me now: escort me—there," she said, and pointed with her sword; and from Gonturan's tip a blue spark jumped, and fell sizzling to the ground, and the cat king paced gravely over to examine the spot where it had fallen.

Then Aerin thought that perhaps it wasn't her nerves after all.

She shook the sword, and the blue light brightened till it lit the air around her, and the pit below her shimmered with it, and the cat king's eyes glinted with it as he looked up at her; and the light made it easier, somehow, to see, for just beyond where Gonturan's tip pointed she saw Kethtaz quite clearly, and Arlbeth on his back; and the blue light seemed to settle around him too, across the eerie ground so far away. It outlined Tor as well, not far from his king; and she wondered where the standard-bearer was, for it was this lack that had made her unsure that she had seen her father aright; but she had no time to think about it now.

"Listen," she said, and many pairs of bright eyes turned to her. "The Crown must fall only into the hands of Arlbeth or Tor. No one else. I will give it to one of them if I can"—she swallowed—"and if I fail, then you must; or if neither should leave this battle alive, then you must carry it far from here—far from here, far from Damar; as far as your feet can bear you." Her voice echoed oddly, as if the blue light reflected it or focused it, or held it together; and she had no doubt, suddenly, of her army, and a great sense of relief came to her, and almost a sort of joy.

"Come on, then," she said. "I'd really best prefer to deliver it myself."

She raised Gonturan, and Talat leaped forward, and the yerig and folstza fanned out around her; and the first Northerner to feel the teeth of Aerin's army fell beneath the dog queen, and the second was beheaded by Gonturan, and the third was pulled down by the tall black cat.

The Northerners had no scouts looking back over the mountains, for they had no reason to think a watch was necessary; they had the best strength of Damar bottled up in the City before them, and what few folk there were still scattered in small towns and mountain villages had been sufficiently terrorized by marauding bands of Northerners that they could be relied on to stay shivering at home. Furthermore, the Northern leaders could hear their enemies from afar, and could tell from whence they came, just as Perlith could turn a handful of nothing into a bouquet of flowers at a court ball.

Or so they had been able to do. They had had no foreknowledge of Aerin's approach, and the Northerners, while no cowards, knew much of magic and perhaps more of *kelar* than the Damarians did; and the unexpectedness of this feat frightened them far more than the simple fact of Aerin's presence. And so they did not rally at once, as they should have, for, had they done so, they might have cut her down and won the day for themselves, and won Damar forever. But they did not. They wheeled their riding beasts, some of them nearly horses but most of them nothing like horses at all, and tried more to get out of her way than to engage her and test her strength.

The common soldiery of the North was more frightened yet.
They saw that their leaders did not like this blue flame that
dazzled their eyes and, if it came too near, parted their queerly
jointed limbs from their thick bodies; and so they scrambled
to be free of the thing, whatever it was; and the blue light only
rippled farther and farther out from its center, and spread all
around them. Frequently it felt like teeth at their throats, and
their brown-and-purple blood soon tinged the ethereal blue a
darker shade; and sometimes it fell from above them, like the
lashing hoofs of a war-horse; and their own dying cries were in
their ears, and a high singing note as well that they had never
heard before, although in it were also the sharp snarls of the
wild mountain cats, and the dangerous baying of a yerig pack,
and the shrill screams of a fighting stallion.

The blue dazzled Aerin's eyes too, but it was a useful sort
of dazzlement because it seemed to break the Northerners'
clumsy movements into arcs whose sweep she could judge so
precisely that as they tried to escape her she knew just where to
let Gonturan fall across them. She did not think of how many
she killed or maimed; she thought of them only as obstacles
that must be overcome that she might rejoin her own people.
Merely to let them part before Talat's trampling hoofs, as they
showed a great willingness to do, was not enough, for they
might then close in again behind her; and so Gonturan fell,
and rose and fell again, and Aerin's blue-brightened eyes
watched and followed, and looked ahead to where the Damarians were making their last stand. She had one landmark to
guide her, one of the tall standing stones that marked the last
uphill stretch of the king's way into the City; the one of the
four stones that did still stand. But she could no longer see Tor
or Arlbeth. Nor did she often dare raise her eyes to look; for
there were those who stood to oppose her, who as they tried to
step out of her way still showed the glint of metal, to disem-
bowel Talat if they could, or hurl a poisoned throwing knife at
her from behind; she could not spare her vigilance. Her army
kept pace with her; a swathe they were cutting through the
Northerners; occasionally she saw, from the corners of her
eyes, a cat body, or a lean dog shape, fling itself on the twisted
helm or misshapen body of a Northerner; but then at once she
had to aim Gonturan for another blow. There was a high-
pitched hum in her ears, though she could still hear the hoarse

shouts of the Northerners, and the harsh ugly sound of the
words of their language in those shouts.

And across the battlefield, near the City, the beleaguered
Damarians looked up to see what was suddenly causing such
consternation in the ranks of their enemies. Looked up: and
strained their eyes, for what they saw was a blue sea rushing
toward them, a white crest at its peak where it reared to break.
But the blue surface rippled more like furry backs than like
water, and the rearing white crest was a war-horse, and a
sword blazed blue in his rider's hand; he carried no shield and
wore no armor, but he seemed not to need it, for the Northerners fled before him, and only his sword's quickness stayed
their flight, and slew them as they sought to escape.

The white horse neighed with war fury, and the yerig bayed,
and the folstza cried their harsh hunting cries, and nearer and
nearer the rushing blue army came; and the Damarians, some
of them, found themselves fearing this unlooked-for succor,
and wondered what the white rider planned for them when he
had cut his way so far; for there was no doubt that he drew
near them, as if their City's gates were his destination; nor was
there any doubt that he would succeed in arriving there.

But there was a muffled exclamation from Tor. "To me!
Quickly!" He urged his tired Dgeth forward, and his excitement gave her new strength. "Follow me! It's Aerin!"

Only a few followed him; but whether this was for weariness
or deafness, or fear of the blue thing, or fear that the blue
thing was or was not Aerin-sol, it was impossible to say; but
one of those who followed close on Dgeth's heels was the
messenger who had once brought news of Maur's terrible waking to the king.

Aerin knew her arm was tired, but it did not seem to matter;
Gonturan found the necks and vitals of the Northerners with
her own keen edge and merely drew Aerin's arm with her.
Then Aerin heard her name called, and she shook her head,
for she was imagining things; but she heard it again. It occurred to her that it sounded like Tor's voice, and that perhaps
she was not imagining things, and she looked up, and there
was Tor indeed. Heavy ranks of Northerners separated them
yet, and even as their eyes met, a riding beast, mottled yellow
and with forked hoofs and the ears of a cat, reared up between
them, and Aerin saw the one-eyed queen hanging from its
throat, and two of her followers leaping for purchase at its

flanks. Hamstrung, it fell kicking, and the queen pulled the rider down, and Aerin watched no further; and then Talat kicked and leaped sideways, and there was work for Gonturan again; and for a moment she lost Tor.

She called his name, this time, and at last she heard him answer; he was to one side of her now, but when she turned Talat that way the battle seemed only to drag him farther away. Then the Crown, which had clung to her shoulder all this time as if by its own volition, shook loose and ran down her arm, and struck Gonturan's hilt with a clang.

"Tor!" she cried again; and as his face turned to her, she tossed the Crown over the hilt, to the tip of the sword, swept the blade upright, and—flung the Hero's Crown across the evil sea that churned between them.

Gonturan blazed up like a falling star as the Crown ran her length, and as it wheeled into the air it in its turn burst into flame, red as the sun at noon, red as a mage's hair; and Tor, dumbly, raised his own sword as if in salute, and the Crown caught its edge, swung, hissing, round the tip, and fell to circle his wrist. Any Northerner might have killed him then, for he dropped his shield, and his sword arm was stretched out immobile as he stared at the glowing red thing hanging from his arm. But the Northerners were afraid of it too; they had seen enough of strange lights, and the blue one they already knew to be fatal. And the white rider had thrown this thing from the wicked Blue Sword.

Aerin shrieked: "It's the Crown, can't you see? PUT IT ON!"

Tor looked up again; Aerin was quite near now, and then she was beside him, banging her calf painfully against his stirrup as Talat pranced and pretended to be taller. She yanked his arm down, pried his fingers loose from his sword hilt, shook the Crown free; pulled his head down toward her and jammed the Crown over his temples.

❧ CHAPTER 23 ❧

AFTER THAT THE DAY belonged to the Damarians, for between the White Rider and the Scarlet there was no hope for the Northerners. But it was nonetheless a long and bitter day for the victors, and they lost many more of their people before it was over, including many simple folk who had never held weapons in their lives before, but who preferred the deadly risk of the battlefield to the terrible passive waiting to hear the final news. The Northerners, too, were slow to acknowledge defeat, even after they knew there was no chance left of their winning. In this war no captives were taken, for a captive demon is a danger to his jailer. It was not till evening drew near, and Talat was limping heavily with weariness, and Aerin held on to her saddle with her shieldless hand, that the remaining Damarians began to be able to gather at the foot of the king's way before the City gates, and lay down their arms, and think about rest. The Northerners were fleeing at last, fleeing as best they might, on three legs, or four, or five; some crawled. What Damarians had yet the strength pursued the slowest and gave them the last blow of mercy, but as darkness fell they left their treacherous enemies to the shadows, and crowded around the fire that had been built near the last standing monolith.

There was little rejoicing, for all were weary, bone-weary, death-weary; and they had had so little hope that morning that now in the evening they had not yet truly begun to believe they had won after all. And there were the wounded to attend to; and all those still left on their legs helped, for there were few enough of them. Many of them were children, for even the healers had taken sword or knife by the end and gone into battle. But the youngest children could at least carry bandages, and collect sticks for the fire, and carry small skins of water to fill the great pot hung over the fire; and as there was no child who had not lost a father or mother or elder brother or sister, the work was the best comfort the weary remaining Damarians could give them.

Aerin and Tor were among those still whole, and they helped as they could. No one noticed particularly at the time, but later it was remembered that most of those who had felt the hands of the first sol, her blue sword still hanging at her side, or of the first sola, the Hero's Crown still set over his forehead, its dull grey still shadowed with red, recovered, however grave their wounds. At the time all those fortunate enough to feel those hands noticed that their touch brought unexpected surcease of pain; and at the time that was all any could think of or appreciate.

Perlith had died on the battlefield. He had led his company of cavalry tirelessly through the last endless weeks, and his men had followed him loyally, with respect if not with love; for they trusted his coolness in battle, and learned to trust his courage; and because even as he grew worn and haggard as the siege progressed, his tongue never lost its cleverness or its cutting edge. He died on the very last day, having come unscathed so far, and his horse came back without him after darkness had fallen, and the saddle still on its back was bloody.

Galanna was holding a bowl of water for a healer when Perlith's horse came back, and someone whispered the news to her where she knelt. She looked up at the messenger, who was too weary himself to have any gentleness left for the breaking of bad news, and said only, "Thank you for telling me." She lowered her eyes to the pink-tinted water again and did not move. The healer, who had known her well in better days, looked at her anxiously, but she showed no sign of distress or of temper; and the healer too was weary beyond gentleness, and thought no more about it. Galanna was conscious that her hair needed washing, that her gown was torn and soiled—that her hands would be trembling were it not for the weight of the bowl she carried; that someone had just told her that Perlith was dead, that his horse had returned with a blood-stained saddle. She tried to think about this, but her mind would revert to her hair, for her scalp itched; and then she thought, I will not see my husband again, it does not matter if my hair is clean or not. I do not care if my hair is ever clean again. And she stared dry-eyed into the bowl she held.

But the second sola was not the worst of their losses. Kethtaz had fallen in battle too, and everyone had lost sight of Arlbeth for a time—just at the time when Aerin and Tor met and Aerin forced the Hero's Crown over Tor's head. They two looked for him anxiously, and it was Aerin who found him, fighting on foot, a long grim wound in his thigh, so that he could not move around much, but could only meet those who came to him. But his sword arm rose and fell as though it were a machine that knew no pain or weariness.

"Up behind me," said Aerin; "I will carry you back to the gates, and they will find you another horse"; but Arlbeth shook his head. "Come," Aerin said feverishly.

"I cannot," said Arlbeth, and turned that his daughter might see the blood that matted his tunic and breeches to his right leg. "I cannot scramble up behind you with only one leg—in your saddle without stirrups."

"Gods," said Aerin, and flung herself out of the saddle, and knelt down before her father. "Get up, then." Arlbeth, with horrible slowness, clambered to Aerin's shoulders, while she bit her lips over the clumsy cruel weight of him, and while her folstza and yerig kept a little space cleared around the three of them, and he got into Talat's saddle, and slumped forward on his old horse's neck.

"Gods," said Aerin again, and her voice broke. "Well, go on, then," she said to Talat; "take him home." But Talat only stood, and looked bewildered, and shivered; and she thumped him on the flank with her closed fist. "Go on! How long can they hold them off for us? Go!" But Talat only swerved away from her and came back, and would not leave, and Arlbeth sank lower and lower across his withers.

"Help me," whispered Aerin, but there was no one to hear; Tor and the rest of them were hard pressed and too far away; and so she raised Gonturan again, and ran forward on foot, and speared the first Northerner she found beyond the little ring of wild dog and cat; and Talat followed her, humbly carrying his burden and keeping close on his lady's heels. And so they brought Arlbeth to the gates of his City, and two old men too crippled to fight helped his daughter pull him down from Talat's saddle. He seemed to come a little awake then, and he smiled at Aerin.

"Can you walk a little?" she said, the tears pouring down her face. "A little," he whispered, and she pulled his arm around her shoulders, and staggered off with him; and the two old men stumbled on before her, and shouted for blankets, and three children came from the shadows, and looked at their bloody king and his daughter with wide panicky eyes. But they brought blankets and cloaks, and Arlbeth was laid down on them by the shadow of one of the fallen monoliths at his City's gates.

"Go on," murmured Arlbeth. "There's no good you can do me." But Aerin stayed by him, weeping, and held his hands in her own; and from her touch a little warmth strayed into the king's cold hands, and the warmth penetrated to his brain. He opened his eyes a little wider. He muttered something she could not hear, and as she bent lower over him he jerked his hands out of hers and said, "Don't waste it on me; I'm too old and too tired. Save Damar for yourself and for Tor. Save Damar." His eyes closed, and Aerin cried, "Father! Father—I brought the Crown back with me." Arlbeth smiled a little, she thought, but did not open his eyes again.

Aerin stood up and ran downhill to where Talat waited, and scrambled onto him and surged back into the battle, and the battle heat took her over at last, and she need think no more, but was become only an extension of a blue sword that she held in her hand; and so she went on, till the battle was over.

Arlbeth was dead when she returned to him. Tor was there already, crouched down beside him, tear marks making muddy stains on his face. And there, facing each other over the king's body, they talked a little, for the first time since Aerin had ridden off in the night to seek Luthe, and her life.

"We've been besieged barely a month," Tor said; "but it seems centuries. But we've been fighting—always retreating, always coming back to the City, riding out again less far; always bringing a few more survivors from more burnt-out villages here for shelter—always fighting, for almost a year. It began . . . shortly after you left."

Aerin shivered.

Tor said, and he sounded bewildered, "Even so, it has not been so very long; wars have lasted years, generations. But this time, somehow, we felt defeated before we began. Always we were weary and discouraged; we never rode out in hope that we could see victory." He paused a minute, and stared down at the shadowed peaceful face of their king. "It's actually been a bit better these last weeks; perhaps we only adjusted finally to despair."

Later they spoke in snatches as they tended their horses and helped elsewhere as they could. Aerin, numb with shock and sorrow, did not think of her father's last words to her, and did not think there might be special healing in her hands, or in the hands of him who wore the Hero's Crown; for that was something else that Luthe had forgotten to teach her. And so she went merely where there was a cry for an extra pair of hands. But somehow she and Tor managed to stay near each other, and the presence of the other was to each a comfort.

Aerin thought of a black tower falling as she tucked blankets, of the Hero's Crown no longer on the head of one who worked to do Damar evil as she pinned bandages; and as she crouched for a moment near the great campfire that threw wild shadows on the walls of her City, she thought of words spoken by another fire: *How could anyone be so stupid as to bring back the Black Dragon's head as a trophy and hang it on a wall for folk to gape at?*

Abruptly she turned to Tor and said: "Where is Maur's head?"

Tor stared at her; he was dazed with grief and exhaustion even as she was, and he could not think who Maur was.

"Before I left, I asked that Maur's head be put somewhere that I need not look at it. Do you know where it was taken?" There was urgency in her question, suddenly, although she herself did not know why; but the urgency penetrated the fog in Tor's mind.

"In—in the treasure hall, I believe," Tor said uncertainly. "I'm not sure."

Aerin reeled to her feet, and a plush-furred black head was at once beneath her hand, propping her up. "I must go there."

"Now?" Tor said unhappily, looking around. "Then I'll go too. . . . We'll have to walk; there isn't a fresh horse in all the City."

It was a brutally long walk, almost all uphill, for the king's

castle stood at the City's peak, a lower flat-topped shoulder
within the encircling mountains. Several of Aerin's army came
with them, and the tallest ones silently supported Tor, and he
wonderingly stroked the heads and backs he found beneath his
fingers. "A long story you have to tell me," Tor said; it was
not a question.

Aerin smiled as much of a smile as her weariness allowed.
"A very long story." She was much too tired to weep any
more, but she sighed, and perhaps Tor heard something in
that sigh, for he edged a yerig out of the way and put an arm
around her, and they toiled up together, leaning on each other.

The castle was deserted. Tomorrow many of the sick and
wounded would be brought here; for this night they would
stay by the fire at the foot of the king's way, for even the hale
and whole had no strength left, and there had been no one in
the City during the last days' fighting; all had been below,
doing what they could.

Tor found candles, and by some wonder he still carried his
flint. The castle was eerie in its silence and solitude and
darkness; and Aerin's tiredness drew little dancing designs at
the corners of her sight and pulled the shadows closer in
around the candlelight. She found she had to follow Tor
blindly; she had spent almost her whole life in these halls, and
yet in but a few months she had forgotten her way through
them; and then horribly she remembered climbing centuries of
stairs in a darkness very like this, and she shivered violently,
and her breath hissed through her teeth. Tor glanced at her
and held out his free hand, and she took it gratefully for she
had been all alone on those other stairs.

"Here we are, I believe," Tor said. She dropped his hand so
that he could attend to the lock, one of the small magics she
had never been able to learn. He muttered a moment, touched
the door in five places, and the door slid open.

A blast of grief, of the deaths of children, of crippling
diseases that took beauty at once but withheld death; of un-
consummated love, of love lost or twisted and grown to hate;
of noble deeds that proved useless, that broke the hearts of
their doers; of betrayal without reason, of guilt without
penance, of all the human miseries that have ever occurred; all
this struck them, like the breath of a slaughterhouse, or the
blow of a murderer. Tor fell to his knees and covered his face
with his hands, and the beasts cringed back, moaning. Aerin

put out her hand, leaned against the doorframe; just this she had feared, had half expected; yet the reality was much worse than what her tired mind had been able to prepare her for.

Greetings, said Maur's head. I did not think to have the pleasure of seeing you again.

It *is* you, responded Aerin. She opened her mouth to gasp, and despair rushed in, bitter as aloes. Tears filled her eyes, but she pushed herself away from the threshold and bent slowly and carefully to pick up the candle Tor had set down before he opened the door. She shook her head to clear her vision, held the candle aloft, and stepped inside the high vaulted room, despite the silent keening of the air. I know despair, she said. There is nothing more that you can show me.

Oh?

The keening changed tone and madness edged it, drifted across her skin, fluttered in her hair like bats' wings; she ducked, and the candle guttered and almost went out. Maur laughed. She remembered that silent hollow laugh.

Angry, she said: Nothing!

"Aerin," a voice said hoarsely behind her: Tor. "Light my —way—I cannot—see you." The words dragged out of him as he dragged himself to his feet. "This—is why—we've been— so—tired—all along."

"Yes." The sibilant hissed in the silence like adders' tongues, but Aerin's anger made a small clear space around her, and her beasts crept to her feet and breathed it gratefully, and Tor staggered to her like a man crossing a narrow bridge to freedom, and put an arm around her again, but this time it was for his own comfort.

"Tor," she said calmly, "we must get rid of Maur's head. Get it out of the City."

Tor shook his head slowly; not in refusal but confusion. "How? It is too huge; we cannot lift it. We must wait. . . ."

Wait, snickered Maur's head.

"*No.*" Aerin looked around wildly. The reek of despair still tingled in her nostrils and in her brain, and her anger was ebbing. She had to think. How?

"We can roll it," she said at last. "It's roundish. We can roll it downstairs, and then downhill—out of the City gates." She thrust the candle at him. "Hold this."

She walked purposefully up to the low platform where Maur's skull lay; the shadows in the eyesockets glinted. Her beasts came after her, clinging to her shadow; and Tor came behind them, just clear-headed enough to hold the light high, and to watch Aerin.

She set her shoulder in one of the ridged hollows at the base of the skull and heaved. Nothing happened but that Maur laughed louder; its laughter crashed in her head like thunder, and her vision was stained red. Then Tor found a niche for the candle and came to help her; they heaved, and heaved again, and barely the massive skull rocked on its base. Then her beasts came, and clawed at the thing, and chipped their teeth on it; their lady's anger and their own fear gave them a wild frenzy, and the skull shuddered where it lay, but they could stir it no further, and Aerin cried at last, "Peace!" and laid her hands on her loyal friends. They calmed under her touch, but they panted where they sat, even the cats, the curved white fangs glinting in the dim light. The candle was burning low.

"It's no use," said Tor heavily. He was still leaning against the skull, pressed up against it as if he loved the touch of it; Aerin grabbed him by the shoulder and yanked him away, and he staggered. He blinked at her, and a little more of Tor crept back into his eyes, and he almost smiled, and with his sleeve he rubbed his face where it had lain against the skull.

Are you finished yet? inquired Maur's head.

No, said Aerin fiercely.

I'm glad. This is the finest amusement I've had since you fled the banqueting-hall. Thank you for opening the door, by the way. Your folk by the City gates should taste me quite clearly by now.

You shall not bully me again! Aerin said, and, almost not knowing what she did, pulled Gonturan free of her scabbard and slapped the flat of her across the base of Maur's head where once the backbone had joined. Blue fire leaped up in sharp tongues that lit the entire vault, with its many shelves and cupboards and niches, and doors into further strong-rooms. It was a ghostly unhealthy color, but the skull shrieked, and there was a crack like a mountain splitting, and the skull fell off its pedestal to the floor.

Aerin hurled herself at it as it was still moving, and grudgingly it rolled another half turn; but as it fell, the thickness of the despair pressing around them weakened suddenly, and with something like hope again Tor and the beasts shoved too, each as they could; and it moved another half circumference.

The moon was high by the time they reached the courtyard, for they could not take the most direct way—the size of the skull precluded all but the widest corridors. The night wind was cold, for they were sweating hard with their labor; and the moon became two moons as Aerin's tired eyes refused to focus. Tor had found rope, and they had tried to drag the thing, but that had worked even less well than rolling it, so they went back to the rolling. It was not nearly round, and it progressed in lumbering half-circle flops, and each flop jarred Tor's and Aerin's muscles painfully; and they had been painfully tired before they began.

"We must rest," murmured Tor.

"Food," said Aerin.

Tor roused himself. "Bring some. Wait."

The slightly moldy dry bread and more than slightly moldy dry cheese he found gave them more strength than they would have thought possible. "Second wind," said Tor, standing up and stretching slowly till his spine cracked.

"Fourth or fifth wind," said Aerin grimly, feeding the end of her cheese to her beasts; "and the strength of panic."

"Yes," said Tor, and they put their shoulders to the work again, the grim echoes of bone against rock ringing terribly in the dark empty City. Depression still gnawed at them, but in a curious way their weariness worked to their advantage, for depression often went with weariness, and so they could ignore the one as a simple unfearsome result of the other. Maur had lost its ascendance once Gonturan had struck it, and while the skull still stank, it seemed almost an organic stench now, under the open sky; no more than the faint rotting smell of ancient carrion.

It was a little easier once they reached the king's way; each heave grew a little less, the fall-over a little hastier, and the crash a little more forceful. Then it began almost to roll; for each circle it lurched seriously twice, but it did not quite come to a complete halt each time; Tor and Aerin needed only to push with their hands. Both Aerin's shoulders were raw beneath her tunic, and there was a long shallow cut along her jaw where one of the dragon's ear spines had caught her briefly; and the old cut on her palm from Gonturan's edge throbbed dimly.

Then, just above the City gates, the vast head broke away from them. It was not merely the incline, which was little greater now than it had been down most of the slope behind them; it was Maur's final moment, and Aerin heard its last scream of gleeful malevolence as it plunged down the road.

"Scatter!" shouted Aerin, just as Tor bellowed, " 'Ware!"

The folk before the gates had indeed smelled Maur's foul miasma after the door of the treasure house was opened, and most of them lay or crouched wherever they had been when that dreadful wind had first blown over them. It had lifted a little since, but the days past had been too much, and once undiluted despair had touched them they found it hard to shake themselves free. They shifted a little now, at the voices, and the desperate urgency in them, and looked up.

The fire had burned down, for no one had had the strength of purpose to feed it since the treasure-house door opened. Maur's skull struck the fire's center, and the still smoldering branches flew in all directions, and the embers splashed like water; and while a few people cried out with sudden pain, there was too little fire to do much harm. The skull crashed into one of the fallen monoliths, which shattered, and then the black skull disappeared into the night, and there was a rumbling and an echo, like an avalanche, and the people, shaken out of their lethargy, looked around fearfully and wondered which way to run; but no mountains fell. The rumbling grew louder, till people put their hands over their ears, and Aerin and Tor knelt down in the roadway with their arms around each other. The rumbling became a roar, and then there was a sudden storm of wind from the battlefield, laden with the smell of death; but the death smell passed them and in its place came a hot, dry, harsh smell like nothing the green Hills of eastern Damar had ever known; but Tor raised his head from Aerin's shoulder and said, "Desert. That's the smell of the western desert." And on the wind were small gritty particles, like sand.

Then the wind died, and the people murmured to one another; but though there was a half moon it shed no light through the thick shadows that hung over the battlefield. They built up the fire again, but not very large, for no one wanted to venture far to look for fuel; and they tended to each other's burns, which all proved slight; and rounded up the horses again, who had been too tired to run far, even in terror.

Aerin and Tor stood up slowly and came into the firelight, and the rest of Aerin's beasts came joyfully up to greet them, those that were still alive, for many of them had not left the battlefield. She blinked up at Tor for a moment and said: "What have you done with the Crown?"

Tor looked blank, then sheepish. "I left it in the treasure hall. Not such a bad place for it; it will be spending most of its time there anyway."

Aerin felt a curious tickling sensation at the back of her throat. When she opened her mouth she discovered it was a laugh.

❧ CHAPTER 24 ❧

AERIN WOKE TWO DAYS later in her own bed in her father's castle—Tor's castle now. It was turning over that woke her; her muscles were so sore and stiff that her weariness was finally less than her aches and pains, and as she rolled onto her right shoulder she woke with a groan.

There was an immediate rustle from somewhere just beyond the bedcurtains, and the curtains themselves were pushed back and daylight flooded in. Aerin couldn't imagine where she was for a moment; her first thoughts were that wherever it was it was doubtless dangerous, and she groped vaguely for Gonturan's hilt; instead her fingers buried themselves in a heavy fur ruff, and a long tongue licked her hand. She tried to sit up, and a voice, attached to the hands that had just parted the curtains, said brokenly, "Oh, my lady." Aerin recognized Teka first, and then realized where she was, and then Teka bent down and buried her face in the bedclothes and sobbed.

"Teka," Aerin said, horrified by her tears.

"My lady, I thought I should never see you again," Teka muttered without lifting her face, but when Aerin tentatively patted a shoulder and smoothed the sleek black-and-grey head, Teka sat back on her heels, sniffed, and said, "Well, I *am* seeing you again, and have been seeing you again now for two and a half days, and I am very sorry to have been so silly. You'll want food and a bath."

"Two and a half days?" Aerin repeated.

"Two and a half days. Tor-sola is not awake yet."

Aerin smiled. "And, of course, you've been sitting in that chair"—she nodded at a high-backed wooden chair with a pillow propped up for the waiter's back and neck, and a cushioned footrest, and a small table with sewing paraphernalia tidily arranged on it—"the whole time."

Teka opened her eyes wide in the old way that had so terrorized the very young Aerin caught out at some misbehavior. "Of course. Bath or a meal first?"

Aerin considered. Even the muscles that made her tongue move and her jaw open and shut to speak and her lips smile hurt. "Malak, very hot, and a very hot bath first, and then food." There was a thrashing behind her and a long pointed face poked over her shoulder. "And food for this one, too. She'll skip the bath. Where are the rest of them?"

Teka scowled. "Wherever it pleases them to lay themselves. I did manage to herd them all into your rooms, lady, and the back hall; they terrify all the staff and most of the court. But they won't leave—and, well, I for one am capable of acknowledging that we owe them a debt, and loyalty is very admirable even in mute beasts, but," she said in a tone of suppressed rage, "I do not approve of animals sharing their sol's bed." The yerig queen yawned widely, and then a long piece of black shadow stood up from the still curtained foot of the bed, stretched himself, and flowed off the bed to the floor. He leaned against the backs of Teka's legs and began to purr and, to Aerin's delight, a slow flush crept up Teka's throat and face.

"I'm glad not everyone in my father's house is terrified by my friends," said Aerin.

"No, my lady," Teka said in a low voice. The king cat poked his head around Teka's waist to smile smugly at Aerin, and Aerin said, "You know, my wild friends, if you are planning to move in with me permanently, you will have to have names. If you live in a house, you are domesticated, and if you are domesticated, you must be named." The yerig sitting beside her licked her ear.

Aerin began the long excruciating process of getting out of bed; she felt that she would never move easily again. "I'll help you, my lady," said Teka, as Aerin touched her feet to the floor and hissed involuntarily. Teka was thinner than she had

been when Aerin saw her last, and as Teka put out a hand to
help her, Aerin saw a long bandage wrapped around her
forearm under her sleeve. She jerked her eyes away and looked
up at Teka's face again. "Must you call me lady?" she said
crossly. "You never did before."

Teka looked at her oddly. "I know that perfectly well," she
said. "If you're up. I'll look to your bath."

The hot water helped the deeper aches but just about killed
the blisters, and Aerin herself with them. She padded the back
of the bath with two or three towels so that she could at least
lie softly; and after three cups of very strong malak she dared
climb out of the bath. Teka laid her down on a cushioned
bench and rubbed a little more of the soreness out with the
help of some astringent solution (that smelled, of course, very
strongly of herbs) that was even worse than the hot water on
blisters; Aerin shrieked.

"Quiet," said Teka remorselessly. She finished by
smoothing on a silky pale ointment that almost made up for
the astringent, as Aerin told her. "Your adventures have made
you no more polite, Aerin-sol," Teka said with asperity.

"You could not possibly have hoped for so much," Aerin
responded as she eased into the undershift Teka had laid out
for her.

"No," Teka admitted, and turned down the corners of her
mouth, which meant she was suppressing a smile.

Aerin turned to pick up the tunic. "Why am I getting all
dressed up to eat breakfast?" she inquired. The tunic was new
to her, blue and heavy, with a lot of gold thread worked into
it.

"It's mid-afternoon," Teka said repressively. "The honor
of your company for an early dinner has been requested by
Tor-sola."

Aerin grunted, and put the tunic on—and grunted again.
"He woke up, then."

"So it would appear. There is nothing that can be done with
your hair."

Aerin grinned and shook her head so that the fine not-quite-
shoulder-length tips swung across her cheeks. "Nothing at all.
It doesn't seem to want to grow."

Tor looked haggard but convalescent, as Aerin felt she probably looked as well. She'd worn Gonturan as a way of ac-

knowledging the formality of the occasion, but the swordbelt only reminded her more intensely of certain of her blisters, and she was glad to hang it on the tall back of her chair. Tor came to her at once and put his arms around her, and they stood, leaning against each other, for a long time.

He put her away from him only an arm's length then and looked down at her. "I—" He broke off, and dropped his arms, and paced around the room once. He turned back like a man nerving himself for a valorous deed, and said, "I'm to be made king tomorrow. They seem to think I already am, you know, but there's a ceremony . . ." His voice trailed off.

"Yes, I know," Aerin said gently. "Of course you're king. It's what my—what Arlbeth wanted. We both know that. And," she said with only a little more difficulty, "it's what the people want as well."

Tor stared at her fiercely. "You should be queen. We both know it. You brought the Crown back; you've won the right to wear it so. They can't doubt you now. Arlbeth would agree. You won the war for them."

Aerin shook her head.

"The gods give me patience. You *did*. Stop being stubborn."

"Tor—calm down. Yes, I know I helped get the Northerners off our doorstep. It doesn't really matter. Come to that, I'd rather you were king."

Tor shook his head.

Aerin smiled sadly. "It's true."

"It shouldn't be."

Aerin shrugged. "I thought you invited me here to feed me. I'm much too hungry to want to stand around and argue."

"Marry me," said Tor. "Then you'll be queen."

Aerin looked up, startled at the suddenness of it.

"I mean, I'll marry you as queen, none of this Honored Wife nonsense. Please I—I need you." He looked at her and bit his lip. "You can't mean that you didn't know that I would ask. I've known for years. Arlbeth knew, too. He hoped for it.

"It's the easy way out, I know," he said, hope and hurt both in his eyes. "I would have asked you even if you hadn't brought the Crown back—believe me. If you'd never killed a dragon, if you broke all the dishes in the castle. If you were the daughter of a farmer. I've loved you—I've loved you, to know it, since your eighteenth birthday, but I think I've loved you all my life. I will marry no one if you'll not have me."

Aerin swallowed hard. "Yes, of course," she said, and found she couldn't say anything else. It had not been only her doom and her duty that had brought her back to the City, and to Tor, for she loved Damar, and she loved its new king, and a part of her that belonged to nothing and no one else belonged to him. She had misunderstood what her fate truly was a few days ago, as she rode to the City to deliver up the Crown into the king's hands; it was not that she left what she loved to go where she must, but that her destiny, like her love, like her heritage, was double. And so the choice at last was an easy one, for Tor could not wait, and the other part of her—the not quite mortal part, the part that owed no loyalty to her father's land—might sleep peacefully for many long years. She smiled.

"Yes-of-course what?" said Tor in anguish.

"Yes-of-course-I'll-marry-you," said Aerin, and when he caught her up in his arms to kiss her she didn't even notice the shrill pain of burst blisters.

It was a long story she told him after that, for all that there was much of it that she left out; yet she thought that Tor probably guessed some of the more bitter things; for he asked her many questions, yet none that she might not have been able to answer, like what face Agsded had worn, or what her second parting from Luthe had been.

They ate at length and in great quantity, and their privacy was disturbed only by the occasional soft-footed hafor bearing fresh plates of food; yet somehow by the end of the meal the shadows on the floor, especially those near Aerin's chair, had grown unusually thick, and some of those shadows had ears and tails.

Tor looked thoughtfully at the yerig queen, who looked thoughtfully back at him. "Something must be done for—or with—your army, Aerin."

"I know," Aerin said, embarrassed. "Teka's been feeding them only bread and milk these last two days, since she says she refuses to have the rooms smelling like a butcher's shop, and fortunately there's that back stair nobody uses—the way I used to sneak off and see Talat. But I never knew why they came to me in the first place, and so I don't know how long they plan to stay, or—or how to get rid of them." She gulped, and found herself staring into two steady yellow eyes; the folstza king's tail twitched. "Nor, indeed, do I wish to be rid of them, although I know they aren't particularly welcome here. I would be lonesome without them." She remembered how they had huddled around her the night after she had left Luthe, and stopped speaking abruptly; the yellow eyes blinked slowly, and Tor became very busy refilling their goblets. She picked hers up and looked into it, and saw not Luthe, but the long years in her father's house of not being particularly welcome; and she thought that perhaps she would enjoy filling the castle with not particularly welcome visitors that were too many and too alarming to be ignored.

"They shall stay here just as long as they wish," Tor said. "Damar owes you any price you feel like asking, and," he said dryly, "I don't think it will hurt anyone to find you and your army just a little fear-inspiring."

Aerin grinned.

He told then of what had come to them during her absence; much of it she knew or guessed already. Nyrlol had rebelled for once and for all soon after she had ridden into Luthe's mountains; and immediately the local sols and villages near him had either gone over to him or been razed. The divison of his army Arlbeth had left to help Nyrlol patrol the Border had been caught in a Northern trap; less than half of their number survived to rejoin their king. Arlbeth had ridden out there in haste, leaving Tor in the City to prepare for what they now knew was to come; and it had come. It had come already, for when Arlbeth met Nyrlol in battle, the man's face had been stiff with fear, but with the fear of what rode behind him, not what he faced; and when Arlbeth killed him, the fear, in his last moments of life, slid away, and a look of exhausted peace closed his eyes forever.

"Arlbeth wasn't surprised, though," Tor said. "We had known we were fighting a lost war since Maur first awoke."

"I didn't know," said Aerin.

"Arlbeth saw no reason that you should," said Tor. "We— we both knew you were dying." He swallowed, and tapped his fingers on the tabletop. "I thought you would not likely live to see us fail, so why further shadow what time remained to you?

"When you left I felt hope for the first time. That note you left me—it wasn't the words, it was just the feeling of the scrap of paper in my hands. I took it out often, just to touch it, and always I felt that hope again." He smiled faintly. "I infected both Arlbeth and Teka with hope." He paused, sighed,

and went on. "I even chewed a leaf of surka, and asked to
dream of you; and I saw you by the shore of a great silver lake,
with a tall blond man beside you, and you were smiling out
across the water, and you looked well and strong." He looked
up at her. "Any price is worth paying to have you here again,
and cured of that which would have killed you long since. Any
price. . . . Neither Arlbeth nor Teka was sure, as I was. I knew
you would come back."

"I hope at least the Crown was a surprise," said Aerin.

Tor laughed. "The Crown was a surprise."

The lifting of Maur's evil influence was as important a relief to
the beleaguered City as the unexpected final victory in the war;
but there was still much healing to be done, and little time for
merrymaking. Arlbeth was buried with quiet state. Tor and
Aerin stood together at the funeral, as they had been almost
always together since Aerin had ridden across the battlefield to
give Tor the Crown; as the two of them had never publicly
been together before. But the people, now, seemed to accept
it, and they simply gave Aerin the same quiet undemonstrative
respect that the first sola had received since the battle; it was as
if they did not even differentiate between the two.

Everyone still felt more than a little grey, and perhaps in the
aftermath of the Northerners a witchwoman's daughter whom
they had, after all, grown used to seeing for over twenty years
past seemed a small thing to worry about; and she was, after
all, their Arlbeth's daughter too, and Arlbeth they sincerely
mourned, and they read in her face that she mourned too. She
stood at Tor's side while Arlbeth's final bonfire burned up
wildly as the incense and spices were thrown on it, and the
tears streamed down her face; and her tears did more good for
her in her people's eyes than the Crown did, for few of them
really understood about the Crown. But she wept not only for
Arlbeth, but for Tor and for herself, and for their fatal ignorance; the wound that had killed the king had not been so
serious a one, had he had any strength left. Maur's weight on
the king of the country it oppressed had been the heaviest, and
the king had been old.

When Tor was proclaimed king in the long Damarian ceremony of sovereignty officially bestowed, it was the first
time in many generations that a Damarian king wore a crown,
the Hero's Crown, for it had been tradition that the kings

went bare-headed in memory of that Crown that was the heart of Damar's strength and unity, and had been lost. After the ceremony the Crown was placed carefully back in the treasure hall.

When Aerin and Tor had gone to look for it three days after they hurled Maur's skull out of the City, they had found it lying on the low vast pedestal where the head had lain. They had looked at it, and at each other, and had left it there. It was a small, flat, dull-grey object, and there was no reason to leave it on a low platform, little more than knee high, and wide enough for several horses to stand on; but they did. And when the treasure keeper, a courtier with a very high opinion of his own artistic integrity, tried to open the subject of a more suitable keeping-place, Aerin protested before the words were all out of his mouth, although they had been directed at Tor.

Tor simply forbade that the Crown be moved, and that was the end of it; and the treasure keeper, offended, bowed low to each of them in turn, and left. He might not have wished to be quite so polite to the witchwoman's daughter, for the courtiers were inclined to take a more stringent view of such things than the rest of Damar. But any lack of courtesy that survived the highborn Damarians' knowledge that Aerin-sol had fought fiercely in the last battle against the Northerners (although of course since she'd shown up only on the last day she'd had more energy left to spend), and the inalterable fact that their new king was planning to marry her, tended to back down in the face of the baleful glare of her four-legged henchmen. Not that they ever did anything but glare. But the treasure keeper's visit had been watched with interest by nine quite large hairy beasts disposed about Aerin's feet and various corners of the audience chamber.

❧ CHAPTER 25 ❧

TOR HAD WANTED to marry her as part of the celebration of
his kingship, and have her acknowledged queen as he was acknowledged king, but Aerin insisted they wait.

"One might almost think you didn't want to be queen,"
Tor said glumly.

"One might almost be right," replied Aerin. "But it's more
that I don't want anybody to have the opportunity to say that
I slipped in the back door. That I was assuming everyone
would be so preoccupied with you that no one would notice I
was being declared official queen by the way."

"Mm," said Tor.

"It was Arlbeth who told me that once royalty commits
itself it can't go back into hiding," Aerin said.

Tor nodded his head slowly. "Very well. But I think you're
doing your people an injustice."

"Ha," said Aerin.

But Tor was right, although not for the reasons he would
have preferred; it had little to do with her fighting in the last
battle, and almost nothing to do with the Crown. By the time
the three months' betrothal that Aerin demanded was up and
the marriage was performed, thirteen weeks after what had
come mysteriously to be called Maur's battle, most Damarians
(all but a few hidebound courtiers) seemed to have more or

222

less forgotten that they had ever held the last king's daughter in so lively an antipathy; and affectionately they called her Fire-hair, and Dragon-Killer. They even seemed to enjoy the prospect of Aerin as their new queen; certainly the wedding was a livelier meeting than Tor's crowning had been, and the crowd cheered when Tor declared Aerin his queen, which startled them both. But many things that had happened before the day Maur's head had been dragged into the City had faded from people's memory, and at the wedding they said comfortably to one another that it was true that the first sol's mother had been a commoner from some outlandish village in the North, and that Aerin-sol had always been an odd sort of child; but she had grown into her rank quite satisfactorily, and she had certainly helped turn the Northern tide with that funny foreign sword of hers and those wild animals that were so fond of her (there are worse spells than those that make wild animals tame).

Besides, while Tor had remained obstinately single, all the other sols of his generation had gotten themselves married off; and Aerin was, whatever her faults, a first sol.

And when Aerin understood at last what had happened, she laughed. So Maur did me a good turn after all, she thought. That's the finest victory of all.

It was called Maur's battle perhaps because it had been fought on what was now known as Maur's plain. While much else had been forgotten, or at least become a little blurry, of the events before the seasons the City had borne with Maur's head held in the king's castle like an enormous jewel, everyone well remembered that at the end of the battle the stretch of earth at the foot of the king's way was a destroyed forest, and that bodies of people and beasts, and of half-beasts and half-people, lay everywhere, with broken bits of war gear mixed with the broken landscape. And they remembered Maur's skull rushing down on them—flaming, they said, like a living dragon, its jaws open to spew fire—and spinning past them in the darkness.

And in the morning, when they awoke, instead of low rolling hills despoiled by war, they found a plain, flat as a table, stretching from the burnt-out fire where the survivors had slept huddled together to the feet of Vasth and Kar and the pass where Aerin had paused and seen what awaited her and gathered herself and her army together. It was a desert plain, and it remained a desert; nothing grew there, nor would grow, but a little low scrub. Desert creatures came to live there, and a new sort of hunting dog was bred to run by sight, and the City dwellers came to love the wild sweet song of the britti, the desert lark. They took to holding horse races on the plain after the first few years of staring at it nervously had worn off, and the uncanniness was lost in familiarity; and then various games of skill were pursued there, mock battles and sword-play, and it became a much better practice ground than the old cramped space behind the castle and the royal stables at the peak of the City. It was a handy spot for the drilling of cavalry, and Tor paid much attention to the rebuilding of his cavalry, for he, like his wife, if perhaps no one else in the City, remembered very clearly what had happened in the months preceding Maur's battle. The Laprun trials therefore grew in size and importance, which was all to the good; what was less good was the growing popularity of the churakak, the duel of honor, fought by those a little too proud of their ability to fight.

The first year's harvest after the battle was a scanty one, but Arlbeth had grain set aside for just such an occurrence, and as there were fewer Damarians to be fed than when he had built his warehouses, the winter was no harder than a winter after a good harvest, although everyone was thoroughly sick of por-ridge by the time spring came.

But spring did come, and people stirred themselves, and many of them felt quite like their old selves, and went out to dig in the ground or refurbish their shops or look to their stock and their holdings with good heart. Those who had remained in the City over the winter, to nurse their wounds and regain their strength, went home to their villages and began the long process of rebuilding, and most of the rebuilding went on cheerfully. Tor and Aerin sent aid where they could, and some of the new villages were handsomer (and better drained) than the old ones had been.

It was during the first winter that Aerin, wandering vaguely one day in the center-court garden of the castle, felt that there was something at the gate she had entered by. She frowned at it till she remembered what it was: the great oil green surka vine was gone. She stared round at all the gates to be sure she had not mistaken it, but it was not there; and she went in search of Tor, and asked what had happened to it.

Tor shook his head. "There isn't any surka any more—anywhere. One day—a fortnight, maybe, before Maur's battle, they all went. I saw this one; the smoke came from nowhere, but when it cleared, the surka was a charred skeleton. It was such a weird sort of thing, and everyone was preoccupied with weird sorts of things that always turned out to be unpleasant, that the remains were rooted out and buried.

"Arlbeth said it was a sign too clear to be ignored, even if we didn't know what it meant, and so we carried no standard during the final days of the siege of the City." He frowned. "The surka seems to be something I want to remind people of; we're probably better off without it. No more Merths." He smiled at her.

"And no more Aerins," said Aerin feelingly.

Some who had lost too much stayed on in the City when spring came; Katah had lost her husband, and she and her six children asked to stay on in the king's castle, where she had grown up. Tor and Aerin were glad to say yes, for the castle was a little too empty; not only Perlith was gone, but Thurny and Gebeth and Orin, and many others. And Aerin found the reliable and practical Katah invaluable in sorting out which petitions and complaints to bend her royal judgment on, and which to ignore. "I have found my calling," said poor Katah, who missed her husband: "I was meant to be a royal secretary."

"You were meant to be the power behind the throne," said Aerin. "I shall cover you with a velvet drape and you can whisper to me what to tell the people as they come." Katah laughed, as she was supposed to.

Katah was not the only one that the passing of time did not heal. Galanna's hair had gone grey during that first winter, and was white by the time the second spring after the battle came. She was quieter, and slower, and while she looked with no love upon Damar's new queen, she caused, and wished to cause, no more trouble.

As Katah was a hard and honest worker, Aerin could contrive to steal a little time to chase dragons—whose numbers had greatly fallen off since the Northerners' defeat—and to teach a suddenly considerable number of interested young men

and women what she knew about dragon-hunting. Among
other things, she found out what she had known all along, that
she had a superior horse. No horse liked wearing kenet, and
most of them were much nastier about it than Talat had ever
been; and then there was the fact that Aerin had no idea what
to tell her students to do with their reins while they were trying
to pin a dragon with their spears. Somehow or other Aerin's
dragon-hunting lessons began to spill into horsemanship lessons, and she taught her pupils first about riding without stirrups, and later without reins. By trial and error she trained a
few young horses to go as Talat had gone for her—to prove to
herself as much as to anyone else that it could be done with
other horses—and she learned to have an eye for the horses
who could learn what she wished to teach them, and those who
could not. Soon the queen of Damar was rumored to be an
uncanny judge of horseflesh, and her opinion on this colt or
or that mare was frequently sought.

Hornmar had taken a bad wound in his side, and he was
older than the king he had served, and Arlbeth's death weakened him almost as much as his own hurt. He had to retire
from his post as the head of the sofor; but he lived in the castle
still, and at his request he was permitted to have the care of his
old friend Talat. Aerin was forced to be grateful for this, for
she had too much work, now, to be able to attend to Talat as
frequently as she had been accustomed to do, and was yet
jealous of who tended him in her place. She would not have
wished to leave him to any ordinary groom, however skilled
and worthy.

Talat himself was as vain and cheerful as ever after a few
weeks' holiday, and had as bottomless a hunger for mik-bars,
but he was beginning to feel his age at last, and Aerin or Hornmar had to chase him around with a stick to make him exercise
his weak leg on the days Aerin did not have time to ride. But
the leg was strong enough that when a few mares were cautiously introduced to him in his pasture, desirable results were
born eleven months later. His foals were all bright-eyed and
bouncy from their first breath, and Hornmar and Aerin were
very careful about who had the handling of them; and all of
them grew up to go bridleless like their sire, and many of them
had his courage.

The royal kennels were expanded, and the yerig and folstza

who chose to stay near their lady were given their own quarters, although the door to the back stairs that led to Aerin's old rooms was always left open. It was observed, though the thotar kennel-masters were at first too timid to do any cross-breeding deliberately, that some of the royal bitches gave birth to taller and hairier puppies than any official royal bloodlines could explain; and it was from these crosses that the long-legged desert dogs eventually came. And after a few generations of kittens grew up and had more kittens, the folstza began to accept more human masters than Aerin, and to hunt on command, at least mostly. Even tamed cats have minds of their own.

Having her own quarters did not stop the yerig queen, now Kala, from bearing her first City litter in the middle of Aerin and Tor's bed. "Oh, gods," said Aerin, who found her, or them: five excellent puppies, and a very proud Kala. "Teka will flay you alive." Teka, so far from flaying anyone alive, adopted one of the puppies, named it Ursha after a small pink wildflower, and it grew up to be a great hulking beast, bigger than its mother, with a singularly wicked look, and a disposition as gentle as a featherbed.

Tor had been king less than three years when he was first called the Just, for the even-handedness of his wisdom; a wisdom, they said, that was never cold, and that sat strangely in the eyes of a man not yet forty. Aerin knew where some of that old wisdom came from, for she had first seen it the afternoon that he had told her she should be queen, had asked her to marry him; the same afternoon that he had not asked her about Luthe. She hoped that she might never be careless of Tor's feelings: Tor, who had been her best friend all her life, and sometimes her only friend. Perhaps the memory of the reek of Maur's despair made her a little forgetful too, for she began to think of the wide silver lake as a place she had visited only in dreams, and of the tall blond man she had once known as a creature of those dreams; for the not quite mortal part of her did sleep, that she might love her country and her husband.